C♥MICS WILL BREAK YOUR HEART

Also by Faith Erin Hicks:

Brain Camp (with Susan Kim
and Laurence Klavan)

Friends with Boys

Nothing Can Possibly Go Wrong
(with Prudence Shen)

The Nameless City trilogy:
The Nameless City
The Stone Heart
The Divided Earth

The Adventures of Superhero Girl

A NOVEL BY **FAITH ERIN HICKS**

COMICS WILL BREAK YOUR HEART

Roaring Brook Press
New York

Library of Congress Control Number: 2018944872

ISBN: 978-1-62672-364-1

Our books may be purchased in bulk for promotional, educational,
or business use. Please contact your local bookseller or the Macmillan
Corporate and Premium Sales Department at (800) 221-7945 ext. 5442
or by e-mail at MacmillanSpecialMarkets@macmillan.com.

First edition, 2019
Book design by Aimee Fleck
Printed in the United States of America

1 3 5 7 9 10 8 6 4 2

For my parents, who always supported
my strange comic-making habit

"Kid, comics will break your heart."

—Jack Kirby

CHAPTER ONE

Miriam rolled up the sleeves of her too-large work shirt and stood with her hands on her hips, staring at the towering bookshelf in front of her. Someone had been messing with her carefully alphabetized comic book display. Mir eyed the disaster before her: memoir comics by Lynda Barry and Alison Bechdel shoved next to various X-Men trade collections, early volumes of Naruto carelessly shelved beside arty French comics. There was even a copy of a popular kids' graphic novel stuffed between two copies of *From Hell*, a bloody retelling of Jack the Ripper. With a sigh, Mir tugged the kids' comic off the shelf and stared at the cover. A round yellow smiley face stared back, grinning. *Smile*, said the comic's title. Mir frowned at it.

"Don't tell me to smile," Mir muttered. She placed the comic on a nearby shelf and started pulling out the other mis-shelved comics, stacking them in neat piles. Superhero comics to her right, science fiction and horror comics to her left, slice of life and memoir in the middle.

The bell above the Emporium of Wonders' front door jangled. Mir looked up, her hands full of the latest run of *Uncanny X-Men*. A teenage boy about her age was stepping through the door, looking around curiously. Mir beamed her best smile at him.

"Welcome to the Emporium of Wonders, Sandford's one-stop entertainment shopping spot! If you need help with anything—" Mir glanced down at the piles of comics surrounding her. She was practically walled in.

"Uh, well, just yell if you need help. My boss is in the back, he can give you a hand. Or I'll find a way, somehow," she finished, gesturing at the stacks of books. The boy nodded, his gray eyes crinkling in amusement. He stood in the store's entrance, staring at the displays in front of him. Mir didn't recognize him, which meant he was probably a tourist. It was only the last weekend in April, early for tourists in Sandford, but Mir knew most of the locals her age. Sandford was a very small town.

"This place is . . . interesting," the boy said. Mir followed his gaze around the store. The Emporium of Wonders was technically a bookstore, but recently its owner (and Mir's boss), Berg, had decided he wanted to sell toys and games alongside the books, so the inventory could most kindly be referred to as a mishmash. One half of the store was bright and gleaming, superhero action figures and limited-edition vinyl toys stacked neatly on clear glass displays. The book section was shabbier— Mir waging her personal war against improperly shelved books—and slightly dusty paintings of lighthouses and seascapes hung along the back wall. The paintings were all by local Sandford artists, those who weren't quite good enough at painting lighthouses and seascapes to earn a spot at the small galleries down on the waterfront.

"Yep," said Mir cheerfully. "If there's a book or action figure or comic you want, we've probably got it. We have all kinds of things."

The boy took a step forward. Instead of heading into the shiny, toy-centric section, he walked toward the wall hung with local artwork. He stopped in front of a painting of a battered boat at sea and peered at it. The boy's back was to Mir, his hands stuffed in his jacket pockets. He was tall, and bent forward at the waist so he could better see the paintings. Curious, Mir stared at the back of his head. Paintings of artfully distressed maritime objects from the Canadian East Coast were popular among a certain kind of Sandford tourist, but this boy didn't look anything like that demographic.

The boy straightened and quickly stepped to his right, to study another painting. Mir blinked, then tore herself away from staring. These comics wouldn't alphabetize themselves.

Mir pulled the remaining mis-shelved comics from the bookcase, carefully slipping each book back in its appropriate spot. She lined up the cheerful, brightly colored spines of the kids' graphic novels, stacked the Hellboy collections in a neat row of black and red, and was just finishing sorting the superhero comics when the boy spoke behind her.

"Is this the TomorrowMen?"

Mir looked up. He was still bent forward, peering intently at a painting of two superheroes, a man and a woman, standing on the edge of a building. The man seemed to shine like a beacon in the painting. He was dressed in red and gold, and his red cape swirled around him, caught by an unseen breeze. His face was bare; he didn't hide his identity with a mask. The woman was painted with more subtle colors, her costume muted purples and golds. She wore a cat's-eye mask, and her dark hair swirled upward in a fantastic 1960s updo.

Mir's mother, Stella, had made the painting.

Mir stood up, rolled down the sleeves on her work shirt, and walked toward the boy.

"Yeah, it's Skylark and Skybound, the two most powerful TomorrowMen." Mir felt a twinge of annoyance at his interest in the painting. She remembered the fight she'd had with her mother over it, how she'd yelled that it didn't make sense for Stella to sell her artwork if she was going to charge so little. Stella could charge hundreds of dollars if she wanted to; she knew that there were TomorrowMen-mad collectors out there, eager to spend real money on original artwork of Skylark and Skybound. But Mir's mother had remained resolute, stubbornly devoted to her price no matter how much Mir yelled.

"You have a bunch of TomorrowMen stuff here," the boy said, his arm sweeping back to take in the shiny, toy-infested section of the Emporium of Wonders, "but I wasn't expecting original art. It's really cool."

"Yeah, it is," said Mir. She did think the painting was cool.

She loved how her mother painted, how she mixed her colors and used reds and browns and purples to blend the perfect skin tone. How she edged her figures with the tiniest bit of yellow, like they were radiating light. She wished she could stop fighting with her mother about her art.

"I like that they're in their original costumes," the boy said. He pointed at Skylark's outfit, a snug bodysuit with tall boots and a waist-length cape. "They've had, what, like fifty costumes in the comics over the last forty years? But there's something perfect about the original costumes. Definitely my favorite."

"They're pretty great," agreed Mir.

The boy turned away from her, hands stuck back in his jacket pockets, and stared at the two figures in the painting.

"I wish they were using these costumes in the movie," he said.

Mir smiled, grateful. "I wish they were too," she said. "Have you seen the latest stills from the movie? They got rid of Skybound's cape." Mir had seen every leaked image from the upcoming movie, every stolen shot of the actors filming on the streets of New York. She'd cringed at Skylark's dull gray-and-black costume and Skybound's cape-less shoulders. They hadn't looked anything like the characters she knew, the comic-book weirdness and bright colors leached out of them.

"It's a tragedy," the boy said, solemnly shaking his head. "He just doesn't look right without the cape."

"He doesn't," Mir said.

"I keep hoping the filmmakers will change the costumes

before the movie comes out," he said. "It's not out until next year, so there's still time."

The boy smiled at her, and the hairs on the back of Mir's neck stood up. His smile was wide and gorgeous, and the air around him seemed to brighten because of it.

"Maybe," Mir said, feeling generous so close to this boy's smile.

"I don't normally care about comic book movies, I swear," the boy laughed. "But I grew up with TomorrowMen comics. They deserve a good movie. Like, Sam Raimi *Spider-Man 2* good. Or *Superman II* good. Those are my favorites."

"I like *Superman II*," Mir agreed.

"Everyone likes *Superman II*." Again the boy grinned, catching Mir in the brightness of his smile.

The boy turned back to the painting.

"How much is it?"

"I'm sorry?" Mir asked blankly.

"The painting," said the boy, pointing up at it. "How much is it?"

Mir stared. "You want to buy it?"

The boy blinked, confused at Mir's question.

"It's not for sale?" he asked. "I just thought—y'know, it's here with all these other paintings and they all seem to be for sale, so I thought maybe it was for sale too. I really like it."

"It's for sale," Mir said, "but it's not—" Suddenly she realized what she was going to say and got nervous. Who was this boy? She didn't know anything about him.

"It's—it's an original painting, but it's . . . unlicensed, I guess? It's not from Warrick Studios, the TomorrowMen comics publisher . . ." She trailed off.

Mir and the boy stared at each other, and in a rush she noticed three things about him: one, he was at least four inches taller than her. Two, he had a slightly crooked nose that made him terribly cute; and three, he was dressed expensively. She hadn't noticed his clothes at first, but now that she was really looking at him, trying to figure out if he was going to cause a problem for Stella, who almost exclusively painted (and sometimes sold) portraits of the TomorrowMen, she saw how well fitted his jacket and jeans were. How they had nice seams and were cut as though someone had made them specifically for his body.

"Hey, what's your name?" said the boy.

"Mir," she said.

"Meer?"

"Miriam. Mir for short."

"Cool," he said. "I'm Weldon, and I think that painting is awesome. Whoever painted it is really great at painting the TomorrowMen, and I'm not going to rat them out to Warrick Studios because something that awesome isn't piracy, it's art."

"Okay, cool," Mir said, relieved.

"Seriously, Mir," said Weldon. "It's completely amazing. You gonna tell me how much you want for it?"

Mir took a deep breath. *Here we go*, she thought.

"Twenty-eight dollars and seventy cents."

Weldon's eyebrows shot up.

"But it's an original. I mean, whoever painted it must've spent hours—"

"Yeah, well." Mir sighed. "My mo—the artist charges the exact amount of money they spent making the painting. So, canvas, sixteen dollars. Paints, eight dollars. And so on. Because, y'know, they think charging for art is . . . not cool, I guess."

"Doing it for love, not money," Weldon said, nodding seriously. "I admire that." Mir felt a white-hot flash of annoyance. Of course the boy in the designer jeans would approve of Stella's pricing system. People who had money always thought it was noble not to care about it.

She unhooked the painting from the wall, sneaking one last look at it as she rang up Weldon's purchase and slipped the canvas into a paper bag. She'd miss it. It had been comforting to look up at Skylark and Skybound at the end of a long day and imagine there was something powerfully good in the world.

Mir watched Weldon leave the store, the painting tucked under his arm. The car he headed toward was a beat-up Hyundai, not a rich-kid car. Mir felt herself warming to him again when he opened the door to the Hyundai. Maybe she'd misjudged him. Maybe his parents bought his clothes, but he had to work for his car. She liked the idea of him toiling away somewhere to pay for gas, changing the oil on the Hyundai himself to save money.

Another car skidded into the parking lot, tires shrieking in protest. Everything happened very fast: three teenage boys slid from the car, fists clenched, ready for violence. Mir recognized them from her high school, older boys known for getting into fights and cutting class. She'd always tried to avoid them, and eventually they'd stopped coming to school. Mir wasn't sure if they'd graduated or not. Now, Weldon turned toward the three boys, as though he'd been expecting them. He leaned Stella's painting against the car and walked straight at them, his step almost jaunty. They all came together in a furious clash.

Mir was already clawing her way over the store counter, screeching at Berg to call the police. This was a fight that meant business. She skidded through the front door and stopped short, trying to figure out what to do.

Weldon's hands blurred as he swung. Mir could tell he would lose; three to one wasn't a fair fight and the other boys were bigger than him. The group came in close, then went down in a pile of arms and legs. One of the boys ended up crouched on top of Weldon, pummeling him. Weldon twisted, his arms curled protectively over his face. It occurred to Mir as she scrambled toward the little utility shed next to the Emporium of Wonders that Weldon's nose might not have been originally so crooked, but had been smashed into its particular shape through violence.

Mir saw Weldon wiggle out from under his assailant and wrap his arms around the boy's torso, heaving him off the ground. The force of the lift propelled the pair onto the hood of the Hyundai. As the other two boys charged the car, Mir caught them full in the face with a torrent of water from the garden hose. They staggered backward, hands held up against the water.

The boy on the hood of the Hyundai grabbed a fistful of Weldon's collar and bent his head back. Mir turned and hit both of them with the water from the hose, and they slid down the car, drenched. Weldon's attacker was on his feet first, face murderous. He wheeled toward Mir. Someone was screaming "Stopstopstopstopstop!!" and Mir realized with surprise that it was her.

The boy came at her. Mir saw his angry hands reaching for her—and he jerked up short as Weldon grabbed his legs from behind.

Sirens wailed in the distance, and the three boys' heads snapped up. The one snared by Weldon kicked backward and wrestled free. Another boy grabbed the car keys off the ground and swung into the Hyundai. The two cars peeled out of the Emporium of Wonders parking lot, tires blowing smoke. Stella's painting thumped softly on the pavement.

Mir shut off the hose. It suddenly seemed very quiet.

Weldon was still on the ground. He rolled onto his side and stared up at Mir. His eye was swelling, but otherwise he seemed unharmed. He grinned a shining, gorgeous smile.

"Thanks."

"The police—the police are coming," Mir said. Her hands, still clutching the hose, were shaking.

"Oh, that's not so good. I'm not really keen on talking to them," Weldon said.

Mir stared at him.

"Why?"

Still on the ground, Weldon stared dreamily toward where the two cars had sped off.

"Because I kind of stole that Hyundai."

The police car skidded into the Emporium of Wonders' parking lot, two officers hopping out of the vehicle with barely disguised glee. Not much happened in Sandford, and Mir could tell the officers were delighted at the chance to use their siren.

"You gonna tell the police?" said Weldon, pushing himself onto his hands and knees. Mir looked down at the back of his head. She remembered him wrapping his arms around the legs of the boy charging at her.

"They got their car back, didn't they?" Mir said, nodding in the direction the three boys had driven off. She tossed the garden hose away, then bent and picked up her mother's painting, inspecting it for damage. To her relief, Mir saw the brown paper she'd wrapped it in had protected it when it had hit the pavement. She tucked the painting under her arm and reached out her free hand to help Weldon up. He wobbled when he stood, his hand flailing briefly, then settling onto her shoulder for balance. She moved her hand under his elbow, ready to grab him if he fell. The hand on her shoulder was very warm, she noted absently.

"What happened here?"

One of the police officers was attempting to loom over them. He wasn't particularly tall, which made the looming seem more like rude crowding. Mir fought the urge to roll her eyes. She'd seen this officer before, napping in his cruiser on one of Sandford's sparsely traveled back roads. Now he looked as excited as a kid on his birthday. The other officer, a woman Mir didn't recognize, had her notepad out, pencil poised over a blank page.

"A fight," said Weldon. He wobbled again as he pointed toward the Emporium of Wonders. "I bought something in that store, and when I came out three guys pulled into the parking lot. We . . . exchanged some words."

Mir stood next to Weldon, watching him out of the corner of her eye. He looked directly at the police officers when he talked, his face open and earnest. Except for the occasional wobble, his hand tightening not-unpleasantly on Mir's shoulder, he seemed completely relaxed. She was amazed at his calm, as though he hadn't been nearly beaten to a pulp by three other boys and wasn't currently lying to the police.

When Weldon was done telling his story, the two cops turned to confer with each other. Weldon, no longer wobbling but still with his hand on Mir's shoulder, reached for the painting.

"Here," he said. "I'll hold it."

"I don't mind," said Mir, but handed the painting over anyway.

"Oh," said the male officer, looking flustered as he riffled through his notes, "we never got your name."

"Weldon Warrick," said Weldon. The officer's eyebrows climbed his forehead.

"Weldon . . . Warrick," repeated the police officer. His partner glanced sideways at him, uncomprehending.

Mir froze. An icy hand didn't so much clutch at her heart as punch it.

"Yeah," said Weldon, half smiling. "That Warrick."

Warrick Studios, thought Mir. *Publisher of the TomorrowMen comics. I just saved the ass of the TomorrowMen heir.*

CHAPTER TWO

Weldon continued his conversation with the police officer, but Mir couldn't make out the words. He suddenly seemed both very far away and much too close to her, the warmth of his hand on her shoulder dragging her downward. She took a single, deliberate step to her right, away from Weldon. He glanced in her direction as his hand slipped off her shoulder. Mir ignored him, crouching next to the discarded garden hose, winding it around her arm. She picked up the coiled plastic and walked toward the utility shed, throwing the hose inside.

Berg was standing at the Emporium of Wonders' front door, staring at the scene in the parking lot. Mir looked over at her boss, face turned away from Weldon.

"I was in the middle of calling the police when I heard the siren. They got here fast," Berg said, shading one hand over his eyes. "Is everything okay?"

"I think so," Mir said, still carefully not looking in Weldon's direction. She turned to squeeze past Berg and caught a glimpse of Weldon, standing in front of the cops as they scribbled furiously in their notepads. He was looking at her, one hand hanging limply by his side, her mother's painting tucked under his other arm. Their eyes met and he smiled, but his face had swollen and all he managed was a lopsided smirk. Mir ducked her head and stepped back inside the Emporium of Wonders. A queasy feeling was sliding around in the pit of her stomach.

Mir walked toward the bookshelf she'd been organizing and picked up the remaining stack of comics. The cover of *New TomorrowMen* volume six was on the top of the pile, Skybound locked in mortal combat with a villainous-looking character Mir didn't recognize. Mir stared at the cover, the queasiness in her stomach hardening into a clenched fist.

"Weldon Warrick of Warrick Studios," she whispered to the battling superheroes. "You've got to be kidding me."

———

That evening, Mir called her dad from the store.

"You don't have to pick me up from work; I'm going to walk home," she said.

"What is this?" Henry said. "My only daughter, my favorite daughter, who always begs for a ride to the place of her employment mere minutes from our home, voluntarily using her legs? I don't believe it."

"You're so funny," Mir said, sighing.

"I am," said Henry. "I am very funny. When will you be home?"

"I'm leaving now, so half an hour."

"Enjoy your walk," said Henry. "I will remember this moment. The Moment Miriam Decided to Use Her Own Legs. It will become legend."

"Ugh," Mir said, hanging up. She rolled her eyes at Berg, who was locking up the store. "Dads."

"Dads indeed," said Berg absently.

Mir had known Berg since she was six years old. Ten years ago, he had long curly hair and grew organic vegetables, which meant when he gave her a carrot from his garden, it didn't quite look the same as the ones from the grocery store. Five years ago, he cut his hair and decided to open the Emporium of Wonders, where Miriam had worked for the past year.

"Weird day, huh?" Mir said, waiting for Berg to finish locking the outer door.

"Lots of excitement," Berg agreed. "Um . . ." He paused like he was going to tell her something. Mir waited. Despite the professional haircut, Berg would always look like he should be farming organic carrots, not managing an entertainment store. He still had dreamy hippie eyes and a fumbling way of talking. He always looked out of place amid the filing cabinets and stacks of order forms in the small office at the back of the store. Secretly, Mir worried about him. He'd never seemed like a proper adult to her, even when she was six years old.

That's not fair to Berg, Mir chided herself. *He might make you wear a work shirt with too-long sleeves, but it's because of him that your bank account has more than babysitting money in it. So be nice.*

"Never mind. It's nothing," Berg said. "I'll see you tomorrow." He had wanted to tell her something, Mir realized, but couldn't bring himself to do it yet. Berg was kind of a chicken sometimes.

The Emporium of Wonders was perched at the edge of Sandford's tiny downtown. Over the last two years, a Starbucks and a high-end sporting apparel store had sprung up nearby, replacing the old hardware store and a convenience store where Miriam had bought candy as a kid. The sporting apparel store sold designer yoga pants and had a window display that exhorted passersby to sweat every day, accompanied by an eight-foot-tall poster of a meditating woman who looked like she'd never sweated in her life. The sports apparel store and its pushy display bugged Mir, but she didn't mind the Starbucks. Sometimes she and her best friend, Raleigh, would go in and get the cheapest thing possible, a cup of hot water with a tea bag in it, and sit for hours on the creaky faux-leather couches at the back of the café, watching coffee drinkers come and go. The rest of downtown was a mixture of touristy souvenir shops, make-your-own-pottery studios, and local businesses slowly sliding into disrepair.

As she walked past the apparel store, Mir looked apprehensively at the distance between it and the Emporium of Wonders. Sometimes it felt like the gap between the two stores was narrowing, the yoga pants store intent on conquering the space occupied by its neighbor. Mir frowned at the towering display of the meditating woman and silently vowed to defend her workplace with everything she had. The Emporium of Wonders was a weird retail mishmash, but working there was easy and uncomplicated. Her job was the one thing in Mir's life that didn't feel like it was about to shift unexpectedly under her feet, dumping her to the ground.

Mir gave the yoga pants store one last pointed look and turned down a side street, toward home. Unbidden, Weldon Warrick popped into her head: his crooked nose and gorgeous grin, the way he'd looked at her, baffled but still smiling, as she stepped emphatically away from him in the parking lot.

"Of all the comic book stores in all the world, Weldon Warrick walks into mine," Mir muttered. She glanced up hurriedly, almost expecting a smirking Weldon to appear behind her, as though she'd said his name three times in a mirror. She wasn't sure if the cops had arrested him. She didn't think so. The three boys who'd nearly pummeled him into applesauce had their car back, so they weren't complaining. She was probably the only one who knew what he'd done, and she'd chosen not to tell.

I wish I'd taken my mom's painting back from him, Mir thought. *It deserves better than to be owned by a thief, even one with a gorgeous smile.* She shook her head, attempting to clear it of Weldon Warrick.

Mir's house was a half hour walk from Sandford's tiny downtown, at the dead end of a street that declined in niceness the farther she walked down it. The houses at the beginning of the road were brightly painted Nova Scotian historical homes, slowly becoming more and more ramshackle until the road dead-ended on Miriam's house, the most ramshackle of them all.

Mir loved her house. She loved the sloping roof and the faded orange paint that her mother liked to touch up with different shades of orange or yellow. She loved the windows with their ancient wooden shutters, the overgrown garden that kept her family in vegetables throughout the summer and autumn, and the wide front porch with its double columns supporting the jutting overhang that always seemed on the verge of collapsing. Mir had lived in the house since she was five years old and could barely remember living anywhere else.

The floorboards creaked under Mir's feet as she walked across the porch and slouched into one of the battered wicker chairs by the front door. Sandford's skyline stretched in front of her, stark against the brightness of the setting sun. The shape of the town was so familiar to Mir: the stubby square buildings, the arch of the bridge over the river that wound into the ocean. A knot of worry started to twist in the pit of Mir's stomach.

The front door banged open and Stella stuck her head around the door.

"Oh," she said, "you're here! Your father said you were walking home, even though he'd offered you a ride. I said we should check and make sure you hadn't been replaced by a pod person."

Miriam made a face at her mother.

"I just wanted to walk—"

"You never walk," said Stella.

"I'll never walk home again if it means you'll stop picking on me," Mir said. "You're mean. Dad's mean."

Stella smiled. Her clothes were splattered with bright paint. She'd wrapped a bandana, also splattered with paint, around her closely shaved head. When Mir was a little girl she would rub her palms wonderingly against the clipped stubble of her mother's head, and think about how different Stella was from her friends' mothers.

"How was today? How is Berg?"

"Berg's okay; today was okay," Mir said, pulling herself out of the chair. She brushed off the butt of her jeans; the porch chairs were always dusty.

"Tell Berg we miss him. He hasn't come to visit in so long."

"I'll tell him," Mir said. "He's really busy with the store, that's probably why he hasn't come by."

Stella swept an arm out for Mir, drawing her into a hug.

"Come inside. I bet you're hungry."

The kitchen was like the outside of Mir's parents' house: slowly sliding toward disrepair, painted with cheerful colors that didn't quite match. Stella pulled a Saran-wrapped plate of food out of the fridge, placing it on the kitchen table in front of Mir.

"Want it heated up?"

"It's fine," said Mir, pulling the plastic off the plate. "It still tastes good cold."

Stella sat down beside Miriam, leaning forward on the table to watch her daughter eat.

"You sure you're okay? You seem a little distant."

"I'm sitting right here next to you," said Mir, around a mouthful of chicken.

"You know what I mean. Did anything happen at the store today?"

"No," Mir lied. "Oh, wait, yes. I sold your painting, the one of Skylark and Skybound standing on that building."

Stella looked impressed.

"Did you? That's fantastic, thank you."

Mir shoved her hand into her jeans pocket and pulled out Weldon Warrick's money. She dropped the various bills and coins onto the table. They sat there between her and Stella.

"I'm so glad that one sold. I'm almost out of burnt umber gouache. I can buy a new tube with this," Stella said, sorting the small pile of cash.

Mir looked down at her plate. It was one of the half dozen mismatched plates Stella had found at the local Goodwill. This one had small blue, green, and brown foxes running an endless loop around the edge of the plate. There were six foxes, but a crack in the plate had cut one of them in half, the fault line snaking through his fox body.

"I wish you'd charge more for your paintings," Mir said softly. Stella's hand stilled over the small pile of coins she was sorting.

"Are we going to fight again?" Stella said.

Mir could remember being very small and sitting on the floor of the studio where Stella painted. The studio was really just the garage in her parents' backyard, the door wedged shut against winter weather. Stella was kneeling beside her. The two of them were moving paintbrushes in unison across the canvas surface. Their brushstrokes scored a red path across the whiteness of the canvas. Stella was smiling as she painted beside Mir. There were no figures on the canvas, just colors. The painting still hung in Stella's studio, a remnant of a time when art felt much less complicated to Mir.

Stella reached out and put her hand on Mir's. Her fingers were cool against Mir's wrist. Mir let her; she didn't really want to fight. She'd been angry all week, but today's violence at the Emporium of Wonders had made her tired instead. She shook her head.

"I just want you to know—"

"I do know," said Stella. "I don't want to abandon material things and go back to living in the woods. I think indoor plumbing is a very fine thing. But we have enough that I don't have to charge more for my paintings. I can keep the art I make just art, rather than something I need to sell to support our family."

"Then why sell them at all?" Mir said, annoyed at the whine in her voice.

"Because art supplies cost, Miriam, and we have enough, but not quite enough."

"No, not quite enough," Mir echoed. Stella's face tensed, and Mir felt that tension in her mother's hand.

"What would be enough for you, Miriam?"

Mir stared hard at the fragmented fox running around the plate on the table in front of her. Poor fox; he didn't know his hind end was in the process of being separated from his shoulders. He ran on and on, completely oblivious.

Mir thought of Weldon Warrick's smile. *He's the heir to the TomorrowMen fortune. What's that worth? Royalties from comics and toys and animated shows and bedsheets and a TomorrowMen movie with a two-hundred-million-dollar budget coming out next year. He's gotta be getting a few bucks from that.* Weldon Warrick's future was paved smooth and endless, no potholes, no bumps in the road. If anyone had enough, it was him.

"The guy who bought your painting recognized that Skylark and Skybound were wearing their original costumes. He said they were his favorite."

Mir felt relief ease Stella's fingers. Stella knew an olive branch when she saw one.

"Was he one of those old-school comic collectors? He wasn't horrible, was he? I respect having an obsessive passion, but collectors can be so nitpicky. You remember that one from a few years ago who had a tantrum because I painted Skylark's belt purple instead of blue—"

"No," Mir interrupted. "It was someone my age."

Stella's elegantly arched eyebrows shot up.

"Interesting. Who was he?"

Mir picked up her fork, scraping a few grains of brown rice across her plate.

"Just some rich kid," she lied. "I think he was a tourist, maybe off a cruise ship. We talked a bit about the Tomorrow-Men movie. He said he grew up reading the comics."

"Was he cute?" Stella asked, smiling.

Mir saw Weldon walk jauntily across the Emporium of Wonders' parking lot, ready for violence. She saw his smile slide across his face. It didn't quite touch his eyes. The thought of the car-stealing heir to the Warrick Comics empire taking Stella's meticulously detailed painting of Skylark and Skybound back to his castle was almost unbearable. *I should have offered him a refund, done something to try to get him to return it*, Mir thought. *That painting deserves a better home than what he could give it.*

"Not really my type." Mir stood up from the table and took her plate to the kitchen sink. "I think he was just passing through town, anyway. I don't think I'll see him again." *I hope I'll never see him again*, Mir thought uneasily. *Whatever reason he's in Sandford, it'd better not keep him here longer than the weekend.*

"What an unusual encounter," said Stella, her nose crinkling as she smiled. The setting sun was shining red through the kitchen window, lighting the soft curve of her head. "If you do see this young man again, sell him another painting. He seems to have good taste."

There was a clatter on the porch outside, and Mir's father and younger brother, Nate, charged through the door. Stella grabbed Nate and kissed him on the top of his head before he had the chance to wriggle free of her grasp. Annoyed, he stomped through the kitchen and into the living room. At twelve, Nate considered himself much too old for mothering.

"Hi," said Henry to Stella, and they tangled together affectionately. Stella was a head shorter than Henry, and he wrapped his arms around her, resting his bearded chin on top of her shaved head. At the sink, Mir watched her parents out of the corner of her eye: their embrace fit them perfectly into each other like puzzle pieces.

Arm in arm, Henry and Stella turned toward her, and Miriam looked up at them.

"Hey, you made it home on your own two legs," said Henry, smiling. Mir let annoyance and frustration slide off her, and grinned at her father.

"I know, it's like some kind of miracle."

CHAPTER THREE

Weldon stood in his aunt and uncle's guest bathroom, staring at his face in the mirror. His eye was nearly swollen shut, the bruise around it beginning to change from angry red to purple. There was a cut on his chin he didn't even remember getting and his ribs felt like someone was leaning a booted foot against his side. It hurt to take more than a shallow breath.

"Weldon Warrick," he said to his reflection in the mirror, "I, David Warrick, your long-suffering father, would like to know: Why do you keep getting yourself into this kind of shit?"

It wasn't a great imitation of his dad. Despite spending the past thirty years in California, David Warrick still had a hint of an East Coast Canadian accent, which became more pronounced the angrier he got. Weldon was used to that accent battering furiously at him whenever he screwed up.

"Don't you know what I'm dealing with this week?" Weldon said. "Licensing and movie budgets and filming schedules and aliens taking over the world. Don't you know how much I have on my plate, Weldon?"

Weldon frowned at the mirror.

"I, David Warrick, god-king of the TomorrowMen empire, have ten million things to deal with right now, so if you could just sit down and not move or speak or breathe, I'd appreciate that, Weldon."

Weldon looked away from his reflection. He stared down at his bare feet, half disappearing into the plush bathroom mat. He looked back up at the mirror, and flashed a slightly crooked but passable version of his usual smile at his reflection. The smile would be back to normal in a few days. It would be like the fight never happened.

Weldon walked out of the bathroom, into the guest bedroom. His suitcase was shoved in a corner, half open, his clothes strewn around it. Tilted against the wall was the painting he'd bought from that girl in the sad little geek store in Sandford's meager downtown. The painting was still wrapped in paper and leaning against the guest bed, where he'd left it the night before.

The girl's face came to him: skeptical brown eyes, freckles dotting her cheeks, and a halo of dark curly hair that spiraled out from her head like her thoughts were exploding outward. He remembered her skinny elbow sticking out of the sleeve of her too-large work shirt as she handed him the change for the painting. He also remembered the way she'd bolted into the parking lot, garden hose held in front of her like she was an action hero in a movie, mowing down the boys he'd stolen that car from. Her hand on his arm, steadying him as he wobbled after the fight. The look of strange animosity creeping across her face as she stepped away from him.

"Weldon! Breakfast!" his aunt yelled from downstairs.

"Coming!" he yelled back.

He hadn't brought many clothes. The trip had been hastily arranged—not so much a "trip," more a "dumping." Two weeks ago, his dad had decided that having Weldon in Los Angeles the summer before the TomorrowMen movie came out was a risk he wasn't willing to take, especially after Weldon was suspended from school for stealing the groundskeeper's truck and driving it through the football field. The punishment seemed like an overreaction to Weldon. He hadn't even gotten off the school campus.

I've done worse things that didn't get me shipped off to the ass-end of Canada, Weldon thought, pulling a T-shirt over his head. *It was just a suspension.*

But this summer was different. This was the summer the hype machine for the TomorrowMen movie kicked into gear. This was the summer the movie trailer premiered at San Diego Comic-Con, to the orgasmic excitement of every geek with a keyboard.

"I, David Warrick, overlord of the TomorrowMen comic empire, have my entire future riding on this film," muttered Weldon. "If it makes north of five hundred million domestically, I will finally have legitimacy. No more scraping by with comic books and animated TV shows. This movie hits big, and I'll be the one talked about in hushed tones at every industry party."

Weldon pulled a green T-shirt from his small pile of clothes, grimacing. His father had put everything into the movie—all of Warrick Studios' resources, millions in financing. David Warrick was finally going to realize his dream of bringing his father's greatest comic book creations, the superheroic Skybound and Skylark, to life.

So it had been decided: Weldon would be shipped off to his father's boyhood town, to live with his aunt and uncle. He would finish off the school year online, since it was too late to look into transferring to a school in Sandford. And if Weldon ever wanted to return to Los Angeles, ever wanted to look upon the hallowed halls of Warrick Studios and take a selfie with the life-sized statue of Skybound outside the studio's main building, if he ever wanted to sleep in his own bed again, he would be good for the summer. He wouldn't steal cars. He wouldn't get into fights. He would write passable essays on his laptop and email them to his internet teacher on time. He would be good. And then maybe David Warrick would let him come home.

"So, thanks, Grampa Warrick," Weldon muttered, trotting downstairs. "You just had to create the comic that got me banished to the far corner of this Canadian wasteland."

The kitchen smelled good.

"Hi," Weldon said, walking over to the pink table tucked neatly in a corner of the kitchen. Wide bay windows looked out over a neatly tended front lawn. Weldon's aunt and uncle had no children, so he guessed the lawn was kind of like their kid. He figured they'd gotten a better deal than his parents: lawns didn't steal cars or get suspended from school.

"Every time I look at that eye of yours, I cringe," said Aunt Kay, reaching up to touch his cheek. He smiled at her. She'd always been soft on him. "Are you sure you don't want a nice cold steak for it? Bag of frozen peas? Aspirin? Anything?"

"It's good," Weldon said. "Doesn't hurt much."

"This town is changing for the worse," said Uncle Alex, sitting at the kitchen table. "When your father and I were kids here, the crime rate was minuscule. A chief of police and a deputy—that was all this town needed. Now, there's too much nonsense."

Weldon nodded solemnly, giving his uncle as much eye contact as he could manage, to show how seriously he was taking the lecture. His uncle continued.

"Nowadays a young man can be walking down the street and just be attacked. It's appalling. I really wish you'd been able to identify who did it, so those kids could be brought to justice. But you did the best you could under the circumstances."

Alex Warrick didn't look much like his brother, David. Weldon had seen photos of them together as teenagers, both of them trim and tan, arms looped around each other's shoulders. David Warrick had kept the tan and the trimness, but between him and Alex, Alex looked younger. David Warrick looked like he hadn't had a good night's sleep in years, the stress of transforming Warrick Studios from mere comic publisher to a movie industry titan pushing him to the breaking point.

Aunt Kay piled eggs and bacon on Weldon's plate.

"We need to talk about the summer," she said. "Your father was very concerned we keep you busy, so I've been looking into various programs you can join."

Are they going to ship me off to summer camp? thought Weldon, dismayed. *I really like showering in a normal bathroom. I like drinking things that don't exclusively come in toxic shades of orange.*

"Your father said you like to run," his aunt continued. "I know there's a cross-country running club at that exercise store downtown, the one that sells those famous yoga pants. It's called the Running Realm, I think."

Relief washed over Weldon. He dug his fork into the small mountain of scrambled eggs in front of him and beamed at his aunt.

"That sounds fantastic, Aunt Kay."

"Sandford is a good place to live," his aunt said, and Weldon saw real concern on her face. He was amused she'd taken his alleged assault so personally. "It's not normally filled with awful people. I've lived here my whole life and I've never seen or experienced anything like what happened to you yesterday. Please don't judge Sandford by what happened. I really want you to have a good summer."

"I do too," Weldon said. He liked his aunt and uncle, but they had been a little too eager to accept his made-up story about the fight yesterday. David Warrick would've pried the truth out of Weldon using the vowels in his East Coast accent. *Someday I'll tell my dad something and he'll actually believe me*, Weldon thought, spooning eggs into his mouth. *Maybe it'll be the truth, maybe it'll be something I made up, but I'll tell him and he'll believe me.*

"Are you all right, dear?" his aunt said. Weldon looked up at her, aware he hadn't been paying attention. "You had the oddest look on your face."

Weldon beamed his smile at her.

"I'm great, Aunt Kay."

After his aunt and uncle left for work, Weldon laced up his running shoes and walked down their long driveway, heading downtown. The asphalt was wet, and water splashed over his shoes as he stretched into a loping run. The air still smelled like spring here. Los Angeles had been hot and hazy when he'd left, eternally summer. *Bring jackets*, his aunt had said when it was decided he would move in with them for the summer. *Jackets, jeans, and rain boots. Not sure what the weather's like in Los Angeles, but here we get four seasons, three of them winter.*

Weldon lifted his head and sucked in a breath. His ribs throbbed, and it occurred to him that going for a run the day after he'd been pounded into applesauce was probably a stupid idea. He took another breath and kept going.

He always ran too fast at the beginning. He'd gotten better at it recently, learning to pace himself for longer distances, but the beginning of a run felt so good. Nervous energy bubbled in his chest, spurring him to run faster. He allowed himself to stretch out, feeling the ground churn under his feet.

There were no sidewalks in his aunt and uncle's part of town, just the road and large houses alongside it. *The rich part of town*, he thought. Funny how similar the rich part of any town looked: carefully groomed lawns, tidy gardens, sleek cars with less than ten thousand miles on the odometer. Weldon eyed a mint-green BMW as he jogged past, wondering if it was unlocked.

I'm going to be good this summer, he reminded himself. *Aunt Kay and Uncle Alex don't need that damage. And I want to go back to LA. The only reason I took that Hyundai is because the driver was an idiot and left the keys in it. That won't happen again.*

Weldon followed the road as it curved away from the houses. In the distance was the bridge into downtown Sandford. He jogged across the bridge, looking down at the wide, slowly moving river below. There was some kind of history to the river, something to do with the fur trade hundreds of years ago, beaver-hat-wearing trappers paddling down it in bark canoes. Weldon couldn't remember the exact story. Canada's history was completely mysterious to him. Did they fight any wars for their independence? *Were* they independent? They had the queen on their money, so maybe not. Weldon jogged off the bridge and onto a sidewalk, mentally making a note to look up Canadian history on Wikipedia.

Weldon turned onto a street, missing a step as he recognized where he was. It was the only street in Sandford that had much of anything: a Starbucks, a couple of tourist-trap shops, and the exercise store his aunt had mentioned. There were a few shabbier local businesses clinging to the street too. Weldon wondered how Sandford locals felt about their gentrifying downtown: Did they like the Starbucks, or did they prefer whatever it had replaced, some broken-down diner that only served black coffee for a dollar a cup?

Down the street, he saw the run-down geek store, the one he'd stopped into yesterday. He always liked seeing Tomorrow-Men merchandise in the wild, and the large poster of Skybound in the store window had attracted his attention as he drove the stolen Hyundai through town. Weldon remembered the painting he'd bought, wrapped carefully in brown paper by that girl. She'd looked a little sad when she'd sold it to him.

I wonder why she didn't tell the cops I stole that car, Weldon thought. He remembered the way the girl had stepped away from him as he'd been interviewed by the police. She hadn't seemed bothered by his confession that he'd stolen the Hyundai, but something had changed in the minutes that followed, something he didn't understand.

Weldon turned and walked across the street and into the Running Realm. A girl behind the counter, her body burned lean from long-distance running, looked up when he entered. He smiled at her, hoping the smile would make up for his eye. From the approving way she smirked back at him, her eyes sliding down his body just a bit, the smile was working.

"Hi," he said. "I heard you had a cross-country club."

"You heard right," said the girl. Her eyes were slightly hooded. Weldon wasn't sure if that made her look predatory or sleepy, but either way, he liked it. "We run twice a week, mostly in the park down the road. It has lots of trails and you get to run beside the river. We do a 5K and a 10K. Sound like something you're up for?"

"Most definitely," Weldon said, crossing his arms and leaning on the counter. The girl with the hooded eyes smiled and pushed a clipboard toward him.

"Sign up here. My name's Ellie, by the way."

Weldon smiled back.

"I'm Weldon Warrick. Very nice to meet you."

CHAPTER FOUR

From the rocky beach beside Sandford's only lake, Mir and Raleigh watched as their friend Evan cannon-balled into the water, sending up a massive splash. He bobbed to the surface, howling, "IT'S COLD!!!"

"His body hair will prevent him from freezing," Raleigh said. Mir nodded.

"Boys have an extra layer of insulation," Mir said. "It's not fat, it's like an extra layer of boy. It's why I'm always cold and Evan never is. He's got an extra layer of boyness."

In the lake, Evan flailed melodramatically, wailing about the water's temperature.

"He seems kinda cold now," Raleigh said.

"He's faking for attention," Mir said, and Raleigh laughed.

The lake was a small horseshoe-shaped body of water lined with evergreen trees, its southeast edge giving way to a tiny, sandy beach where Mir and Raleigh were sitting. A rickety dock extended out from the beach. Just moments ago, Evan had pounded down the length of the dock and launched himself into the water.

"I'm glad you came out today," Raleigh said.

"Yeah, I'm glad too. It's been so long since we hung out."

"You're so busy," said Raleigh. "You have, like, all the jobs."

"Just the one," said Mir.

"Well, you work a lot of hours at the one job. And you have all the homework since you're in all the advanced classes. And then you help your parents grow all the things in your garden on the weekend. My mom says thanks for the squash, by the way. I'm not going to say thanks, because now I have to eat squash for dinner all next week."

Mir giggled. Raleigh glanced over at Mir and they grinned at each other.

"It's the price of being friends with me: you risk my parents gifting you a metric ton of vegetables," said Mir.

"Why doesn't pizza grow on trees? I would love a metric ton of pizza."

"Pizza tree," Mir said. "I bet my mom can grow that. She's a plant wizard."

"Tell her to grow a money tree too," Raleigh said. "Then you won't have to work and can just be lazy your entire life. And also buy your awesome friend Raleigh an iPad."

Evan emerged from the lake like a triumphant Wookiee, water streaming from his swim trunks. He struck a heroic pose on the tiny beach, fists on his hips, head thrown back. Water dripped from his hair and beard. *I swear he's had that beard since sixth grade*, Miriam thought.

"Ladies!" said Evan, waggling an eyebrow at Mir and Raleigh. "Tremble at the sight of the wild Nova Scotian man in his native element! Behold my pristine majesty!"

Evan flexed his arms mightily. What skin wasn't covered with hair blazed white in the sun. Mir and Raleigh burst out laughing. In sixth grade, Raleigh and Mir had gotten over their childhood suspicion of boys and agreed they'd be his friend for one simple reason: Evan was the best.

Raleigh held her hands over her eyes, blocking Evan from view.

"Too much sexy, Evan," she laughed. "I admit to being weak in the knees. You win."

Mir watched her two friends, smiling. For as long as Mir could remember, Raleigh had been beside her, her stride matching Mir's as they went out in search of adventure. They had been locked in friendship, needing only each other until they discovered Evan.

"Am I too late for the Evan show?" said Jamie, Raleigh's boyfriend. He was walking around the bend in the trail that led to the tiny beach, backpack slung over one shoulder. Raleigh squealed when she saw him, leaping to her feet to fling her freckled arms around his neck. Encouraged, Evan also squealed and lumbered toward Jamie, intent on wrapping him in a wet hug.

"Hey, Mir," said Jamie, managing to kiss Raleigh hello and fend off Evan's attempt to hug him. "It's been, like, years since I saw you."

"Years and years," Mir said, smiling, ignoring the tiny twist of guilt in her gut. If Jamie had noticed her absence, then it really had been ages since she'd seen her friends. Jamie and Mir's friendship was one of proximity: she knew he was friends with her only because she was his girlfriend's best friend. Jamie and Raleigh had been together for a year, and Mir was still trying to adjust to his presence. She always felt a little uneasy when he was around. Jamie had sharp edges, and sometimes Mir seemed to catch on them.

Jamie linked hands with Raleigh, and the two of them sat on the sand next to Miriam. Evan sat on Mir's other side, still glistening from the lake water.

"It's too cold for swimming, Evan," said Jamie. "You'll freeze your tiny brain."

"Brains are like fleshy computers," Evan said. "And computers work best in a cold environment. Therefore, my brain will be improved by the coldness of the water."

"If you talked smart like that to the teachers at school they'd stop trying to put you in the special class," Jamie said.

Evan grinned and looked out over the lake, resting his forearms on his knees. He always deflected Jamie's needling that way: get in, make a quick joke, then smile and retreat. And Jamie would let him be, which from Jamie was a sign of friendship.

"Why aren't you working, Mir? It's Wednesday. You always

work on Wednesday," Jamie said. Raleigh had her arm draped over him, comfortable and adorable.

"Berg gave me the afternoon off," Mir said. Berg had actually given her the whole week off, stopping her as she stepped into the maintenance closet to change into her work uniform. He had seemed distracted, like something was bothering him but he couldn't bring himself to say out loud what it was.

"Do you want—um . . ." Berg had trailed off. Mir waited, one hand on the closet doorknob, the other clutching her threadbare Emporium of Wonders T-shirt.

"It's nice out today," Berg continued. "I don't think the store will be busy. Why don't you take the afternoon off? You can go do something with your friends. Enjoy the spring weather."

Lately the Emporium of Wonders had been quiet, even for the lull before the beginning of tourism season. All week, only a handful of customers had wandered into the store, and most hadn't bought anything.

"Is everything okay?" Mir asked Berg. There was something upsetting in the way he wouldn't quite look at her.

"Everything will be fine," Berg said. He smiled. "Things are just slow now, and there's no point in you coming in. We have a new shipment of TomorrowMen merchandise coming in next week, so business should pick up then. That stuff always flies off the shelves." And he had continued to smile in a way that Miriam didn't like.

"I haven't seen Berg since he had that vegetable stand at the farmers' market," Raleigh said now, resting the side of her cheek against Jamie's shoulder. Mir still remembered the day Raleigh told her she'd seen a new boy in her English class, a boy who was all edges, skinny, with dark hair and dark eyes. A boy who didn't seem to pay attention, but always had the right answer when the teacher called on him. He'd said hello to Raleigh as he'd passed by her in the hall the next day, and Raleigh had breathlessly relayed the encounter to Miriam. Mir had listened, smiling but feeling slightly queasy. First it had been only her and Raleigh. Then they'd added Evan. Maybe adding a fourth would make things very different for Raleigh and Mir.

Evan smoothed out his towel and lay down on it, reaching into his messenger bag. He pulled out a well-thumbed comic— *New TomorrowMen* #67—and flipped it open, bending the pages back at the spine. Miriam lay down beside him, looking up at the comic. She liked the artwork in this issue, superhero faces drawn with graceful black lines, fine details left to the imagination.

"Who drew this, Evan?"

"Stuart Samuel," Evan said. "I like his art a lot. He drew a reboot of *Daredevil* for Marvel a few years ago, and after that he drew a TomorrowMen spin-off comic about Tristan Terrific. Now he's drawing the main book."

"Which one is Tristan Terrific? Is he the one who can teleport through time?" Raleigh asked.

"No," said Evan patiently, "that's the Mage of Ages."

"Comics are so weird." Raleigh sighed.

"Comics are incredibly weird," said Evan. "That's why they're awesome."

41

"I liked the TomorrowMen animated show when I was a kid," said Raleigh.

"Which show? *The TomorrowMen: Earth's Mighty Defenders*, *TomorrowMen GO!*, or *TomorrowMen Through Time*?"

"Oh my god, Evan," groaned Jamie. "I'd call you a nerd, but I know you like that."

"Nerds run the world," Evan declared. "Because of nerds, we get five superhero movies a year. And there's going to be a TomorrowMen movie next year."

Evan turned to Mir.

"You're going to see the movie, right?"

Mir stared at her feet, wishing he hadn't asked her that.

"I'm not sure—"

"But you have to!" Evan said, his face bright and earnest. Mir cringed, willing him to stop talking about the TomorrowMen movie. "You have history with those characters! Your grandfather literally created most of them!"

"Wait, what?" said Jamie, his gaze darting toward Mir. Beside him, Raleigh sighed, pressing her face into the hollow of Jamie's shoulder.

"I've told you about this before, I swear I did," Raleigh said. Jamie was frowning, still staring at Mir. She looked back at him, unnerved by the intensity of his gaze.

"No. Or if you did, I don't remember."

"Years and years ago, Mir's grandfather drew the very first TomorrowMen comics," said Raleigh, her voice nonchalant. "Mir told us back in, what? Sixth grade? You should've seen

Evan's face when he found out. I thought his head was going to explode."

"It's not a big deal," Mir said.

"It's absolutely a big deal!" Evan roared. He was already climbing to his feet, arms spread wide, intent on telling the story. Mir watched him with growing horror.

"Listen well, and hear the story of the TomorrowMen! How Joseph Warrick, writer of the TomorrowMen, was born in New York, the only son of immigrant parents from Poland. He grew up on the hardscrabble streets of New York, as the world rebuilt itself after World War Two."

"Why am I imagining the cast of *Annie*?" said Raleigh, grinning.

"But when Joseph Warrick was ten, his family moved to none other than Sandford, Nova Scotia. There he met a young artist, Micah Kendrick, grandfather of our very own Miriam Kendrick! Little did these two men know that together they would create one of the most popular and long-running comic books in the world: *The TomorrowMen*!"

Evan struck a classic superhero pose, fists on his hips, chest thrust out.

"Skybound! Leader of the TomorrowMen! An ordinary American soldier experimented on by his own government, he defied the cruel organization that gave him superstrength and chose to use his superpowers for good."

Evan changed his pose, teetering on one leg, arms extended in front of him like he was flying.

"Skylark! An alien queen who came to Earth to warn us of an impending threat. She fell in love with Skybound and abandoned her empire to stay with him. Superpowers: flight, the ability to harness energy into psionic bursts, looking really good in spandex."

"Sexist," Raleigh snorted.

Evan pressed two fingers to his temples, glowering down at Raleigh, Jamie, and Mir. Mir smirked despite herself. He looked ridiculous.

"Tristan Terrific! A former villain with the power of pure persuasion. He can convince a person to do anything just by talking to them. He caused all sorts of trouble for Skybound and Skylark before changing his ways and joining their side."

"Wasn't there also a teleporting wizard?" said Jamie.

"I'm getting to him. The Mage of Ages! A New York businessman plucked from the modern day and whisked back to the era of King Arthur, he uses the magic of Excalibur to teleport through time."

"And I guess they're called the TomorrowMEN because they're pretty much all dudes," Raleigh said.

"There are other members of the team, some of them women, but they switch in and out," admitted Evan. "Skybound, Skylark, Tristan Terrific, and the Mage of Ages are the core four."

"And your grandfather created them," Jamie said, his eyes narrowed at Mir. His tone was light, but Mir thought she saw suspicion in his glance.

"Co-created," she said. "But, I mean, it's not a big deal—"

"It's such a big deal," Evan muttered defiantly, resuming his heroic pose, fists on his hips, staring out over the lake. "It is the biggest deal."

Mir sighed, looking downward at the sand underneath her feet.

"I never got to meet my grandfather," she said. "He died a few years before I was born. My mom's told me a bit about him, though. He drew lots of comics, not just the TomorrowMen."

Mir remembered the first time she'd seen a photo of her grandfather in a book about the history of superhero comics. He looked shockingly young, smiling and standing next to an equally young Joseph Warrick. There was only one photo of her grandfather at home, a small framed family portrait of him, her grandmother, and a very young Stella held between them. Micah Kendrick looked so much older in that photo, as though something had been taken from him. A year ago Mir had searched for her grandfather's name online, and discovered pages of links to a court case settled ten years earlier, when Micah Kendrick's daughter, Stella, ended a twenty-year legal battle over the rights to the TomorrowMen with the TomorrowMen's longtime publisher, Warrick Comics. Micah Kendrick had died eight years before that.

"And now they're making a movie out of these comics," said Jamie, still looking at Mir with narrowed eyes. "I've been reading about it. Warrick Studios is worth millions, and when the TomorrowMen movie drops, they might be worth billions.

The merchandising alone makes them a ton of cash. You're not secretly a rich kid, are you? You haven't been hiding that from us all these years?"

All these years? Mir thought. *You've been a part of this group for a year. Next to Raleigh and Evan, you don't know me at all.*

"I'm not a rich kid," said Mir. "My family doesn't get anything from the TomorrowMen merchandise or the movie. There was a legal case over the rights to the characters years ago, but my mom settled with Warrick Studios after my grandfather died."

"Settled," said Jamie. His face seemed sharper than usual, and Mir thought she caught a note of disgust in his voice. "Warrick Studios must've paid a lot of money to make your family go away."

Mir made a show of adjusting her sitting position, carefully folding her legs underneath her. Raleigh looked worried, glancing from her boyfriend to Mir. Mir knew Raleigh's expression; she hated it when there was weirdness in the group. *When it was just the three of us there was never any weirdness*, Mir thought, picking at a blade of grass so she wouldn't have to look at Jamie.

"I don't know—I don't think it was that much money. I know my parents bought our house with what they got from the settlement, but . . ." Mir's voice trailed off.

Jamie chuckled, the sound like a knife scraping on pavement.

"Your mom doesn't even have to work. She does those

paintings, which she sells for like zero dollars. I mean, both my parents work, and they don't own their own house."

Mir stared at him, not sure what to say. A slick, awful feeling sloshed in her stomach. Jamie's gaze seemed to pin her against the sky.

"I'm not rich," Mir said. Her words felt thin and ineffectual.

Jamie continued to stare at her, then turned away, leaning his cheek against the top of Raleigh's head.

"I guess not," he said. "If you were a rich kid, your parents probably wouldn't still have dial-up internet. At least my parents have high speed."

Raleigh laughed, which Mir knew was her choosing to believe the moment of weirdness had passed. She wrapped her arms tighter around Jamie's torso, and in the early evening light they seemed to fuse together. Mir forced the edges of her mouth up in a semblance of a smile. She glanced at Evan, who was staring at Jamie. Evan caught Mir's eye, but didn't smile.

He can see how messed up things are too, Mir thought. She looked away, staring over the tops of the pine trees on the other side of the lake.

CHAPTER FIVE

Weldon's phone rang at 1:45 a.m. He jerked awake, startled, then lunged for the phone on the side table beside his bed. He stared at the phone, unable to read the call display, then put it to his ear.

"Hello?"

"Hey, kiddo, it's me," Emma Sanders said. Weldon closed his eyes, cradling the phone by his ear. Of course it was his mom. She was the only person who would call without thinking about the four-hour time difference between Nova Scotia and California. He should've called her the day he'd landed in Sandford, but he'd been so angry about her refusing to let him spend the summer with her. He hated being angry with her.

"Sorry I didn't call earlier. I was having some problems with—anyway, it doesn't matter."

"It's fine," said Weldon. "I'm glad you called."

"You're so forgiving of your forgetful mother," Weldon's mom chuckled. He could see her sitting at the table in her tiny kitchen in her tiny house in San Diego, her blond-going-ashy hair falling in a perfect cascade around her face. Weldon wondered if she'd changed anything in the house or if it still looked the same: faded patterned curtains hanging in the living room, cheap Formica toilet in the lone full bathroom.

"How're the Warricks?" Weldon's mom said. "Have they started counting down to the movie yet?"

"No," said Weldon. "Well, Dad's going kind of nuts. The trailer's premiering at Comic-Con and he's a little freaked out about it. Having a good initial trailer is really important, I guess."

"Gotta impress the nerds," Emma said, and Weldon felt her smile reach through the phone. He could tell she was in a listening mood, and his heart pulsed with joy.

"Certain nerds. Nerds with blogs. Important nerds."

"Remember when Comic-Con was just a room in a hotel, all these rickety little tables set up, vendors selling back issues for a nickel?"

"I remember when the back issues were a dollar," said Weldon.

"Oh, right," Emma laughed, and Weldon thrilled at the warmth in her voice. "I forget how young you are, kiddo. You've only known that massive convention center, choked full of cosplayers and people who don't even read comics. All the fake nerds."

"Everyone's a nerd nowadays," said Weldon.

"No, honey," Emma said. "They aren't nerds the way I was a nerd."

Emma Sanders was a science fiction movie queen, the star of dozens of low-budget movies from the eighties and nineties. Weldon remembered bits and pieces from his childhood, his mother gone for days, coming home to San Diego with smears of blue makeup in the creases behind her ears. "I've showered twice since I got off work and it still won't all come off," she would laugh, shaking her perfect cascade of blond hair. Emma Sanders was tall but delicate, like a much smaller person stretched out over an Amazon's frame. Weldon remembered the way his dad reached for her when she came home, the way they affectionately folded into each other. He always felt left out, and would wind his way around their legs as they embraced, looking up at them anxiously. "I missed you," his father would whisper to his mother. "Someday I'll be in Los Angeles too. We'll move all of Warrick Comics there. When we make the TomorrowMen movie, we'll change the name and call it Warrick Studios."

In his aunt and uncle's guest room in Sandford, Weldon squeezed his eyes shut, loneliness pressing him downward.

"Oh yeah?" Weldon said. "You want to nerd fight? Okay, name me the first appearance of Tristan Terrific."

"Oh, honey," said Emma, "you are so foolish to tangle with me. Which Tristan Terrific? Because there's the original Tristan Terrific, and then there's Jordan Nash, who took over the mantle of Tristan Terrific after the original Tristan died fighting the planet-killing robot Ymir. Jordan Nash inherited Tristan

Terrific's power of pure persuasion when the original Tristan Terrific implanted his consciousness into an artificial brain."

Weldon rubbed the back of his wrist across his eyes and laughed.

"Mom, you are an entirely different class of nerd."

"A better class of nerd," Weldon's mother said.

Weldon pulled his wrist away from his eyes and stared at the ceiling. There was a shadow reaching along it, splintering across the cream expanse. Weldon remembered the lie Emma had told him three years ago, when she left Los Angeles and moved back to her tiny house in San Diego: "Your dad and I . . . we just need a little time apart." There had been lines on his mother's forehead as she'd told him she was leaving. She was no longer a towering, shining creature, a science fiction queen of the cinema. She was a woman with sorrow etched on her face, who wrapped her arms tightly around her only son. He remembered the feeling of her chest heaving as she swallowed a sob. And then she left LA, the movie industry, and him.

"Psst, Charlie," his mother said, her voice tilted away from the phone. "Stop that, Charlie. Leave the couch alone." There was the sound of thumping in the background, followed by an irritated meow.

"Jeez, that cat is still around?" Weldon said. Charlie was Emma's overweight Persian, a yellow-eyed nightmare creature that communicated in a cascade of raspy meows. Charlie had been Emma's pet for as long as Weldon could remember, and he suspected the beast would outlive them all. Charlie had barely tolerated Weldon and David when they lived together as a family. Weldon suspected the cat was thrilled when his parents broke up: no more husband and son vying for Emma's affection.

"Still kicking. Better than a watchdog, my Charlie. He'd make short work of anyone who tried to set foot in this house without permission."

"I can believe it," Weldon said, thinking of Charlie's malevolent stare.

"Ah, kiddo, I miss you sometimes," sighed Emma.

"Miss you too," said Weldon, choosing to ignore the "sometimes." He squeezed his eyes shut, willing himself not to think badly of her. *She had to do what was right for her*, he thought. *She needed to leave LA, it's as simple as that. It had nothing to do with me.* But the words felt thin and hollow, and he didn't think he believed them.

"So, tell me about Sandford," Emma said.

Weldon sighed.

"It's boring."

"You need a little less excitement in your life, according to your father," Emma said.

Weldon cringed.

"Did he . . . um, tell you?"

"Yes, Weldon, he told me. We are still your parents, despite everything. I know you took a groundskeeper's cart without permission and drove it in doughnuts around a football field. Why would you do that?"

"I don't know," he said softly. "I hated that school."

There was silence on Emma's end of the phone. Weldon waited, holding his breath.

"I wish I could've spent the summer with you." It was the wrong thing to say. There was no sound on the other end of the phone, but he felt his mother fold up into herself, closing off her sympathy.

"I'm sorry I couldn't do that for you, kid," she said. There was ice in her voice.

"No, it's not—"

"Not my fault? Of course it is."

"Mom—"

"Your father made it clear it was most definitely my fault. You only started up with this nonsense after I left, according to him."

Weldon kept staring at the ceiling and tried to think of a way to unravel her anger. David Warrick was hot and loud when he was angry. Emma Sanders froze people out. Weldon remembered the fights they had in the last few years of their marriage, Emma silent and cold, his father always yelling. *You should have broken up a long time ago*, Weldon thought. *Then maybe you wouldn't hate each other so much. It's like you're each other's archnemeses.*

"I joined a running group yesterday," Weldon said, hoping a change in subject would distract his mother.

"Hm," said Emma, not particularly distracted.

"They do 5Ks and 10Ks in the big park by the river. I'm going to try to do a regular 10K this summer."

"That'd be good for you," Emma said. The ice in her voice was starting to melt, replaced by weariness. Weldon suspected she knew he was trying to deflect.

"Are you still running?"

"Of course," Emma said. "Can't get fat, not if I want to start working again. Not allowed if you act for a living. No aging either." She laughed lightly, but he heard the sadness behind it. She hadn't acted since breaking up with David Warrick and moving away from Los Angeles. He clenched a fist and ground it into his eye socket. Every subject was a minefield with his mother. He was never sure what would remind her of some horrible thing or some sad thing. Or his father.

"Do you still run at the San Diego waterfront?" Weldon said. "By the convention center?" He was hanging on to the conversation by a fingernail. At any moment his mother would change her mind about talking to him and put down the phone. Even when he was little, she never seemed to want him around the way most kids' moms did. It was as though her son was an amusing sidekick: fun to have around on occasion, but not an essential part of her narrative. Weldon always felt like he was chasing her, desperate to prove to her that he was interesting and integral. *Maybe I did start getting into trouble when she left*, Weldon thought. *Maybe I thought it was something she might find interesting.* He wished he didn't care so much about her opinion of him. It was the distance between them that made him care; he was always reaching for her, Emma always pulling away.

"Sometimes," said Emma, her voice thoughtful. "I have a lot

of good memories of that convention. It's nice to remember sometimes."

"Yeah," said Weldon.

"Kid, I gotta go," said Emma. Weldon's heart lurched.

"Okay," he said. *At least she doesn't sound angry anymore*, he thought.

"Be good, kid."

"Okay," said Weldon. The connection went dead on the other end.

Weldon swung his legs over the side of the bed and sat there, staring at the inoffensive cream walls in his aunt and uncle's spare bedroom. After a few minutes he stood, dressed in jeans and a T-shirt, laced up his running shoes, and slipped out the bedroom door.

The house was quiet. Weldon walked carefully down the stairs toward the front door. Nothing creaked as he moved, the plush carpet draping everything in silence. In the foyer, Weldon paused, looking around. There was a small table with a basket of odds and ends pushed against the wall to his right. On top of the pile of gum packets, receipts, and bills were his uncle's car keys. Weldon carefully plucked the keys from the basket. They jingled slightly, the tiny noise reverberating throughout the silent house. Weldon held his breath. No other noise followed.

The front door opened silently. He stood on the front steps of the house and looked out over his aunt and uncle's lawn. It shone wet and dewy under the down-turned sliver of the moon. Weldon felt strangely calm, as he always did when he'd made up his mind to do something terrible. He was caught in the inevitability of the moment, no other path to take but the one in front of him.

Weldon walked toward his uncle's car. It was a large SUV, glowing silver in the half-light. Weldon stuck the key in the lock and opened the door, swinging into the driver's seat. He popped the parking brake and slid the car into neutral. It rolled silently down the gentle slope of his aunt and uncle's driveway. On the road, Weldon turned on the engine and pulled away from the house. The neighborhood was cloaked in moonlight, houses with curtains drawn over their windows like closed eyelids. Weldon leaned back in the driver's seat, adjusting the incline of the chair slightly. No one was awake to see him leave.

Weldon guided the car in a lazy loop through the neighborhood, passing house after sleeping house. The bridge into town lay before him, the water underneath it black and endless. He slowed the SUV as he drove across the bridge, bringing it to a stop in the middle. Weldon rolled down the car window and leaned out. Above him hung the moon, carved to a sickle shape. The river slid by, ignoring him. He could see a few lights ahead in Sandford's tiny downtown, and there were several large streetlamps attached to the bridge. But here in the exact middle of the bridge there was nothing but blackness. Weldon looked at the river for a few more seconds, then put the car into gear and drove across the bridge.

Weldon didn't see a single person as he drove down

Sandford's main street. No late-night partyers, no homeless people trying to stay warm in some corner, no one who'd worked the night shift and was now on their way home. He was completely alone.

Out of the corner of his eye, Weldon saw a flash of red and yellow. He stepped on the brake and the SUV obligingly jerked to a halt. It was the Skybound poster in the window of the sad little geek store. There was a small spotlight illuminating the poster, and the bright colors of Skybound's costume blazed in the dim storefront. Weldon steered the SUV over to the side of the road and stared hard at the poster. Technically it was a fantastic drawing, every detail lovingly rendered. Skybound's cape seemed to flap in the wind, every muscle in his body etched with precision. Weldon thought of the painting he'd bought, the quick brushstrokes patterned across the faces of Skylark and Skybound. When he peered closely at the painting, the brushstrokes broke apart and became individual color blobs, but when he stood back, everything combined into a beautiful whole. He thought he liked his painting better than this realistically rendered poster.

I'd like to see that girl again, Weldon thought.

Weldon turned away from the geek store, looking at his hands on the SUV's steering wheel. He still had time, hours before anyone woke up and saw what he'd done. He could return the car and try to find that girl, and solve the mystery of why she'd suddenly wanted nothing to do with him. *But . . . I'm already here*, Weldon thought. *I've stolen this car. I'm going to get caught in the morning and then things will happen. This is what I've decided to do.* Weldon waited, still looking at the steering wheel, rolling the idea around in his head. He glanced to his right and saw the red and yellow of Skybound's costume. *Be good, kid*, Emma Sanders whispered.

Weldon turned the steering wheel and drove the SUV back across the bridge. He cringed at the noise of the engine as he drove the car up the gently sloping driveway, but nothing in the house stirred. He put his uncle's car keys back in the basket by the front door and slipped into his bedroom. The clock on the nightstand read 3:14 a.m. He'd been gone barely longer than an hour.

He didn't think he'd sleep, but when the clock flipped over to 5:00 a.m., Weldon was facedown in his bed, snoring softly.

CHAPTER SIX

Mir stood outside Sandford High School, a feeling of dread settling over her shoulders. Evan had called her last night, after Mir had returned home from the lake. He had been brief: "I'm starting to think it's really screwed up how Jamie keeps picking on you." Mir had tried to laugh, but she was relieved that someone other than her had seen it.

"It's not a big deal," she'd said.

"Yeah, it kinda is," Evan said. "He's not mean to Raleigh, but he's mean to you, and that's messed up."

"He's mean to you too," Mir pointed out.

"He just thinks I'm an idiot and I think he's full of shit. Plus, we're both guys." Mir could almost hear Evan's nonchalant shrug through the phone line. "It's different with you. You're Raleigh's best friend. You've known her forever, and her boyfriend picks on you any chance he gets. It's a lot messed up, Mir."

Mir hadn't said anything. She'd just stood in her parents' kitchen, winding the cord of the old landline phone around her hand.

"It doesn't matter, Evan," Mir said finally. She'd stared at the knot of phone cord twisted around her hand. *That's my parents*, she'd thought. *So tightfisted they can't even spring for a cordless phone. They cost, what, thirty dollars? But I bet this ancient contraption was free.*

"It does matter," Evan said. "We're Raleigh's friends. We should matter."

She would choose him over us, Mir thought, then felt wretched for thinking so little of Raleigh's loyalty.

"I gotta go, Evan. See you tomorrow."

———

Mir stared at the school entrance, hands tight on her backpack straps. She'd see Raleigh at her locker, unless Mir went straight to class. But she always put her coat and extra books away before first period, and it would be obvious to Raleigh that she was being avoided if Mir wasn't there.

Mir squared her shoulders and stepped into the stream of students heading toward the school.

Raleigh was waiting by Mir's locker, swaying anxiously from foot to foot. Her round face split into a relieved grin when she saw Mir.

"Hey!"

"Hi," Mir said, using the motion of taking off her jacket to avoid eye contact with Raleigh.

"You're okay, right? Things felt kind of weird yesterday," Raleigh said, reaching out to touch Mir's arm.

"Yeah, I'm fine," Mir said. The cheerfulness sounded hollow to her ears, but maybe Raleigh couldn't tell. Raleigh beamed, and Mir could practically smell the anxiety radiating from her friend.

"I just wanted to make sure. Last night . . . it was just weird. You know Jamie doesn't mean anything, right? He's just kinda blunt sometimes."

"It's okay, Raleigh," Mir said. "It's fine. For real."

"Good, I'm glad," Raleigh said.

It isn't okay, Mir thought, packing her afternoon schoolbooks into the locker. *Nothing about this is okay. You're my best friend, so why can't I tell you that?*

Mir caught a glimpse of herself in the small mirror she'd taped to the locker door. She'd wound her hair up into a bun this morning, pulling it back tightly. She'd felt like she needed the hairdo, something that wasn't her usual messy-hair-somewhat-constrained-by-a-ponytail look. Stella had sensed something was off, and dug a small jar of styling gel out from the linen closet, wordlessly working over Mir's hair so every piece of it was tucked perfectly into the bun.

Raleigh fell into step with her.

"What book are you reading in Advanced English?" Raleigh asked.

"*The Stone Angel*. Just finished it this morning," Mir lied. She'd finished it two weeks ago, several days after it was assigned. Mir and Raleigh hadn't been in the same classes since grade nine, when Mir went into the advanced stream and Raleigh remained behind in the general stream. Mir remembered how lonely it had been to start grade ten without Raleigh sitting next to her, as she had all throughout elementary school. The first few weeks she kept looking to her left, expecting to see Raleigh's familiar shape beside her. They would see each other at lunch and after school and on the weekends, but it hadn't been the same. And now there was Jamie pulling Raleigh even farther away, in a way that felt permanent.

"Was it boring?"

"Yeah, pretty much," said Mir, forcing out a laugh. "It was a book about an angry old woman who lives in Manitoba. Riveting stuff." *It was, kinda*, Mir thought. *All I could feel while I read was this woman's regret and her anger. It was amazing.*

"You make school look so easy," said Raleigh. "I remember in grade nine, you read all of *Brave New World* in an afternoon. I thought the teacher's eyes were going to fall out of his head when you told him."

"It's only, like, two hundred pages," Mir said. "And I was really bored that night. The only source of entertainment at my house besides reading is gardening, and that's way too much work for me."

"Whenever you came over to my place to watch TV, you'd get completely mesmerized. I had to practically yell your name before you'd hear me," Raleigh said. "It didn't matter what show we watched, you were enthralled. Even those tacky old game shows were like magic to you. God forbid anything get between you and *The Price is Right*."

Mir laughed. She remembered her feeling of awe when she first sat in front of Raleigh's towering television, how the images on the screen closed off the world around her, making everything else inconsequential. She remembered the look of amusement on Raleigh's face when she finally turned toward her. "Seriously, Mir," Raleigh had said. "I said your name like five times. You didn't hear me?"

"I don't have any defense against TV," Mir said now. "If I had regular access, I'd sit in front of the screen all day, every day, and do absolutely nothing else. So maybe it's good I don't have one."

"Maybe it is," Raleigh said. "Because then you wouldn't have the excuse to practically live at my place."

"My best memories are of sitting in front of your TV, completely in thrall to its power," Mir said.

"Oh, Mir, that's just so sad," laughed Raleigh, pressing her hands to her face in mock despair. Mir smiled and with all her might willed the weirdness of last night to be wiped clean. But the feeling of it remained, a current of unease running beneath the sound of Raleigh's laughter.

The first bell rang and the halls swelled with students. Mir and Raleigh pushed past a group of ninth graders standing in a semicircle, their heads bent over their phones. *First thing I do when*

I grow up is get a phone and high-speed internet and cable television, Mir thought. *Five million channels, I want every single one of them.*

Mir and Raleigh climbed the stairs leading to the school's upper level, where all the English classes met, both the general and advanced streams. Raleigh turned to say goodbye to Mir, then hesitated, thinking about something.

"I swear I used to enjoy reading when I was a kid," Raleigh said. "Then I got to high school. Why can't we have an English class on *The Princess Diaries* or *Goosebumps* or *The Magic Tree House?* Or any of the manga we read when we were twelve? I could discuss the literary merit of *Fruits Basket* for hours. Then we could both be in the same classes."

"I remember you sneaking me those *Goosebumps* books," Mir said. Raleigh laughed.

"I was your crappy horror book dealer. Wanna buy the latest R. L. Stine? I can hook you up." Raleigh mimed opening a trench coat, illicit literary wares on display. "Hot off the press."

"My mom hated those books," Mir sighed. "She got so excited when she found out I was reading *The Stone Angel.* She thinks Margaret Laurence is the ultimate Canadian writer."

"But look what it got you," said Raleigh, and her voice almost sounded wistful. "You had a mom who pushed you to be better, and now you're the one in the advanced classes. You're going to university. You'll leave us all behind."

Mir stared at Raleigh, surprised.

"Raleigh, I would never—"

Mir's English teacher walked briskly past her toward the

classroom, trailing loose-leaf paper and randomly escaping pens. Mr. Kean had an impressive walrus mustache and was one of the few teachers who could elicit participation out of a class of sleepy first-period eleventh graders. He was a legend.

"You've gotta go," said Raleigh. She turned and walked away from Mir. Mir watched her go, uneasy.

During second period, Mir had an appointment with the school guidance counselor. She arrived seven minutes early and sat in the small waiting room outside Ms. Archer's door, turning her tattered school copy of *The Stone Angel* over and over in her hands. On the inside of the back cover of the book, someone had written *this book is fucking stupid* in pencil. Mir dug through her backpack and pulled out an eraser, scrubbing at the words until only a faint impression of them remained.

Ms. Archer's door opened, and she stuck her head out, smiling at Mir.

"Come on in, Miriam."

Mir dumped her backpack on one of the two chairs opposite Ms. Archer's desk and plopped herself in the other one.

"How've you been?" Ms. Archer looked up at Mir, the lines around her eyes crinkling warmly. Mir smiled back. She'd always liked Ms. Archer. She liked the counselor's short, matter-of-fact haircut, her practical footwear, and the vibrant, patterned sweaters she often wore.

"Fine, Ms. Archer," Mir said.

"School going well?"

"Yep. Same as always."

"Your grades reflect that. You've done amazing work this year, Miriam, excelling in many subjects. Which is why I wanted to see you. I wanted to ask if you've given any consideration to university or college."

Mir stared at her knees. *You'll leave us all behind*, Raleigh whispered in the back of her mind, and Mir felt cold. She remembered her first day of grade ten, feeling lost in a classroom without Raleigh beside her. It had been nearly two years since their paths split, but Mir always believed they'd meet up again, maybe on the other side of high school. They had been friends for so long Mir couldn't remember herself without Raleigh. Mir had read a thousand *Goosebumps* novels with her, competing to see who could finish their book first. They had watched thousands of hours of cheesy game show TV together, the rest of the world walled off and unimportant.

But she thinks I'm going to leave, Mir thought, and her chest felt hollow with loneliness. *I don't even know what I want to do after high school, but she thinks I've already made my decision. How could she think that?*

"I don't know," she finally said.

"Can you tell me what subjects you're most interested in?" Ms. Archer asked. "You've done a lot of English courses, and you've done very well in all of them. You've also kept up with biology, though not so much with the math."

"I like things . . ." Mir hesitated. "I guess I like subjects where I can use words to explain things. I want to keep going with some math so I can have those credits, but I don't like it as much."

"Using words, all right," Ms. Archer said. "You might want to consider a general bachelor's degree, Miriam. That will allow you to take many different subjects and discover what you're genuinely interested in pursuing."

Mir looked down again. Words were crowding her throat, and she swallowed hard, forcing them downward.

"I don't know," she said again. Ms. Archer looked up at her, curious. "University's expensive."

"There is assistance available to exceptional students who demonstrate financial need. There's also the possibility of scholarships."

"Everyone I know is staying here after graduation," Mir whispered. "I'd have to leave Sandford if I wanted to go to university."

Ms. Archer leaned toward Mir, who stared at her knees, ashamed of the kindness in the guidance counselor's face.

"Would leaving be so bad?" Ms. Archer said.

Mir thought of Raleigh. She imagined leaving to attend school in Toronto or Montreal. She imagined coming home for summer break and seeing Raleigh walking past her on the street, face closed and unwelcoming, one hand looped through Jamie's arm.

Maybe it would be, Mir thought.

CHAPTER SEVEN

Saturday morning broke gray and overcast. Weldon was woken at 7:00 a.m. by the sound of his uncle hauling his riding lawn mower out of the garage. Weldon lay in bed for another half hour, staring at the ceiling and listening to the roar of the mower before finally pulling himself out of bed. His aches from the fight were mostly gone, but his eye was healing slowly. When he looked in the mirror, he was startled at how angry the dark purple bruise made him look.

Weldon dressed for running. He thought about Ellie and the way her eyes had skimmed admiringly over him when he'd entered the running store. She was cute and might be fun to hang out with. She didn't seem that much older than him.

He was lacing up his running shoes when the painting, still leaning against the side table by the bed, caught his eye. Weldon pulled the painting from behind the table, peering at it. Skylark in particular was painted with exquisite care. The alien queen's hair was swept upward, brown mixed with purple and the smallest touch of gold. Her face looked alive, eyes wide, staring boldly. Weldon remembered the girl he had bought the painting from (Miriam, he reminded himself). He hadn't lied to Miriam; he did really love Skylark and Skybound's original costumes. There was something tough but seductive about the cut of Skylark's bodysuit and the tall boots she wore. Weldon drew his thumb across the swirl of Skylark's hair, tracing the upward curve of it. There was something almost familiar about the alien queen's face.

Outside, the lawn mower stuttered, then started up again. Weldon returned the painting to its spot beside his night table and walked downstairs.

In the kitchen, Weldon ate a bowl of cereal and fended off his aunt's concern.

"Your eye isn't healing very quickly, is it? The doctor did say there wasn't anything to do but leave it alone . . ." His aunt sighed. To Weldon's relief, she kept her hands to herself. He was tired of her manhandling his face.

"It really doesn't hurt, Aunt Kay," Weldon said, trying to eat and talk at the same time. "Bruises take a while to heal."

"It's so terrible to look at," his aunt said. Her hands fluttered at her waist, as though they itched to grasp his face and turn it every which way. *You stay over there for another five minutes, then I can escape*, Weldon thought. His spoon clattered in his empty bowl, and he stood up.

"How long will your run be?" his aunt asked.

"Not long," Weldon said. "It's only a 5K, so twenty minutes

over to the park, half an hour for the run, and twenty minutes for the run back. An hour and a half, maybe?"

His aunt nodded, pleased.

"I'm glad you found a running group. I hope they're good to you."

"I'm sure they will be," Weldon said, thinking of Ellie's runner's body.

He jogged into town, the exercise fading his annoyance over being woken up early. A small group of runners was already gathered at the park when he arrived. He walked casually in circles at the edge of the group as they pretended not to notice him.

"Hey," said Ellie, appearing behind him. "Good to see you came out to join us."

"I did," Weldon said, nodding at her. She smiled, and he noticed she had freckles dusted across the bridge of her nose. She turned toward the group of runners, who were now eyeing Weldon with open suspicion.

"Hey, guys, this is Weldon," Ellie said, gesturing at him. "He's new. He'll be running with us today, and maybe a few other days. If he likes us." Weldon thought she'd turn and smirk at him after saying that line, but she didn't. *All business*, Weldon thought approvingly.

Ellie sketched out the running route for him while the other runners fidgeted impatiently, eager to start. The route was easy enough: through the park, along the river, down the waterfront, and up the main road of Sandford to conclude at the Running Realm. Five point three K, no problem at all.

"Got it?" Ellie said, and when Weldon nodded, she flashed him a wide grin and jogged off. The group of runners snapped into ordered rows and ran after Ellie in near-unison. Weldon followed, content to trail behind the pack.

The park was a large wooded area between a residential area of Sandford and the river. The running group circled the park once, then jogged beside the river, heading back into town. The gravel path gave way to wooden planks, and finally a boardwalk rose up before them, dotted with the occasional early morning walker. There were half a dozen ship berths, filled with ships of varying historical accuracy. Most advertised cruises on the river, where you could enjoy the historic sight of Sandford from the vantage point of the water. Weldon suspected that by the time the ships got out far enough to appreciate Sandford's historic skyline, most of the passengers would be too drunk to enjoy the view. Right now the ships were empty, bobbing gently in their berths as they waited for tourist season.

Ellie picked up the pace as they ran along the boardwalk. She turned toward the heart of town, and the group streamed behind her like the tail of a kite. Out of the corner of his eye, Weldon spotted a familiar figure. His step hitched and he slowed. The group of runners continued on, leaving him behind.

Miriam was walking along the boardwalk, trailing behind two people: a woman with a shaved head and a bearded man with blond hair. They were obviously a couple, holding hands and stopping to consult whenever something on the boardwalk interested them. Ahead of them, a boy about twelve years old ran down the waterfront, his dark curly hair bouncing with each step.

Weldon glanced after the running group. They were a half block away from him by now, Ellie's ponytail bobbing gently, a beacon worth following. He hesitated. He had wanted to see Miriam again. And there she was, right in front of him, a coincidence he couldn't pass up. He turned and walked toward Miriam's family.

———

Mir watched her parents inspecting a vendor's wares on the harbor boardwalk, feeling deeply annoyed with them. Stella had woken her up at an ungodly hour, insisting it was going to be a beautiful day and the entire family should go down to the waterfront market. Mir had allowed herself to be dragged along, bouncing sleepily in the backseat of Henry's truck, while Nate talked endlessly about the cartoons he'd watched the past week at his best friend Eli's house.

At the waterfront, Mir watched her parents wander from one vendor to another, her sleepiness deepening to grumpiness. Did they have to hold hands everywhere they went? Did her dad have to make stupid jokes that made her mom roar with laughter? Did they have to be so couple-y all the time?

Mir glowered at the back of her dad's head. There was a photo of her parents on their wedding day, framed and hung in the hallway of their house: Henry in a goofy 1970s suit, although it was years past the seventies, Stella with her shaved head, wearing a snug red dress. When she was little, Miriam had asked: "Why red? Why not white?" Stella replied: "I look good in red." They always had to be different.

"Miriam, hi," said a voice behind her.

Mir turned, stared, and Weldon Warrick stared back.

Oh, no, Mir thought.

Weldon beamed at her. He was sweaty and glowing. He'd probably been running, Mir guessed, glancing at his sneakers and shorts. He looked mostly healed from the fight the previous weekend, although his eye was still puffy and purple. His hair was awfully cute, the longer top part of it flopping down into his eyes. Mir had to admit he looked pretty good.

"Hi," Mir said grudgingly. *Curse you, Canadian genes*, she seethed inwardly. *I always have to be so polite.*

"Nice to see you again," Weldon said. "Especially under better circumstances. Is that your family?" He pointed at her parents' backs and at Nate, who was waving furiously at one of the boats pushing away from the dock.

"Yes," said Mir.

They stood opposite each other in silence for a good ten seconds, Mir counting the seconds down, Weldon smiling winningly at her the whole time. *I bet he's never had an awkward moment in his entire life*, Mir thought, gritting her teeth.

"I wanted to thank you," Weldon said finally. "I didn't get a chance to, at the store. After that stuff with those guys. What you did to break up the fight."

Mir shifted in place, staring at Weldon.

Weldon stopped smiling. He looked away and scrubbed at the back of his head with his hand. The gesture seemed genuine and awkward.

"You were like . . . I don't know, you were like a superhero, going to the rescue of some idiot who didn't deserve it."

"I'm not a superhero," Mir said. "Superheroes are the worst. Have you seen what they do when they supposedly save the day? Whole cities, smashed to bits. Imagine being that one person who was working late and suddenly you get your head bashed in by falling debris because Skybound punched a robot through your office building."

Weldon looked startled. The hand he'd raised to the back of his head hovered uncertainly in place. Mir was surprised at the words that had come out of her mouth. She wasn't really sure she believed what she'd just said. Up until this point, she'd thought superheroes were pretty okay.

"Miriam, who's your friend?" said Stella. Mir grimaced, then turned toward her parents. They were standing arm in arm, Henry holding a brightly colored paper parasol over his head, some cheap thing he'd probably bought from a harbor-front vendor. Henry collected tourist-bait tchotchkes that cluttered up their home until Stella threw them away or Nate buried them in the backyard, never to be seen again.

Mir waved a hand at Weldon, resigned to making the introduction.

"Mom, Dad, this is Weldon Warrick. Weldon Warrick, this is my mom and dad. I guess you can call them Henry and Stella."

"Hello! I'm Stella," beamed Mir's dad. "It's fantastic to meet you, Weldon."

"My dad thinks he's funny," said Mir.

"What did you say your name was?" Stella asked.

"Weldon Warrick," Weldon said. Mir saw he was waiting for the connection, expecting some exclamation of surprise, a confession of love for the TomorrowMen comics, excitement about the upcoming movie.

"Oh," said Stella, her voice very small. She looked away from Henry, who glanced down at her, uncomprehending. In a rush Henry understood, and his head snapped up. He stared at Weldon, astonished.

"You're—"

"You're David's son," Stella finished for him. For a moment she looked sad, then gathered herself and smiled at Weldon. Weldon looked confused.

"You know my dad?" he asked. "Did you know him when he was a teenager? He used to live in Sandford. I think he left pretty soon after high school graduation . . ."

"Your grandfather knew my father," said Stella. "He created the TomorrowMen with my father, Micah Kendrick."

"What?" said Weldon. He stared at Stella, his mouth hanging open in a perfect O shape. Mir felt the tiniest spark of sympathy for him.

"So I guess we have a bit of history," Stella said. "We're related through comics. Are you visiting Alex and Katherine? Is that why you're in Sandford?"

"No, I——" Weldon stared at her, his eyebrows beating a hasty retreat up his forehead. "I mean, yes, I'm visiting—no, wait, I'm staying with them. For the summer. Because, um, well, my dad's busy because there's going to be a movie——"

"I heard about that," said Stella. "A movie about the TomorrowMen. I think that's wonderful."

Weldon stared at her, clearly at a loss for what to say. He glanced at Mir, his eyebrows still skirting the border of his hairline. Mir shrugged. She wasn't about to help him out. Stella's eyes darted from Weldon to Mir.

"You two know each other? Miriam, you didn't tell me that."

Mir opened her mouth to explain, but Weldon spoke first.

"I went to that store? The one . . . um, I bought a painting. Um, from her. From Miriam," Weldon said, squinting at Mir as though he was trying to remember who she was. Mir stared back at him, trying her hardest to keep her expression impassive. Weldon's confusion was causing a bubble of nervous laughter to start working its way up from her stomach. She clenched her jaw in an effort to keep from breaking out in hysterics.

"Oh!" said Stella, suddenly delighted. "Miriam told me about you. You're the boy who bought my TomorrowMen painting. That makes so much more sense now. She told me you knew Skylark and Skybound's original costumes. Of course you did; you're a part of them."

"You painted the painting I bought," Weldon said. "The To-morrowMen painting." Each sentence was a statement, not a question, Weldon's brain trying to process the information.

"I did," Stella said. "This is so funny, you buying my painting. And now we're here, meeting for the first time. Isn't this funny, Miriam?"

"Hilarious," Mir said.

"Henry—" Stella turned toward her husband, who was watching the exchange from under the shade of his paper parasol. "I'd like to invite Weldon over for dinner sometime, feed him something good and maybe show him some more of my paintings. Does that sound okay?"

Henry shrugged, smiling. "Okay by me."

"Wait, what?" Mir said, the bubble of laughter dissolving in her stomach.

"Will you come over for dinner, Weldon?" Stella asked.

Weldon's gaze moved from Stella, to Henry, to Nate off in the distance, inspecting something at the edge of the boardwalk, before finally settling on Mir. Mir suspected her expression was a mask of horror, but she couldn't summon the energy to try to hide it.

"You'd . . . really like me to come to your house?"

"I really would," said Stella.

"I . . ." Weldon rubbed the back of his head with his hand again. "Well, okay. That's very nice of you. I'd like to see more of your paintings."

Mir heard them making plans, but only vaguely, like she was

listening to their conversation from a great distance. She barely heard when Weldon and her parents said their goodbyes and he jogged away from them, heading back downtown. She jerked when Stella touched her shoulder.

"Miriam?" said Stella. Mir walked away from her mom, already practicing all the things she'd say later on, when they fought about inviting Weldon Warrick to dinner.

CHAPTER EIGHT

When they got home, Henry grabbed Nate by the hood of his jacket, muttered something about going for a walk, and half dragged him out of the house. Mir and her mother were left alone in the kitchen.

Stella sighed.

"Well, have at it, I guess," she said.

Mir sharpened the words she'd practiced saying in her head. She'd sat in stunned silence during the ride home, half listening to Nate and her dad babble about something. Hockey, maybe. Nate was newly into hockey and very patriotic about it. Stella hadn't said anything, the female half of the family locked in silence while the male half chattered on.

"You invited Weldon Warrick over for dinner, Mom. To our house."

"You're right, I did," Stella said, opening the fridge and pulling out several carrots and an onion. The onion was from the local farmers' market. The carrots Stella had grown in their garden.

"I don't understand you," Mir said. "After everything he's done to us."

"Stop," said Stella, turning toward Mir. She held a carrot out defiantly in front of her, like a Sunday school pointer. "I want you to stop that right now, Miriam. Weldon Warrick has done absolutely nothing to us. Joseph Warrick is an entirely different matter, but unless the boy we met on the waterfront is secretly his grandfather reincarnated, I don't see why we shouldn't have him over to break bread."

"He's a Warrick!" Mir howled. Her carefully practiced words flew from her mind. All she could think about was the unfairness of Stella's reaction, inviting a thief over for dinner. "They stole from us!"

"I said stop." Stella feinted the carrot at Mir. "Don't go down that road, Miriam. That road made your grandfather a stranger to me. Those damn characters, those superheroes, they meant more to him than his own family. He spent twenty years in court, fighting for each piece of the TomorrowMen, while my mother left him and his kids grew up without him."

Stella's tone was tightly controlled. She continued:

"And in the end he got his name in the credits of all the TomorrowMen comics, and his name will be in the credits of that TomorrowMen movie, but so what? It wasn't enough for him. He wanted money for every little thing related to the TomorrowMen—"

"That was his right," Mir said furiously. "He created them with Joseph Warrick. The Warricks get a piece of every TomorrowMen thing that's sold. Granddad should've gotten that too. Why do the Warricks get to be rich and we don't—"

"*Because he was too proud to compromise!*" Stella screamed. Mir flinched, taking a step backward.

"What the studio offered him, his name on all the credits, a yearly stipend, it was never going to be *enough* for him. He wanted full ownership, full partnership, whatever. He wouldn't even back down after he got sick. And then I was supposed to give up my life to keep fighting *his* fight."

Mir sat down at the kitchen table and put her head in her hands, digging her fingers deep into the roots of her hair. Sometimes she would pick up a comic book from a display table at the Emporium of Wonders and look for her grandfather's name in the credits: *Based on characters created by Joseph Warrick and Micah Kendrick*. She would put her finger over Joseph Warrick's name and stare at her grandfather's name. She imagined him at a drawing desk, ink flowing from the brush he was moving across a sheet of white paper. She imagined him drawing the face of Skylark, a face with wide eyes and full lips, a face that looked so much like Stella's. The face of an alien queen who fell in love with a superhuman man.

"He died before you were born," said Stella, her voice wobbling. "I don't know why you've decided what happened to him is something that you want to be angry about."

Mir pulled her hands from her hair and let large chunks of

curls fall around her head, blocking off the sight of her mother. Anger was ebbing out of her, leaving behind a feeling like someone had wiped a dirty hand across her heart.

"I made my choice after he died," Stella said. She took a deep breath, as though shaking something heavy from her shoulders. "I took the buyout Warrick Studios was offering. I dropped the legal case over ownership of the TomorrowMen, and I got on with my life. What the studio paid was enough."

"Not quite enough," Mir whispered.

Stella sighed. The hand holding the carrot dropped to her side, and she turned toward the kitchen counter. She started washing the carrots in the sink, scraping their outer skin with a knife.

"I'm guessing that comment has something to do with you being unsure about what you're going to do after graduation next year. I know this is a scary time for you, Miriam, and maybe it seems like having lots of money would make this transition easier. If you want to go to university, we'll figure out how to pay for it. There are options."

"I'll be paying off student loans for the rest of my life," Mir muttered into the table. Stella started chopping the carrots too vigorously and a small orange piece rolled across the floor.

"Yep, you'll be just like everyone else. Maybe that's the worst thing about this whole TomorrowMen legacy; all we can see is what might have been. But who knew the comics were going to sell so well, that there'd someday be animated shows and merchandise and now this movie? Your grandfather didn't know. He was an artist who wanted his comic book published, so he signed a bad contract. It happens every day of the week, to artists no one knows of. Nobody would give a shit about the TomorrowMen or Micah Kendrick if those comics hadn't continued on for forty years."

Mir threw out the last words she had in this argument, the signal that the fight was over.

"It isn't fair."

Stella slowed her mutilation of the carrot and wiped at her eyes with the back of her hand.

"You're right, it isn't," said Stella. "But this is the way it is. Go call your father and brother in. Tell them to stop hiding. The fireworks are done."

That evening, Mir called Evan.

"Are you busy? Want to go to a movie?"

"Going out will screw up my very important plan to stare at the internet all night, but okay," Evan said. "What kind of movie?"

"I dunno," said Mir, realizing she hadn't thought that far. "Something with . . . uh, explosions? Accents?"

"Exploding accents?" Evan said. Miriam could practically feel his shit-eating grin through the phone. "Maybe something Schwarzenegger-rific?"

"No, he's way too old," Mir sighed. "I'm always afraid he's going to break a hip while beating up bad guys."

"Guess we can just head down to the theater and see what's

playing," Evan said. "Not like there's more than one place to watch movies in Sandford."

"Sounds good," said Mir. "See you there in forty-five minutes?"

"Raleigh and Jamie too?" asked Evan. Mir twisted the old phone cord around her wrist, pressing the soft plastic into her skin.

"Nah, just the two of us."

There was a pause at Evan's end. He recovered quickly, so quickly Mir almost thought she'd imagined the pause.

"Okay. See you in forty-five."

Sandford's only movie theater was a thirty-minute walk from Mir's house, wedged between a slowly dying local grocery store and a brightly lit twenty-four-hour pharmacy. It was a squat building with a faded pink-and-gray color scheme and neon signs bolted to its exterior. Despite the theater's apocalyptic facade and a manager who seemed to hate anyone under the age of fifty, half of Mir's high school was gathered out front. Mir found an empty wall to lean against and propped herself there, waiting for Evan.

If I see Weldon Warrick here, I'll run away screaming, she thought. She looked around furtively, almost expecting to see Weldon's wide smile as he walked toward her. Deciding it would probably be safer not to look in any direction, Mir stared at the pavement between her shoes.

"Hi," said Evan.

Mir looked up, relieved.

"Hi. You made it on time."

"Indeed," Evan said, offering Mir his arm. She smiled and looped her own arm through his, and they walked toward the theater entrance.

"So what'll it be for tonight's entertainment? *If You Could See Me Now*, starring Canada's own Ryan Gosling?"

"Ugh, no." Mir wrinkled her nose in distaste. "I like a good Gosling movie as much as the next girl, but if a movie's got a title that's a sentence, odds are it's a terrible romantic comedy. I could use something action-y tonight. Is there anything with fights?"

Evan scanned the movie titles. Around them the scrum of teenagers churned and whooped, phones held to their chests like talismans.

"What about that one?" Evan said, pointing. "*The Avenging Queen*. Natalie Portman is a clone of Queen Elizabeth brought back to life to fight the Spanish Armada, who are zombies. I think. I watched a trailer online and it seemed pretty insane."

"You had me at 'Natalie Portman,'" said Mir. "Also at 'clone' and 'zombies.' Let's do it."

Arm in arm, they walked into the theater, under the flickering neon signs.

Ninety-six minutes later, Miriam gave *The Avenging Queen* two severed Spanish Armada zombie thumbs up.

"You like anything with Natalie Portman in it," Evan said accusingly.

"She is my nonsexual girl crush," Mir said.

"Aw, I was hoping it was entirely sexual."

"Boys!" sighed Mir, rolling her eyes.

"We do tend to like it when hot girls make out with each other," Evan said, grinning. They walked down Sandford's main street, stopping to stare at the mutated clay bowls and ashtrays in the front window of the make-your-own-pottery store. The stores were closed, but their signs were brightly lit, casting multi-colored reflections on the sidewalk. Small groups of teenagers roamed the street, bored but not ready to return home so early on a Saturday night. Most of the faces Mir recognized from school, although she didn't know any of them well. A few friendly nods were thrown her way, but the groups mostly ignored Mir and Evan, shouting to each other about how there was nothing to do.

Mir looked at the front of the Emporium of Wonders, a few blocks down from the pottery store. She'd never paid much attention to the store exterior, but now she noticed how run-down it looked compared to the closed but brightly lit Starbucks.

"Evan, what are you going to do next year?" Mir asked, still looking at the Emporium of Wonders. Did Berg ever wash its windows? It looked terrible. She made a mental note to wash them herself on Monday.

Evan shrugged.

"I dunno, graduate like everyone else?"

"Yeah, but after that."

Evan smirked and took a step back from Mir, stuffing his hands in his pants pockets.

"Oh, right, your whole freak-out thing."

Mir stared at him, hurt.

"What freak-out thing?"

"Come on," Evan said. He was still smiling, but his eyebrows were drawn downward, making his smile look deeply annoyed. "You've been doing this for months. You're freaking out because next year is our last year of high school and you're the only one of us who wants to go to university."

"You're not even going to try to get in?" Mir asked. She leaned against the make-your-own-pottery store window, folding her arms across her chest. The spring air suddenly seemed very cold.

Evan shrugged.

"I hate school, Mir. I hate reading things that aren't comics, I hate writing essays. I like seeing people every day; I like making them laugh. Sometimes I like drama class, because that's just fooling around and being stupid. That's what I'm good at: being stupid."

"Evan," Mir said. "You're not stupid."

"Yeah, okay." He looked away from her, putting his hands back in his pockets. "That's probably true, but I don't care about school. Why would I do more of it? I'm fine working for my dad after I graduate. He wants me to work for him."

The electric sign over the entrance to the Emporium of Wonders flickered, then went out. Mir glanced over at it. The store was almost completely dark, a faint edge of light coming from some back room in the store's interior. Mir wondered if Berg was in there, working late.

"Will you be happy doing that?" Mir said.

"Sure," said Evan. "I like landscaping, and my dad'll help me learn the business end of things. Why wouldn't I be happy?"

"That sounds nice," said Mir softly. Evan watched her, waiting. "I don't know what I want."

"You want to go to school," Evan said. "You do this really long slow-motion look around every time we walk by the guidance counselor's office, so you can see if she's got new university pamphlets in."

"The McGill one is really pretty," Mir said. "Have you seen their coat of arms? It's red. It's got birds and crowns on it."

"So what's the big deal?" Evan said. "You go to university after you graduate. I don't see what you're freaking out about."

Mir slid down the store window and crouched on the sidewalk, wrapping her arms around her knees. Her sweater was several sizes too large, and she pulled it over her knees, making herself as small as possible.

"Because I don't know what I want to do in school. I don't know what I like, or what I'm good at, and school is so much money. What if I spend all that money and I can't figure it out? What if I'm still this way after university graduation?"

"How do you think so far ahead?" Evan said wonderingly. He crouched on the sidewalk beside Miriam and they huddled together. He reached out and put his hand on the back of her neck, underneath her hair. Mir forced herself not to flinch at the feeling of his touch, warm and solid.

"You're taking over your dad's business, Raleigh and Jamie

have each other. What do I have? Why am I the only one of all of us who can't figure it out?"

Evan's fingers on the back of Miriam's neck moved a little. His head was so close to hers, their foreheads nearly touching. Since Jamie and Raleigh had started dating, Mir had felt the focus of Evan's feelings shift, centering more directly on her. Over the past year she'd noticed him looking thoughtfully at her out of the corner of his eye, as though he was weighing some new idea in his mind. She'd been careful to keep him at a distance since she first noticed his feelings had changed, but now there was only the two of them on the sidewalk. No Jamie to make some cutting remark and ruin the moment, no Raleigh to remind her that the three of them had been friends since sixth grade. *I watched you grow that beard for the first time*, Mir thought, not daring to look up. *I wish I wanted to be more than your friend. It would make so much sense. But I can't seem to feel that way about you.*

"I'm such a jerk, Evan."

"Nah, you're okay," Evan said, and pulled his hand away from the back of her neck. The warmth of him went with it.

CHAPTER NINE

Weldon had changed his shirt five times and his pants four times. Each time he thought he had his outfit figured out, he caught a glimpse of himself in the mirror and realized it was all wrong.

"Why don't I have any non-asshole clothes?" he muttered, dumping his entire suitcase on the guest bed. He flung an Abercrombie & Fitch T-shirt across the room, and swore at it.

Weldon looked at the clock next to the bed. He had forty-two minutes before he was officially late for dinner at Stella and Henry's house. Was their last name Kendrick? He wasn't sure. It made sense that Micah Kendrick's daughter would have his last name, but if Stella was married, maybe it had changed. Maybe he could ask. He very much wanted to make sure Stella knew how polite he could be, and calling her Ms. Kendrick instead of Stella seemed like a good place to start.

After the encounter with Miriam's family on the waterfront, Weldon had pulled out his laptop and googled Micah Kendrick.

He'd stared for a long time at the first photograph that had popped up: a sepia-tinged snapshot of a young man with a strong jaw and easy, charismatic smile. He could see the resemblance to Stella immediately, especially with her hair cut so short. Weldon's fingers hovered over the laptop keyboard, then typed in "Micah Kendrick comics."

Micah Kendrick's artwork filled the laptop's screen. The drawings looked primitive compared to the photo-realistic art style of modern TomorrowMen comics, but energy bubbled from every line. When drawn by Micah Kendrick, the TomorrowMen were outlandishly superheroic, striking impossibly athletic poses as they fought their way across the galaxy. Skylark, the only female TomorrowMan, was drawn smaller than her male teammates, but no less powerful. She fought alongside her teammates in whatever battle the TomorrowMen were facing, her gaze charged and regal.

Weldon had stared hard at one drawing of Skylark in particular, the cover of *Spectacular Space Stories*, issue number three. The first meeting of Skylark and Skybound, when Skylark came to warn Earth of its impending doom. There was something familiar about the way Skylark's face was drawn, the way her hair swirled upward, the tilt of her nose. Weldon had turned away from his laptop and pulled out the painting he'd bought from Miriam, holding it up next to the digital image of the comic cover. The two faces of Skylark were identical, not just in design but also in character. One was a painting and the other an ink drawing, but otherwise they matched perfectly.

Weldon's hands had hesitated over the keyboard, then googled "TomorrowMen rights lawsuit." Pages of links sprang up, mostly to news sites. He scrolled down the page, clicked to the next page, and kept scrolling. Weldon vaguely remembered his father mentioning the lawsuit when he was younger, usually in cheerful tones. It was some battle from the past that David Warrick had fought and won; Weldon had never before thought about the people on the other side of the lawsuit. He closed the laptop without clicking any of the links.

Weldon stared at the pile of shirts in front of him. He grabbed a plain gray one, pulled it over his head, and stared hopefully at his reflection in the mirror on the back of the bathroom door. The T-shirt and jeans were as close to neutral as anything he owned. *I guess "neutral asshole" is better than total asshole*, he thought. He glanced up at his face, noting with relief that the bruise was nearly gone. All that remained was a purple smudge underneath his eye.

Weldon's aunt stuck her head in the guest bedroom. She glanced, surprised, at the piles of clothes strewn around the room.

"Are you going somewhere, Weldon?"

"Yeah," Weldon said. "I met these people the other day, Henry and Stella . . . Kendrick? They invited me to dinner."

"Stella and Henry," said Aunt Kay, and her warm brown eyes narrowed suddenly. "Oh, yes, I suppose they do have a daughter about your age, don't they?"

"Miriam," said Weldon.

"Well, that's . . ." His aunt's voice faltered. "That's very nice that you're visiting them, Weldon. But please be careful; they're, well, we have some history with them. You're here to avoid trouble, not go looking for it."

"All the comic book stuff, right?" Weldon said.

Weldon's aunt entered the room and quickly invaded his personal space, placing her hands on his shoulders. Her solution to every problem seemed to be to massage it to death.

"Yes, all that comic book nonsense. All of us, your father, your uncle, me and Stella and Henry grew up in this town. We even went to the same high school. I did my best to be nice to the Kendricks, considering . . . everything that happened. But sometimes . . ." His aunt paused, her face darkening. "Sometimes things can be strained in a small town. I just want you to know they might have . . . some underlying hostility."

Weldon watched his aunt talk, fascinated. All this family history he knew so little about. She continued:

"I won't tell you not to see them tonight, but be careful with yourself. All right, Weldon?"

He nodded.

"How are you getting down to the Kendricks' house?"

"I thought I'd walk," Weldon said.

"Ask Alex to drive you; it's a fair distance to their side of town," said his aunt. She hesitated, looking at him, then seemed to decide something, and smiled warmly at him.

"You're a good boy underneath it all, Weldon. I know you are."

"Thank you, Aunt Kay," Weldon said, smiling back.

———

Half an hour later, Weldon stood outside Miriam's house, watching his uncle's car vanish into the Sandford horizon. He turned and walked toward the house, pausing to look at the large garden stretching out beside it. The garden looked overgrown, tomato vines clambering up wire-frame supports, stalks of corn waving gently in the evening breeze.

Miriam clattered out of the house, her face screwed up like she had just eaten something sour. She had a small basket tucked under one arm. She missed the first porch step when she saw Weldon, and stumbled down the remaining steps, regaining her balance by flailing her arms. Weldon quickly plastered a smile across his face.

"Hi!" he said. Miriam stared at him, looking as though she hoped she could will him out of existence.

"Hi," she said, then held up the basket. "I'm getting tomatoes. I guess you can help."

"That sounds cool," Weldon said. Miriam turned away from him, heading toward the garden, and Weldon thought he heard her mutter something like, "Ooh, yeah, so cool, picking tomatoes. Whee."

Weldon stared at the back of Miriam's head as he followed

her into the garden. Her hair was tied at the base of her neck with what looked like string, and she was wearing an oversized sweater, similar to the one he'd seen her wearing on the waterfront the other day. The sweater was so large she was practically swimming in it.

Miriam vigorously threw open the gate to the garden and stomped through, Weldon trailing behind her. The entire garden was surrounded by a large fence, sturdy wooden posts strung with chicken wire. Shiny pie plates hung from the posts, which Weldon assumed were there to scare off birds looking for a free meal. He paused to touch the leaf of a tomato plant, remembering how his mom had loved visiting the local farmers' market in Burbank, close to where they'd lived when they'd moved from San Diego to LA.

"Here," Miriam snapped, shoving the basket into Weldon's arms. He stood, holding it out, as she furiously pulled tomatoes from the vine, tossing them into the basket. She moved quickly from plant to plant, inspecting, selecting, and rejecting certain tomatoes. Soon there was a small pile of slightly misshapen bright red tomatoes in the basket.

"Okay, good," Miriam said, and stormed past him, through the gate, impatiently holding it for him as he followed her. She swung the gate shut, locked it with a small piece of twine, then trotted toward the house. Weldon followed, impressed.

Stella beamed when Weldon came through the door, the basket of tomatoes held in front of him like a gift. Miriam swept through the kitchen, pointedly ignoring her mother.

"Weldon, welcome to our home!" Stella said. Weldon smiled at her, suddenly feeling too tall and out of place in Stella's kitchen, with its yellow-and-orange walls and a dining room table propped up by a phone book under one leg.

Stella reached out and took the basket of tomatoes from Weldon, placing it beside the sink.

"We're not ready to eat yet. Hope you aren't super hungry right this minute."

"Oh, no," Weldon said. "I'm good, I can hold out for a while longer."

"Fantastic," Stella said, pulling the tomatoes out of the basket and starting to rinse them in the sink. "Usually I put to work anyone foolish enough to set foot in the kitchen at dinner time, but since you're a guest, I won't coerce you into helping. MIRIAM!"

Weldon jumped.

"WHAT!" Miriam screamed back from somewhere in the bowels of the house.

"YOUR FATHER'S NOT HOME FROM WORK YET SO YOU GET TO SHOW WELDON AROUND THE HOUSE. COME OUT AND DO THAT PLEASE."

There was a long silence. Stella continued washing the tomatoes as though everything was perfectly normal. Weldon wished he'd worn a sweater over his T-shirt. He had the feeling he'd started sweating copiously and was worried about pit stains.

There was a clatter from the depths of the house, and Miriam reappeared in the kitchen.

"Thank you, Miriam," said Stella, not looking up from the

sink. "You can show Weldon my studio, if you want. He said he wouldn't mind seeing more of my art."

Miriam looked over at Weldon and nodded grimly, a soldier given an unpleasant task. She squared her shoulders and waved a hand at him.

"Follow me."

Weldon trotted after Miriam, through the ramshackle house and out the back door, toward an outbuilding standing behind the house. After some shoving and muttering of curse words, Miriam coaxed the door to the outbuilding open, and they went inside.

The building was a repurposed garage, one side taken up by a car door that had been taped to prevent winter cold from getting in. A small window on another wall filtered in outside light, and tall shelving units took up the entire back section. Paint, canvas, sketchbooks, a drawing desk, and an easel filled the rest of the space. Everywhere Weldon looked, he saw the painted forms of the TomorrowMen. Skybound flew across a long horizontal canvas, his arms stretched out before him. Skylark floated in space, her hands sifting through a nearby galaxy. The Mage of Ages, the hood of his cloak thrown back, knelt beside a river, staring at his reflection. There was a handful of non-TomorrowMen artwork, mostly watercolors of landscapes, but overwhelmingly the thing Stella Kendrick liked to paint best was her father's superhero creations.

"Wow," Weldon whispered, stunned. "Your mom's work is incredible."

"Yeah," said Miriam, and Weldon caught the note of pride in her voice. "She's amazing. Everything she paints is amazing."

There was a painting of Tristan Terrific on the easel, lightning-bolt hair swept back from his forehead, eyes lit with mischief. Weldon walked toward the easel, bending to squint at the painting. Up close, Tristan Terrific's face dematerialized into a thousand smeary brushstrokes.

"What does she do with all her art?" Weldon asked.

Mir shrugged.

"Most of it she gives away. To kids who like the characters, elementary schools, children's hospitals, the odd collector. It used to be that she'd take requests online and give them to the people who asked for them, but some people got really pushy, so she quit doing that."

"Pushy?"

"Yeah," Mir said. "I guess there's a market for this stuff. My grandfather is kind of famous in some circles. An original TomorrowMen drawing by him could sell for thousands of dollars to the right person. So if his daughter starts giving away original TomorrowMen artwork . . ."

"People get pushy," Weldon finished.

Mir nodded.

"A couple of years ago, Mom painted a picture of Skylark for a guy who requested it. He turned around and tried to sell it at auction. It sucks for her, because she just wants to paint and share her work. But people are jerks sometimes."

Mir glanced at Weldon, her brown eyes sliding disapprovingly under her eyelashes.

"If she's worried about people reselling her work, why does she sell it at that . . . uh, that store downtown, where I bought my painting?"

"No one knows she sells paintings at the Emporium of Wonders," Mir said. "Berg, the guy who owns the place, he knows but he'd never tell."

Weldon remembered how there was a layer of grime on the large window at the front of the store. The merchandise had been new and neatly displayed, but there was an air of impending doom about the place. All the shiny vinyl toys and Tomorrow-Men figures couldn't hide the store's worn carpet and peeling exterior paint. He wondered how many more months Stella's paintings would sell there, the Emporium of Wonders hanging on by a fingernail as Starbucks loomed closer.

Weldon realized Mir was still talking, and pulled his attention back to her.

". . . she doesn't even sign them. She sells those paintings because paint costs money and she wants to be able to buy a new tube of burnt umber every now and then."

"I'm glad I was able to contribute to the burnt umber fund," said Weldon, smiling. Miriam snorted and walked toward the metal shelving at the back of the garage, rooting through a tin of half-finished paint tubes.

"She's getting low on all of these," Mir said, turning a

flattened tube over in her hands. Weldon stared at her out of the corner of his eye. He could only see a sliver of her face, the soft curve of her cheek jutting out from behind a mess of curls. Her face suddenly seemed very familiar to him, like he'd known her longer than their two previous brief encounters. He felt content standing near her, surrounded by the painted forms of the TomorrowMen.

Mir tossed the paint tube back in the tin on the shelves with a loud clatter. Weldon stuck his hands in his pockets, thought better of it, put his hands on his hips, decided that looked even more awkward, and finally settled on clasping his hands behind his back. Miriam turned away from the shelves and looked at him curiously. Weldon ducked from her gaze and squinted hard at the Tristan Terrific painting on the easel in front of him, trying to appear as though he'd been examining it studiously during the last few minutes and not thinking how standing near Miriam Kendrick was something he liked doing and might want to do more of in the future.

"Did you know who I was back at your store?" he asked.

"Who you were?"

"You know." Weldon looked up from the Tristan Terrific painting. "Weldon *Warrick*."

"Oh . . ." Mir said.

"I was wondering why you didn't seem to care when I told you I'd stolen that car, but when I told the cops my name, you kinda . . ." Weldon shrugged. "Well, it makes sense why you didn't want anything to do with me after that."

"My grandfather sold the rights for the TomorrowMen to Warrick Comics for nine hundred dollars when he was in his twenties," Miriam said. It came out flatly, a repetition of facts. "And next year Warrick Studios has a two-hundred-million-dollar TomorrowMen movie coming out."

"Yeah," said Weldon. "It's kind of weird, right? Your mom inviting me over for dinner? I'd think she wouldn't want anything to do with anyone named Warrick."

"That's my mom," Mir said. "She wants to be friends with everyone, even the people who stole her inheritance."

She looked up at Weldon, daring him to say something. He waited, letting the silence stretch between them.

"Any particular reason why you steal cars?" Mir said.

Weldon shrugged.

"Trying to get my parents' attention, I guess," he said, curious to see her reaction. It was something he'd never admitted to anyone besides himself.

The admission surprised her. He liked the way her thick eyebrows scrambled up her forehead, then shot back down in an attempt at nonchalance.

"So," she said. "Anything else in here you want to see?"

"No, it's all very nice."

"Uh-huh," Mir said. "Well, I guess we can go back inside. My dad'll probably be home soon, and then we can eat."

"Sounds great."

Miriam narrowed her eyes at Weldon, apparently suspicious of the cheer in his voice.

"Just to warn you, my dad thinks he's funny. He'll probably tell some story or terrible joke and my mom will laugh really hard at it. I think maybe—oh god—" Mir froze, her expression horrified. "I think he might tell the bull castration story. Oh god. Ohhhh god." She dropped her face into her hands, her words muffled by her fingers. "Ohhhh god."

"The what story?"

Miriam raised her head, her face grim.

"You'll see. You're a guest, and guests get my dad at his very best."

Weldon followed Mir back into the house, suddenly feeling nervous about eating with her family. He hoped they wouldn't bring up the TomorrowMen legal case. The lawsuit was ancient history, but from the paintings in Stella's studio, she still felt a connection to the characters. Weldon hoped Mir's parents hadn't invited him to their house just so they could yell at him for what his grandfather had done.

In the kitchen, Stella had finished chopping the tomatoes and everything simmered on the stove, ready for eating. Henry was sitting at the table and rose when Weldon came in, extending a hand. Weldon shook it in what he hoped was a respectful manner.

"Nice to see you again, sir."

"Sir!" Henry yelled, clearly amused. "That's a new one. Mir, did you put him up to this?"

"No, Dad," sighed Mir. She went to a nearby cupboard,

pulled down half a dozen dishes, and began placing them around the kitchen table.

"Call me Henry, Weldon," said Henry, his complexion glowing pink with delight. "I must insist. We're very happy to have you over for dinner, by the way. Thank you so much for coming."

"No problem at all," said Weldon, feeling the nervousness in his stomach sliding away. He saw the evening unfold before him: his anxiety over the dinner, wanting so badly for them to like him, to prove to them he wasn't like the rest of his family. He saw his nervousness reflected in Henry's high energy. He saw it in Stella's eager smile, the way she watched him out of the corner of her eye. They were nervous too.

Miriam shoved a fistful of forks into his hands.

"Here, help me," she said, ignoring her dad. Weldon moved to the table and laid the forks beside the plates. Miriam stood next to him and matched the forks with knives. *She's the only one who's not nervous*, Weldon thought, and wondered why.

At dinner, Henry told the bull castration story. The performance was over fifteen minutes long and included sound effects (a bull bellowing in distress), dramatic gestures (to indicate Henry, his father, and his two brothers chasing a terrified bull around a small pen), and eventually, full-body reenactment, as Henry leaped from the table to mime the final takedown of the bull. The punch line was Henry's father discovering the bull had already been castrated by a previous owner, rendering the whole ordeal moot. Stella roared with laughter, her hands clasped to her stomach. Nate pummeled the table during the parts he liked best, laughing so hard Weldon worried he might fall off his chair. Even Mir, her chin resting on one hand, expression carefully neutral throughout the story, dissolved into giggles at the dramatic finale.

After Henry's theatrics, dinner subsided into less acrobatic conversation. Stella talked about painting and the intricacies of color theory, which confused Weldon. He eventually stopped asking her to explain and just nodded while she talked. Nate wanted to know about Los Angeles, and especially if Weldon knew anyone who worked on his favorite cartoon show, *Mysterious Quest*. Weldon apologetically admitted he didn't. Nate, undeterred, launched into his idea for a *Mysterious Quest* episode, most of which revolved around the show's main characters, a girl named Finley and her talking cat, Muffin, befriending a new character named, coincidentally, Nate.

"I'm writing the script in English class," Nate said proudly. "I have twelve pages written so far."

"That's awesome," said Weldon. "Can I read it when you're done?"

Nate thought deliberately a moment, then agreed.

Twice during the meal, Weldon caught Mir looking at him. The first time their eyes met, she looked away nonchalantly, fiddling with the food on her plate. He assumed it meant nothing until he caught her looking at him a second time, as though she was trying to figure something out.

When dinner was finished, Weldon helped clear the table, despite Stella's protestations. Then he helped wash the dishes, which caused Stella to protest even more. Every dish was washed, table and counters scrubbed, when Henry finally asked if he needed a ride home. Reluctantly, Weldon shook his head.

"Just gotta call my uncle, he'll pick me up."

Stella smiled, the expression a little strained.

"Tell Alex and Kay I say hello."

Before long, Weldon's phone chirped, informing him his uncle was waiting outside in his car. Stella gestured at Mir.

"Mir, walk Weldon outside, will you? Weldon, it's been lovely to have you over. We'll have to do it again sometime, all right?"

"That would be really great," said Weldon.

He and Mir walked out into the near pitch black outdoors, the light from the interior of Mir's house radiating out past them. The air was crisp, in contrast to the brightness and warmth of the Kendricks' kitchen. Weldon felt a tug in the pit of his stomach to turn around and walk back inside. He wanted very much to curl up underneath the kitchen table and stay there forever.

At the top of the driveway, Alex Warrick waited, his SUV's headlights lighting a path through the darkness. There were no streetlamps this far from Sandford's downtown, and the town skyline glowed dimly in the distance.

Mir walked down the driveway beside Weldon, staring at his uncle's truck.

"You don't have to come with me the whole way," Weldon said.

"Okay," said Mir, and stopped. Weldon stopped too, turning to face her.

"Your family is amazing," he said.

"Yeah, I guess," she said. "They work really hard at it."

"You're so lucky," Weldon said, awed. He turned away from her and walked toward the truck. There was a feeling of singing in his chest.

CHAPTER TEN

The Saturday morning after Weldon Warrick came for dinner, there were two people in the Emporium of Wonders, and one of them was Mir. The other was Evan. Over the last hour, seven people had wandered into the store, one person buying a TomorrowMen mug for $5.99, the rest browsing, then leaving without purchasing anything.

Mir sighed.

"You seem becalmed," Evan said.

"Yeah," Mir said. "I'm bored. Thanks for coming by."

"Berg won't mind?"

Mir shook her head.

"It's dead today. Just like yesterday. I guess that's why Berg cut my hours; not much point in having an employee around if there's no customers."

Evan glanced up at Mir, concerned.

"You okay with the cut hours? I could maybe talk to my dad if you wanted to haul sod a couple times a week."

"It's okay for now," Mir said. "It'll pick up soon, when tourist season gets going." She didn't say that Evan's dad intimidated her, with his booming voice and habit of swearing profusely if things didn't shape up exactly how he wanted them to. Evan's dad had always been nice to her, but she felt on edge around him, sure he was going to yell at her for some minor infraction.

"One year of school left after this one," Evan sighed, leaning against the checkout counter. "I feel old. I look at the grade nine kids and I wonder, was I ever so young?"

"You're sixteen," Mir told him. "That's still kinda young."

"And they're thirteen!" Evan said. "We're three years older than them. It feels like just yesterday I was staring at that high school for the first time, hoping some hulking tenth grader wouldn't take a liking to me and make me his personal freshman butler."

"You're right, you're ancient. I can hear your hip creaking from over here," Mir said, pushing lightly on his shoulder. Evan clutched where she'd touched him, let out a dramatic squawk of pretend pain, and fell to the floor. He writhed on the ground, moaning, "Ach, she broke my wee bonny shoulder."

"Your accent is so authentic," Mir said, giggling. "Also, maybe get up off the floor. I haven't vacuumed for a few days."

"Ugh." Evan's disembodied voice floated up from the other side of the counter. "It is definitely gross down here." He sprang to his feet, brushing casually at a smear of dirt on the sleeve of his jacket.

"So . . ." Mir let the word trail off, not sure how to

continue. Evan gave his sleeve one last swipe and folded his hands expectantly on the counter, leaning toward her.

"Yes?"

"Have you seen Raleigh and Jamie recently?"

"Not really," Evan said. "Just in the halls at school."

"It feels extra weird," Mir sighed.

"What, ever since Jamie was a butt to you about your family and the TomorrowMen settlement?"

Mir rubbed at her forehead, squeezing her eyes shut so she wouldn't have to look at Evan.

"It feels so messed up. He's Raleigh's boyfriend. She chose him."

Evan chuckled skeptically.

"So what? She couldn't make a mistake and date a guy who's a jerk? C'mon, it happens. They'll break up when she realizes."

Mir shrugged, looking away. A small, angry part of her wished she believed Evan, that eventually Jamie would fall out of their lives and he would take all the wrongness he brought to their group with him. But when Mir saw the two of them together, Raleigh's profile cradled in the hollow of Jamie's shoulder, she knew Evan was wrong. It would be that way forever. They would never break up.

"Anyway, I gotta go," Evan sighed. "Gotta pick up my sisters at their secret assassin training."

"It's Girl Guides, Evan," Miriam said. "They practice building tents and they sell cookies, dressed in adorable matching uniforms. I really don't think it's a front for a mysterious league of junior assassins."

Evan shook his head sadly.

"How little you know of the world, Miriam Kendrick."

The bell over the Emporium of Wonders' front door jangled. Mir guiltily straightened up from the counter, trying not to look like an employee slacking off at work. Weldon Warrick was half through the entrance, nearly missing a step when he saw she wasn't alone. He recovered quickly, and walked toward Mir and Evan, hands stuck in his jacket pockets. At the sight of him, a not-unpleasant warmth crept into Miriam's stomach.

"Hey," said Weldon, flashing his smile at Evan. "I'm Weldon. I don't think we've met."

Evan eyed Weldon suspiciously.

"Um, okay," said Evan.

Weldon turned his head and aimed his smile at Mir. It was as bright as the headlights on his uncle's car two nights ago. Mir remembered his face in shadow, him saying "You're so lucky." The darkness had prevented her from seeing his expression. She'd thought about the words a lot since then. *What on earth did he mean? He's Weldon Warrick. He has everything.*

"I feel like I introduce you a lot," Miriam said. She waved an open hand at Weldon. "Evan, this is Weldon Warrick. Yes, that Warrick. He's from Los Angeles, but is staying here in Sandford with his aunt and uncle for a while. You probably will not get along."

"You wound me, Mir," said Weldon, placing a shocked hand

on his chest. "Evan and I could be the best of friends, if you'd give us a chance."

"That Warrick?" Evan said, his voice climbing several octaves. "Warrick Studios Warrick? TomorrowMen comics Warrick?"

Weldon nodded modestly at Evan, but Mir saw a glow of pleasure creep across his face. She imagined herself brushing off the excited words of a fan—*yes, I'm that Miriam Kendrick. Yes, my grandfather created the TomorrowMen. Of course I'll be at the movie premiere next summer. It's so exciting seeing the TomorrowMen up on the big screen! My grandfather would have been so proud.*

"Shit, man! I love the TomorrowMen!" Evan laughed. "I've been reading those comics since I was eight! You should see the longboxes in my closet. There's some *X-Men*, yeah, but the rest is all *TomorrowMen*. I mean, holy shit." Evan's hands flailed excitedly at Weldon.

"Thanks," said Weldon. "What's your favorite run on the comic?"

"I dunno, I loved that Tristan Terrific spin-off from two years ago," Evan said. "The one drawn by Stuart Samuel. That was great stuff. Brought this really human element to the TomorrowMen, showed us a side of them we hadn't seen before, you know?"

"Everyone hated that miniseries at the beginning," Weldon said. "All these reviews claiming the publisher was destroying the character by having him deal with his dark side. But now people really like those comics."

Evan gestured at him, bearded face shining. "Stuart Samuel is such a good artist. He draws like . . . like, I don't know. Like he literally lives in the same world as the TomorrowMen, and he's just drawing what he sees. He's amazing."

Miriam watched the two boys standing in the middle of the store, Evan bubbling over with delight, Weldon basking in the glow of his enthusiasm. Weldon's crooked nose looked less crooked in profile, and she could barely see his black eye anymore. A tiny smudge of green beneath his right eye was the only indication of the violence she'd interrupted. *I've seen a lot of Weldon Warrick for only meeting him a short time ago*, Mir thought.

"—and the *World of TomorrowMen* series that ran two years ago, the one written by Kurt Busiek? That was fantastic, a whole new side of the TomorrowMen. You really got to see their world up close."

"I prefer the superhero stuff," Weldon said. "I like to see the TomorrowMen using their superpowers, fighting world threats, really saving the universe. Superhero comics should be about saving the world."

Weldon's gaze slid toward Miriam, and she remembered what she'd said to him on the waterfront, when he'd jogged by her family. *Superheroes are the worst.* She still wasn't sure where her comment had come from. A small voice at the back of her mind piped up: *Maybe you were trying to hurt him? Just a little bit?* Mir looked away from Weldon, feeling guilty.

"For sure," Evan said. "I like the superhero stuff too. But sometimes you want a different spin on that kind of thing, you know? If every story was Skybound punching a supervillain into the sun, that'd get pretty boring eventually. I appreciate a fresh take."

"Yeah, gotta keep the characters evolving," Weldon said, nodding. "I see your point."

"Sure you do!" Evan laughed. He glanced nervously at Mir, then continued. "Uh, okay, totally asking for a friend, but say someone had some ideas for TomorrowMen stories, how would someone go about getting . . . um, hired to write Tomorrow-Men comics? Like say my friend actually had a TomorrowMen script written and he—or she!—wanted to send it some-where—"

"Evan!" Miriam hissed.

Evan grinned, shrugging at Weldon.

"Can't blame a guy for trying to take advantage of an op-portunity."

"Nah, I can't," Weldon said. "You'd be surprised where comic book writers come from. Sometimes it's just being in the right place at the right time. No promises, but if you have a script or a mini-comic, I could pass it on to my dad."

Evan bubbled over with delight, showering Weldon with gratitude. Mir stared at him, remembering the night after they'd seen the *Avenging Queen* movie, Evan shrugging and saying he didn't mind the idea of running his father's business. He'd al-ways been terrible at school; he never knew when to be quiet, when to listen and memorize dates and names. He always handed his assignments in late. But he loved comics. A memory floated into Mir's mind: Evan sitting alone during lunch at school, writing furiously in a spiral notebook, a pile of comics beside him. *Have you been writing stories all this time, and you never told me?* Mir thought. *Why would you hide that from me?*

Evan was practically dancing in place as he and Weldon swapped email addresses, phones cupped in their hands. Weldon assured him that he'd try to get the script in front of his father, but he couldn't do much beyond that. It was typically editors who did the hiring at Warrick Comics, not their CEO. Evan nodded furiously, promising to send Weldon a script, the best script he'd ever written, the best script anyone had ever written, as soon as possible.

The bell on the front door of the Emporium of Wonders clanged as Evan thundered out of the store, shouting his goodbyes over his shoulder. Mir waited until the sound of the bell subsided before turning toward Weldon.

"Can you really do that, give your dad a TomorrowMen script written by someone you don't know? And could he really get hired?"

Weldon leaned one elbow on the counter, and Mir slid backward as he encroached on her personal space. She got a closer glimpse of his jacket: definitely real leather, definitely expensive.

"Sure. Comics are a weird industry; people get hired in strange ways," Weldon said. "The guy writing the current TomorrowMen used to do comics on the internet. He didn't draw them or anything, he just took photographs of his friends and traced the photos. But the writing was really good, and he gained a following. Eventually an editor saw his comics and hired him."

"Really?" Mir said. "They just hired some guy who did free online comics to write a TomorrowMen comic?"

"Like I said, it's a weird, weird industry," Weldon said. "There's no direct path to becoming a comic book writer or artist. I think there are a few schools that offer courses in comic writing or drawing, but it's not like becoming a lawyer. You don't go to school, graduate with a degree, and get hired by a publisher and draw comics for the next thirty years. Some writers have English or creative writing degrees, but you don't need that kind of background to get hired. You just need a knack for writing comic scripts."

"And the artists?"

"The artists," Weldon said darkly, as though contemplating a long-held secret. "The artists come from anywhere, and they're all kinds of crazy. They'll have backgrounds in animation, in illustration or commercial work. When I was a kid, my parents used to have these big barbecues after Comic-Con and invite all of the artists and writers—"

"Comic-Con? Is that the convention in San Diego?"

Weldon nodded.

"Yeah, it used to be a gathering just for comics, an opportunity for creators to meet their fans and hang out with their friends. But then movie studios started turning comics into movies and the whole thing got completely out of hand."

Mir leaned forward on the store counter, trying to imagine

the madness of Comic-Con. A crush of people, all decked out in nerd paraphernalia, drawn to the West Coast like moths to a flame.

"My parents used to live in San Diego, and they'd have this giant get-together for everyone who worked on the Tomorrow-Men comics. They'd, like, roast a pig in our backyard and everyone would stuff their faces. Mom would try to put me to bed before everyone got really drunk, but I'd sneak out to watch the whole thing."

Mir tried to picture a miniature Weldon in footie pajamas, sneaking out of bed to peer down at a crowd of drunken cartoonists.

"Comics were all they talked about," Weldon continued. "Eventually they'd break off into little groups and the artists would sit and draw, and the writers would argue about writing. It was like it consumed them. It was all they could ever imagine doing."

Mir caught the note of wonder in his voice. He wasn't looking at her, rather staring off at something in the distance. She couldn't help but look at his profile again. It would be very easy to admit to herself that Weldon Warrick was nice to look at, and that was something Mir was pretty sure she shouldn't do.

"My mom paints all the time," Mir said. "And it's not like it's easy for her, like she just does it because it's fun. She's always trying to improve, to learn new techniques, and sometimes that's difficult. But I don't think she could ever imagine not painting. It's like painting is an innate part of her, something that can't be removed."

Weldon looked at Mir.

"An innate part of her?"

Mir hesitated. Weldon waited, his gaze direct on her face. She didn't think he was trying to make her uncomfortable, but the directness of his stare was disconcerting. She stared back, and tried to explain.

"It's like . . . it's like painting is something she *needs* to do. It's more than feeling love for something, because love changes. If it's a person you love, sometimes you don't love that person because they're being a jerk to you. Or sometimes you fall out of love. But if you have something that's this . . . *part* of you, losing it would be more than losing something you loved, it would be like losing a limb. It would change how you functioned as a person."

Weldon blinked, his gaze softening.

"I like that explanation," he said, and smiled. Mir felt something in her chest flutter, just a little.

The bell above the front door to the Emporium of Wonders jangled, and Mir and Weldon jerked apart. She hadn't noticed she'd been leaning in as she'd been talking, the distance between them narrowing. A family of four tumbled through the front door, the two children already shouting when they spotted the TomorrowMen merchandise. Miriam fixed a smile to her face and beamed a greeting at them.

"Welcome to the Emporium of Wonders! If there's anything I can help you with, please ask!"

The parents gave her a distracted look and tiredly began following their bellowing children around the store. Mir winced when one of the kids picked up a forty-dollar Skybound action figure and shook the box heartily.

"Kids love that stuff," Weldon said. "The merchandising makes three times what the comics pull in. Kind of unfair, when you think about it. Everything comes from the comics, but the comics bring in a pittance compared to the newest Skybound doll."

"Not a doll," said Miriam. "Action figure."

Weldon grinned at her. "Right. Action figure—oh hey, you don't, um, run, do you?"

"Run?"

"Y'know, jogging. Exercise?"

"Oh, no, I hate exercise. I prefer to sit and be driven places, as God intended."

"That was me a couple years ago," Weldon said. "Then I started running and—"

One of the two children tore up to the counter, the Skybound action figure clutched between his paws. He threw it on the counter and howled, "THIS MOMMY THIS!" His mother joined him, pulling her wallet from her shoulder bag. Weldon backed away to give them room, and waved at Mir.

"Anyway, you're busy now, so I'll—I'll see you around, okay?"

Miriam began ringing up the purchase, nodding an "okay" at Weldon. As she passed the action figure back to the jubilant child she caught another glimpse of Weldon through the Emporium of Wonders' large front window, walking away with his hands in his jacket pockets. His head was down, and his shoulders seemed slumped a little, as though he was disappointed in something.

Did he come to the store just to see me? Mir wondered.

The parent of the demanding child put three twenties on the counter in front of Mir, and she distracted herself with getting change. The family left as quickly as they had entered, their child roaring delightedly over his new toy.

Miriam leaned her forearms on the counter.

He came to see me, she thought. She remembered Weldon stepping through the Emporium of Wonders' front door, his missed step at the sight of Evan. She ducked her head and rubbed a hand across the nape of her neck, under the thicket of her ponytail. The thought of Weldon Warrick coming to visit her at the Emporium of Wonders was not unpleasant.

CHAPTER ELEVEN

The worst thing about being banished from your home and shipped off to the far reaches of Canada was the boredom. Weldon lay on a couch in the front living room and stared at the ceiling, listening to the silence that blanketed his aunt and uncle's huge, empty house. The house had three rooms designated "recreational," plus a large finished basement, which had a pool table. Weldon had tried to practice on the pool table, but playing without a partner wasn't fun and he soon abandoned it. There were nearly six hundred channels on the television, but after watching three episodes of a pawn-shop-based reality show, Weldon decided TV was a lost cause and turned it off. He'd even finished his online homework for the week, handing it in to his mysterious teacher on the other side of the internet.

Weldon checked his phone for the fifteenth time. No messages. He checked a couple of comic blogs and read opinion pieces on the upcoming TomorrowMen movie. According to the internet, the movie was going to be "sick," "awesome," and "worse than the craps I take in the morning."

Weldon rolled onto his stomach, propping his chin up on a pillow. No one had messaged or called him since he'd been in Sandford. But who would? Weldon let his phone drop onto his chest, thinking. He'd always had friends, but his high school friends had been different from the kids he'd known when he was younger. His mother had left the summer before ninth grade, and he had gone into high school angry, looking for people to be angry with. He had abandoned his middle school friends and gotten to know the boys who were always late to class and rude to the teachers. The boys who liked to pick fights with other boys, for no reason other than it was something to do. Weldon had hated how he felt around his friends, but it was better than the exhausted loneliness he felt when he was by himself. When he thought of his family.

His phone rang. He bolted up from the couch and stared at the phone in surprise. The display blinked DAD.

"Hello?"

"Weldon, how are you?" David Warrick sounded almost cheerful. Like he'd had several good nights' sleep. *Possibly because I haven't been around*, Weldon thought.

"I'm good."

"Settling in okay with your aunt and uncle?"

Like I had any choice, Weldon thought.

"Yeah, they're fine. The bed's comfortable, anyway."

A pause.

121

"I appreciate you being willing to do this," his dad said. "Everything is crazy around here. Late nights, constant meetings. Trying to get everything right. It wouldn't have been fun for you."

"I know, it's okay. I'm fine here."

I only stole a car my first day in town. I only got into a fight with a bunch of local assholes. I only started hanging out with the granddaughter of the guy your father ripped off when he created the Tomorrow-Men. Weldon took a deep breath and closed his eyes, willing himself to be calm.

"Are you running at all?"

"Yeah," Weldon said. "I found a running group downtown. They seem pretty dedicated. I'll go with them a few days a week."

"That's good to hear," said his dad. Weldon thought he heard relief in his father's voice, and wondered if maybe David Warrick had felt a bit guilty shipping his son off to Sandford. Weldon hoped so.

"I haven't been back to Sandford in . . . oh, seven years? Eight?" said his dad. "Time flies. I keep trying to get your aunt and uncle down here to California for a visit, but you know how they are." Weldon thought of his aunt and uncle and their immaculate lawn. How his uncle lovingly tended the grass, driving the riding mower in slow, deliberate loops across the yard. He thought of his aunt in a wide-brimmed hat, her hands sunk deep in earth. Everything they seemed to want was here. Of course they weren't curious about what was outside their yard.

"Sometimes I can't believe I grew up there," David Warrick

said, snorting out a laugh. "I was desperate to get away. I blamed my father—your grandfather—for forcing us to live in the middle of nowhere. I was furious with him when we moved back to Sandford after he was pushed out of Warrick Comics. I thought I was destined for greater things. American things."

Weldon sat up, holding the phone tight to his ear. His father never talked about Joseph Warrick being forcibly retired from his own company when his son was a teenager. The whole thing was mysterious; some reports Weldon had read online said that the retirement was Joseph Warrick's idea, that he'd finally had enough of comic books. Others compared the ousting to Steve Jobs being fired from Apple: the company founder tossed away by subordinates grasping at power. But Joseph Warrick never returned triumphant to Warrick Comics, and seemed content to spend the rest of his life living quietly in his hometown, as his old friend Micah Kendrick battled for the rights to characters they had created decades ago. Years after his father's retirement, David Warrick left Canada to join Warrick Comics in California, and he'd been there ever since.

"There's a bar—Bearlys—it's not still downtown, is it?" Weldon's father asked.

"What street's it on?"

"The main street, what's it called? Vernon Street. Named after an old mayor, I think."

Weldon thought of Sandford's one downtown street, the Starbucks and Running Realm towering over it. He couldn't remember a bar named Bearlys.

"I'm not sure. I didn't see anything called that. It might've moved."

"It's probably gone," sighed David Warrick. "Your grandfather took me there the night I turned nineteen. A little father-son celebration. I remember sitting in that bar, sipping a beer and thinking about how I was going to escape Sandford. How I wasn't going to be like him, slinking home with his tail between his legs."

Weldon listened, free arm wrapped around his knees. Everything about this conversation was strange.

"Listen to me," David Warrick chuckled. "I do go on."

"It's okay," said Weldon.

"I'm sorry I shipped you off to your aunt and uncle," said his father. "I didn't know what else to do, especially after your mother—"

"It's okay," said Weldon quickly. He hugged his knees hard, feeling a lonely ache spread across the back of his ribs. He remembered his father on his phone after Weldon had been suspended from school, talking to his mother in low tones that rose in volume until Weldon could pick out the words. Ugly words, both adults hurling them at each other thoughtlessly. Weldon remembered his father hanging up the phone and standing in their kitchen with his back to Weldon, as though he was unable to turn around. Weldon had known then he would not be going to stay with his mother in San Diego.

"Why do you do these things, Weldon?" said his dad now.

"You were doing well at that school. I thought you were making friends. Then I get a call because you've gotten in trouble again."

"I don't know," said Weldon. *Because you don't see me. Because we used to go to San Diego Comic-Con as a family, you and me and Mom. We used to walk down the aisles of the convention center and flip through the dollar bins. Back then everything was just comics. There weren't giant media booths advertising cartoons and* Doctor Who *and vinyl toys. Mom used to pull old issues of the TomorrowMen out of the dollar bins and hold them up, laughing at the ridiculous covers. "The Tomorrow-Men versus The Broccoli People! Humanity hangs in the balance!"*

They had stopped going to Comic-Con together when Weldon was ten, three years before his mother left. At first Weldon had missed it, and then he hadn't anymore. But thinking about it now made the lonely ache in his ribs sharpen.

"Dammit, Weldon. You know that's not an answer, right?"

"Yeah," said Weldon. He could picture his dad in his office at Warrick Studios. The walls were papered with replicas of famous old TomorrowMen covers. The first meeting of Skylark and Skybound. The wedding of Skylark and Skybound, the best-selling TomorrowMen comic of all time. The cover to the issue where Tristan Terrific, old archnemesis of Skybound, joined the TomorrowMen team. The history of the TomorrowMen turned into office wallpaper. The cover with the Broccoli People was nowhere to be found.

David Warrick sighed heavily over the phone.

"I want to make a deal with you," he said. "I don't know if

this makes me a bad parent, like I'm rewarding your past behavior or something, but I'm not sure what else to do. I want you to make me a promise, Weldon, one you're going to keep."

"Okay," said Weldon.

"Don't 'okay' me, son. I want you to think about this, and if it's something you can do for me. You're seventeen, and it's time you started using your brain like you're at least approaching adulthood."

"Okay."

"Ehhgh," David Warrick said into the phone, disgusted. He pressed onward. "I want you to promise you won't be an idiot this summer. No stealing, no acting out. We'll reassess when September comes around, but right now, let's just focus on the summer."

"Okay."

"You be good, and I'll let you come to Comic-Con. You can join me for the movie preview in Hall H along with the six thousand people dedicated enough to sleep in line on the sidewalk the night before. You get to be up there with me, watching history happen. The first look at footage from the TomorrowMen movie released to the public."

Weldon closed his eyes. He could see it in front of him, the sprawling convention center like an alien spaceship crashed on the edge of the San Diego waterfront. The mobs of people in Star Wars and Captain America and Legend of Zelda and TomorrowMen T-shirts crowded around the front doors, bodies pressing forward, desperate to enter. He saw the actors from the TomorrowMen movie, their perfect faces aloof, pretending not to see the scrum of people around them as they were escorted into Hall H, the cavernous room reserved for the most anticipated announcements of Comic-Con. He saw himself trailing after them, his dad a few feet ahead of him. The crowd roared as the actors took the stage, six thousand frenzied voices reaching a deafening crescendo. He was there with David Warrick, who had fought so hard to get a TomorrowMen movie made. Weldon could see his father nearly vibrating with the emotion of the crowd. He turned toward Weldon, his face shining—

"Yes," Weldon said.

"Weldon, I need you to think about this. This is a promise."

"I promise. I won't do it anymore."

"Won't do what?"

"Won't be a jerk."

Let me come with you. Let me stand on the stage with you. Believe me when I say I want this.

David Warrick sighed.

"Okay, Weldon. Okay."

They talked for a few more minutes after that. About the weather in Sandford versus California, about Weldon's aunt and uncle, about the prime minster of Canada, whose name Weldon surprised himself by plucking out of thin air. Eventually the conversation wound down and David Warrick said he had to go.

"I believe you can do this, Weldon," he said. "I trust that you'll make the right decisions."

"Thanks, Dad," said Weldon, meaning it. Maybe them being apart had been good for them.

"Goodbye, son."

"Bye, Dad."

Weldon sat on the couch for a while longer, hugging his knees and feeling the conversation roll around in his head. *He said he trusted me.* Had that really never happened before? Weldon couldn't remember. His body felt explosive and quivery, energy and emotion spilling over. He stretched and got off the couch. The excitement of the moment overwhelmed him, and he let out a loud whoop that echoed through the empty house.

CHAPTER TWELVE

"Help me with my TomorrowMen script."

Mir looked up. Evan was sitting across from her at one of the school library tables, earnestly staring at her over a pile of books. Mir had been at the library for the past three hours, writing her final essay on *The Stone Angel*. The end of school and final exams loomed, and Mir's brain felt overstuffed from endless studying. Evan had showed up half an hour ago and awkwardly hung around Mir, obviously wanting something but too embarrassed to come out and ask for it. Mir decided to ignore him until he got the courage to speak up.

"Your TomorrowMen script?"

"Yeah!" Evan beamed at Mir, his beard practically radiating light. "The one I'm going to give to Weldon Warrick so he can pass it on to his dad and then I'll become the next writer on the TomorrowMen."

Mir leaned back from the table.

"Evan, that is really, really unlikely. You know that, right?"

"Weirder things have happened," Evan said. He was still smiling, but Mir could tell by the way his gaze dropped to the pile of papers in front of him that her comment had hurt. *Why am I so good at hurting him?* she thought. *Mir, stop using practicality as an excuse to shit on your friends' dreams. Not everyone wants to put every penny they earn into a savings account so they can go to university. Some people want different things.*

"You're right," Mir said. "Weldon told us about how strange the comic book industry was. I'm sure people have gotten hired in even weirder ways."

"So will you help me?"

Mir looked at the piles of notepaper in front of her, photocopied articles from literary journals and the well-thumbed school copy of *The Stone Angel*. It was not an appealing mess.

"What do you need help with?"

Evan moved to Mir's side of the table and thunked down in the chair next to her. Mir couldn't remember the last time she'd seen him in the school library. Evan preferred to find his entertainment outdoors, usually something that involved swimming or driving ATVs or jumping off high ledges. Mir remembered Evan complaining as she walked with Raleigh to the local library, telling them it was such a nice day outside, why did they want to spend it inside reading books? Mir and Raleigh had shaken their heads, bonding over their disapproval. Didn't Evan know books were fun?

I wonder if Raleigh still goes to the library, Mir thought. *I'll ask her the next time I see her.* Whenever that was. The thought of

Raleigh made Mir's chest ache. She missed their conversations about the books they read, series that Stella silently disapproved of, pointedly leaving copies of *Anne of Green Gables* on top of the stacks of R. L. Stine Mir brought home from the library. Raleigh was so good at finding the grossest part of any *Goosebumps* book and reading that section aloud in a quavering, sarcastic voice. Mir remembered rolling around on the carpet in Raleigh's family room, laughing until her sides ached.

Evan shoved a jumbled printout at Mir. She stared at it, uncomprehending.

"What's this?"

"That's my outline," Evan said. "I did a lot of research online, and most comic book writers start with a story outline. Then they do panel breakdowns, figure out the flow of the story, and then they write in the dialogue and stuff. Only some writers don't even do panel breakdowns. They leave that up to the artists. It's really confusing, actually. Every writer seems to work differently."

Mir frowned at the chaotic mess of words on the piece of paper in front of her.

"Evan, are you saying you haven't actually written a script?"

"Well, not technically," Evan said. He pointed at the paper. "But I wrote the story down, and it has most of the dialogue in there. The rest is just formatting everything so it looks like an actual script. Super easy!"

"That doesn't sound easy," Mir said.

"That's why I need help," said Evan, grinning sheepishly.

"You're the smartest person I know, so I've chosen to reward you with this task. I just . . . I have everything in there, all the story's there, I just need help to make it look like a script."

It had always been like this with him. He would slide through school, cramming the night before every test, happy with low Cs and Ds. Surviving classes because Mir made him study, the two of them sprawled on the floor of Stella and Henry's living room, Mir shouting at Evan in mock annoyance whenever he got off track. Which was often. She knew he probably had an essay due tomorrow for his English class, a paper he'd slap together at the last minute. *What book would his class be reading?* Mir thought. Something easier than *The Stone Angel*, probably. Something deadly boring to Evan. Something that would further convince him reading anything but a comic book was an exercise in soul-killing.

Mir squinted at the printout. It was practically unreadable, a solid block of words, no paragraph or dialogue breaks. Mir put down the paper and reached for her notebook, flipping it to a blank page at the back.

"Tell me the story you want to write."

Evan stared at Mir, confused. She smiled, gesturing at the area next to the table they were sitting at.

"I mean, act it out. You're good at that stuff. You're the best at drama class and you're really good at explaining things. You act it out, and I'll write it down, and then we'll go from there, cool?"

Understanding dawned on Evan's face. Mir held up a hand.

"But we're still in the library, okay? So maybe keep it as quiet as possible."

Evan stood in front of the table, eyes closed. Mir watched him, her pen poised above the notebook. Evan opened his eyes and reached his hands toward Mir, his voice stage-whisper low.

"This is a story about the choices of Tristan Terrific, the only member of the TomorrowMen who is not a hero. Every day he struggles with his gift: his powers are pure persuasion. He can speak to a person and make that person do anything, convinced it was of his own free will."

Mir scribbled frantically, the story taking shape on the paper as she wrote. Every moment of Tristan Terrific's life was steeped in pain. Every moment he lived, he knew what he could do with his powers, how he could control and manipulate the minds of people around him. And in the past, he had. He'd built an empire on the backs of people who had no idea their will was not their own. Tristan Terrific had seen them as ants. Tiny ants, going about their lives, never knowing they were being manipulated. But one day Tristan Terrific woke up and saw what he was doing, and saw that it was wrong. So he tried to be good. And being good was agony.

Evan's story was fairly simple. "You should tell a complete story in twenty-two pages for a pitch," he explained to Mir. "It can't be one piece of a giant epic space war crossover or something. So I'm doing a day in the life, one day with Tristan Terrific. He saves the world with the TomorrowMen, but he's always afraid. He's seen what he's capable of and he's afraid that some-day he might return to that."

Evan leaned on the table in front of Mir, staring at her seri-ously.

"He's addicted to his powers," said Evan. "Every day he has to choose not to use his powers on people, except when the world's in the balance. And even then it's like, should I take that step? Should I manipulate that bad guy? Is the cost of giving in to his powers worth the lives of innocent civilians?"

Mir finished writing and threw her pen down, massaging her wrist. Evan smiled hopefully at her.

"What did you think?"

Mir stared at the notebook and at her frantic handwriting, the words slanting longer and longer the farther down the page she went.

"It's good, Evan," she said. She liked the idea of seeing a day in a struggling superhero's life, seeing the moral choices he made in order to remain on the side of good. It wasn't all giant robot fights and superpowers on display, the things that Weldon War-rick said he liked in comics. It was something she thought she might enjoy. She nodded, smiling to herself.

"I'd read it."

"Yesss!" Evan fist-pumped the air, earning a hissed "SHHH!" from the librarian eyeing them from the circulation desk. He did a tiny dance, feet thumping softly on the carpeted floor be-fore he sat back down at the table, leaning toward Miriam.

"I know it's stupid," he said. "I know that I won't get hired to write TomorrowMen comics because I give a script to that Warrick guy. I'm sixteen, and there are a million established writers already out there who'd kill to write comics for Warrick Studios. But——" Evan looked up at Mir, and she couldn't help but grin back, his excitement infectious. "It's fun to do this, y'know? I've never written anything important before. Anything to show someone, I mean."

"I'm glad," Mir said, meaning it. For the millionth time, she wished she felt something more for Evan. It would have been so simple. *I have to make everything complicated*, she thought. *Can't fall for the guy I've known since sixth grade, have to fall for . . .* Weldon Warrick's smile was suddenly in her mind, his gaze focused straight on her as he leaned on the counter of the Emporium of Wonders. Mir flinched away from the memory.

"I'm glad too," said Evan, still beaming. Mir pushed Weldon Warrick from her mind and tapped the paper in front of her.

"Have you written other TomorrowMen stories?"

"Oh, yeah, lots. Just for myself, just for fun." Evan reached in his bag, pulling out a spiral notebook. He flipped it open, the pages covered with his awkward writing, small doodles of superheroes in the margins. He grinned at Mir. "Didn't you notice me during free period, hiding in the cafeteria, scribbling away?"

"Yeah, I did, but I guess I thought . . ." Mir trailed off, picking up the notebook and staring at it in awe. "Well, I kinda thought you were studying."

"How long have you known me?" Evan half yelled, earning

another pointed look from the librarian. He dropped his voice to a whisper. "When do I ever study?"

"When I make you!" Mir hissed back.

Mir held the well-thumbed spiral notebook in her hands, carefully flipping through it. She glanced up at Evan once, out of the corner of her eye, and saw his cheeks were pink from embarrassment. But he was smiling, encouraged by her interest. The amount of writing in the notebook was astonishing, pages and pages of words, hardly any paragraph breaks, filled with stories. Evan's stories. She'd never seen him write like this before.

Mir closed the notebook.

"Why didn't you tell me about this?"

Evan shrugged.

"I thought it might be weird. Jamie and Raleigh don't care about comics, so why would I tell them? And you've got history with the TomorrowMen. Really complicated history. I thought you might not like that I write stories about them."

"I think it's awesome, Evan," Mir said. Evan smiled, kind of shyly. The shyness looked strange on him. Mir was so used to him being loud and fearless, the life of every drama class.

"It's nothing," he said, reaching for the notebook. Mir let him take it, stuffing the book back in his bag. She tore the lined sheet with Evan's TomorrowMen story from her notebook, and started to stand up.

"Let's type this up while it's still fresh, okay?"

Evan grabbed Mir's hand and pulled her back down to her chair. His face was serious.

"Can I ask you something?"

"Sure," Mir said, concerned. Evan stared at her for what felt like an agonizingly long time, then plunged forward.

"You and this Warrick guy, is there something . . . um, he came to see you in the store that day, didn't he? Is there something with you and him?"

Mir's stomach lurched. She remembered the way Weldon's face had brightened when he'd seen her behind the Emporium of Wonders' front desk, the way he'd hesitated when he saw she wasn't alone. Evan had noticed that.

"I don't—no, I don't think so," Mir said.

"But you guys had met before, right?"

"Yeah. He came into the store two weeks ago. I think he's spending the summer in Sandford. I've met him maybe three times, I barely know him." Mir gave Evan her best serious expression, the one usually reserved for discussing grades with teachers. Evan let go of her hand, leaning back in his chair. Mir thought she caught an expression of relief flicker across his face, but the moment passed so quickly she wondered if she'd imagined it.

"Cool," said Evan. Mir took the scribbled-on notebook paper to one of the library's terrible computers, a beige box that was probably obsolete the minute the library bought it. She sat down in front of the computer, Evan dragging over a nearby chair to sit beside her. Mir pulled up Microsoft Word and flexed her fingers over the computer keyboard. She typed "Tristan Terrific Script, draft 1, by Evan Willis" at the top of the new document.

"Did you want to put your name in there too? You're helping me," Evan said.

Mir shook her head.

"It's your story, Evan. I'm just your typing monkey. Although I expect compensation when you get hired by Warrick Studios and spend the next thirty years getting rich writing TomorrowMen comics."

"I will buy you a solid gold toilet," Evan said solemnly, scooting his chair closer to Mir. Mir typed the opening words she had scrawled in her notebook:

PAGE 1

PANEL 1: Tristan Terrific catapults backward out of a window, glass breaking all around him. He is tied to a chair, a ticking time bomb strapped to the back of it.

CAPTION (NARRATION): I wish my name wasn't Tristan Terrific.

Evan grinned, leaning over Mir's shoulder.

"This is going to be awesome."

CHAPTER THIRTEEN

The following Saturday, Weldon went running again. He jogged easily into town, over the bridge, through the brief swell of traffic that was Sandford's pitiful downtown, and into the park by the waterfront. There were other joggers dotting the paths, nimbly dodging people walking their dogs, nodding the occasional hello. It all felt cozy and very small town.

Weldon turned his conversation with his father over and over in his head. San Diego Comic-Con floated in the future like a glittering prize. All he had to do was be good for the summer. No stealing cars, no fights, no screwing up. Be good, be good. Weldon sucked in a breath and picked up speed, his feet sweeping over the dirt path.

"I'll trust you to make the right decisions," David Warrick had said.

Has he really never said that to me? Weldon thought. He rewound memories from the past few years. His parents fighting, his mom leaving, her absence like a scab ripped off too soon.

His dad throwing everything into getting the TomorrowMen movie off the ground. Weldon alone in their Burbank house, feeling the emptiness of every room. It made him want to crawl out of his skin, made him want to put his fist through whatever wall was closest to him. Weldon lowered his head, pumped his arms, and made the ground move even faster under his feet. He ran David Warrick's words back through his head: *I'll trust you to make the right decisions. I trust you. I trust you.*

What changed in two weeks that he would say that to me? Weldon dug his feet into the dirt path as he jogged up an incline. The park wasn't flat; it sloped up and away from the water. Weldon liked the extra challenge of the hills.

Maybe Dad's just happier now. His movie's nearly finished, the trailer will be premiering soon. Everything's finally coming up Warrick.

Weldon reached the top of the hill and paused, turning to look down toward the water. Sandford weather was dreary and gray even in late May, but a bit of sunlight had managed to creep through the ceiling of clouds. The water sparkled for a moment.

Weldon turned away and resumed his jog. *Kinda getting fond of this awful place*, he thought, shaking his head.

He was jogging through downtown, heading for the bridge and home, when he spotted the boys. At first he wasn't sure why they looked so familiar; then one of them aggressively punched another boy in the shoulder and Weldon recognized the arc of the boy's swing. That same boy had swung his fist toward Weldon's face in payback for stealing his car. Ice shot down his spine and he froze, not sure what to do. He decided hiding was his best option and scurried ahead of the group of boys, toward the Running Realm. He pulled the front door open and slid inside in what he hoped was a nonchalant manner. If the boys spotted him, he'd be cornered.

Weldon watched from behind a blank-faced mannequin as the boys sauntered by, shoving and shouting at one another. He realized he was clenching his fists, and deliberately opened his hands, pressing his palms against his thighs. Blood pounded in his ears, a violent staccato. He imagined stepping outside the store, calling out to them. He imagined recognition lighting their faces. He saw himself buried under a hail of blows, saw his nose break, his forehead split open, saw booted feet descend to blacken his vision. There was no Miriam flying out the doors of the Emporium of Wonders to save his life.

"Hey," said a voice behind him. Weldon turned to see Ellie leaning on the store counter, her chin in her hands. "You hiding?"

Weldon took a breath, his stomach lurching.

"Yeah. That okay?"

Ellie walked out from behind the counter and joined him at the window, staring out at the group of boys across the street.

"Oh, those douchebags," she sighed, shaking her head. "Yeah, hide all you want. I hate those guys." She extended her hand, flipping her middle finger toward the boys.

"Thanks for letting me hide," said Weldon.

"Anything I can do to mess with those guys," Ellie said, still staring out the window. "Typical Sandford losers. There's nothing to do in this shitty town, so all they do is go around beating people up and getting drunk. They're the worst.

"What'd you do to them? Something good?" Ellie grinned, her eyes narrowing happily.

"One of them left his car running and unlocked, so I took it."

Ellie laughed and clapped her hands, delighted. Weldon shook his head to hide the smile creeping across his face. Ellie would've bought him a drink after the fight, congratulating him on his fine adventure.

"You're not from around here, are you? I remember a lady came in a couple weeks back, saying her nephew would be staying for the summer, and he jogged, so . . ." Ellie left the sentence hanging.

"My dad's from here," said Weldon. "He moved to California after high school. That's where I'm from."

"Really," said Ellie. The word came out liquid and full of intrigue. Her eyes dipped up and down Weldon, impressed. "I've always wanted to go to the West Coast."

"Canadian West Coast or American?" said Weldon.

"Either. Both. That side is where things happen. All the artists are there, all the people who make things. It's like there's something in the Pacific water; everyone who wants to be someone or do something interesting gets drawn there."

"You can do things or be somebody on the East Coast as well," said Weldon. "Lots of artists in New York. Stephen King's in Maine, that's East Coast."

"Not this East Coast," said Ellie, her mouth smiling, her eyes angry. "Not this shitty town."

Ellie moved away from him, walking toward the store counter. She stood behind it and pretended to arrange a pile of metal water bottles. Weldon walked over to her, drawn by the bitterness in her voice.

"You don't like it here?"

"Sandford is fine," Ellie said, peering intently at one of the bottles in the display. "It's fine if you have money and can live across the bridge in the nice section of town. But it's a terrible place to live if you're just starting out, because there's nothing to start out with. No jobs that aren't working in retail or slinging booze on one of the tourist cruises."

Ellie sighed, leaning back from her bottle display.

"Listen to me, griping about prospects in this town. I am so old."

Weldon looked at her, the freckles spread across her nose, the fit lines of her body. She didn't look older than twenty, but she might be. The store she stood in was gleaming and new, mannequins posed immaculately, showing off their designer running clothes. But he saw it through her eyes, this feeling of being stuck in one place while the rest of the world moved on without you.

"So why are you here, instead of in LA where things actually happen?" Ellie asked, looking up at Weldon.

"I'm in exile," Weldon said. "My dad is making a superhero

movie, and I'm a distraction. So I got sent to the ass-end of Canada until the movie's done."

Ellie's eyes lit up.

"A superhero movie? Which one?"

"The TomorrowMen."

"Oh, I loved them as a kid," Ellie said, delighted, a hand fluttering to her mouth. Weldon smiled, feeling a familiar flush of recognition and pride. Everyone loved the TomorrowMen. Even if they'd never read a comic, they still remembered the shows or owned some toy or T-shirt with the TomorrowMen insignia on it. "I dressed up as Skylark for Halloween one year. I think I was in grade four. God, I loved her."

"She's the best one," Weldon agreed.

"So are you going to make movies too?" Ellie said. She leaned forward a little, her expression openly envious. "If your dad is making them, you must want to as well. He could get you a job. You could be the next Steven Spielberg. Or Quentin Tarantino."

She laughed.

"Or, I don't know, a famous screenwriter. I don't know the names of any screenwriters, but I'm sure there are some famous ones."

Weldon hesitated. He remembered Miriam describing her mother's relationship to her paintings. To Stella, making art was something she needed to do, a necessity for living. Losing that part of her would be like losing a limb. He remembered the comic artists and writers clumped together in small, drunken groups in his parents' house in San Diego. Talking about comics, only comics, like there was nothing else in the world. *I've never felt that way about anything*, Weldon thought.

"No," said Weldon, "I don't want to make movies." He was surprised at the decisiveness of his words, but he knew they were true. If the TomorrowMen movie was as successful as expected, David Warrick had a slate of films ready to follow the first movie. Solo films starring each individual TomorrowMan waited in the wings. If Weldon behaved himself and earned his father's trust, there might be a job for him in the Warrick Studio universe. Weldon flinched at the thought of being forever chained to his father's comic book universe, his career dependent on David Warrick. *I want to be with my dad at Comic-Con this year, to see the TomorrowMen movie trailer premiere*, he thought. *And then I want to figure out what I want to do with my life. Which will be different from what he does with his life.*

"You're just going to throw away that opportunity?" Ellie said. Her voice had an edge. Weldon saw the envy had transformed into anger. He was dismissing opportunities she would never have.

"It's just . . . It's just a coincidence, it's not an opportunity," Weldon said. He felt resentful of her anger. She didn't know his father, or the tangled world of the TomorrowMen. "I just happen to be related to someone who makes movies. Some people are incredibly talented and love filmmaking, but they're not related to people who run a movie studio. Why should I take the career of someone who really wants to work in movies just because my dad is David Warrick?"

Ellie turned her face away, rubbing her arms as though she was suddenly cold. A tension hung between them. Weldon waited, wondering if she would continue to argue. She moved away from him, walking behind the store counter. Weldon straightened, feeling like he was being dismissed.

"I'll see you around," he said. Ellie nodded, still not looking at him. Weldon left the store, the small, quaint bell hanging from the front door jangling with his exit.

Outside on the sidewalk, he scanned quickly for the gang of boys. There was no sign of them. He jogged back to his aunt and uncle's house, checking carefully behind him every five minutes.

CHAPTER FOURTEEN

Something felt wrong. It was Sunday, and Mir's shift at the Emporium of Wonders was six hours, the longest shift she'd worked since Berg asked her to take a week off. Mir walked toward the back of the Emporium of Wonders, trying to put her finger on the feeling that something in the store was off. She had just started to re-alphabetize the graphic novels when Berg called her name. He was standing in the door-way to his office, his eyes sadder and droopier than normal.

"Miriam, can I talk to you?"

"Sure, but no one's watching the store and it's still an hour before closing."

"Put up the closed sign," Berg said. "It's important."

Miriam felt cold. She walked to the front of the store and flipped the OPEN/CLOSED sign around. In Berg's office, she sat on a chair opposite his desk, feeling like an intruder. Like she hadn't spent hours in that office over the past year, helping Berg stack and sort papers, laughing with him about weird customers.

Berg always asked about her family, especially about her mother's garden. How big was it this summer? Were there new plants? What kind of fertilizer was Stella using? Mir would bug him to visit: "Mom and Dad would love to have you over, Berg! Like old times"—but he always brushed her off. "Too busy, Mir. Tell them I'm sorry. Send them my love."

"The store is closing, Miriam," said Berg.

Mir waited to feel something, but nothing came. All the small puzzling moments from the past months fell firmly into place. Berg cutting her hours, the disorganization in the store, the dirty front window. The look of giving up had been draped over the Emporium of Wonders for months. She'd seen the end coming without even realizing it.

"There's something else," Berg continued. "I can't pay you for the last two weeks of work."

"But—" The protest hung on Mir's lips. She couldn't think of words to follow it, her mouth pushing out the "But" prematurely, no argument to back it up. "But I . . . I . . . worked! I worked today!" she finished, lamely.

"I'm sorry, Mir, but everything's gone," Berg said. "My creditors ate it all, and it still wasn't enough. There's nothing left to pay you. I'm really sorry. I know you were saving your money for school."

"I guess I *was* saving for school," Mir said, more to herself than Berg. She had already counted the money in her head. She had counted forward a year, counted out her work hours times her hourly pay, adding it all up. She had already imagined putting all the money she was going to earn in her bank account, had counted it in her head against the cost of tuition to McGill, to the University of Toronto, to any other university that caught her eye. The money she didn't have yet had made her feel safe. And now it was gone.

Berg reached out his hand and placed it on top of Mir's hand, which was wringing the life out of her work shirt.

"You're a good kid," he said. "You worked hard for me, and you deserve better. I really wanted to hang on for another year, just so you could earn a little more money. And now I can't even pay you for the last two weeks. Please forgive me."

It was horrible to hear him say that, and she pulled her hand away from his. Mir stood and walked out of the office. She grabbed her backpack and walked out of the store. On the sidewalk she struggled with the straps of her backpack, putting the wrong arm through one strap, trying to correct, and putting the wrong arm through the strap again. After two tries, she managed to get the backpack on. Mir drew in a shaky breath and looked down the street. The make-your-own-pottery store had a new sign in the window, advertising evening classes for beginner artisans. Two women were leaving the designer yoga pants store, brown paper shopping bags dangling from their arms.

Mir walked toward the Starbucks at the end of the road, past the SWEAT EVERY DAY sign in the yoga pants store's window. She pushed open the door to Starbucks and stood in line, looking at the other people in the coffee shop, their faces bent to laptops or phones, mugs left forgotten on the tables in front of them.

"What can I get you?" said the girl behind the counter, her short dark hair spiked artfully in every direction. Mir remembered her as the older sister of a boy a grade ahead of her. She'd left Sandford for art school in Halifax. It looked like she was back for the summer, bringing a little bit of city style with her. For a moment, Mir lost her train of thought, staring at the girl's hair. She wondered how her own hair would look cut so short. It would probably still be curly. Probably not spikeable.

"A large coffee," Mir said.

The spiky-haired girl handed Mir the coffee, the white-and-green cup warm in her hand. She piled as much sugar and two-percent milk into the coffee as she could, then walked out of the Starbucks. When she was back on the sidewalk, Mir took a careful sip of the coffee. Despite the sugar and milk, it still tasted too much like coffee, and she screwed up her face against the bitterness.

She turned toward the designer yoga pants store and hurled the coffee at it. The paper cup hit the store's front window with a satisfying smack and exploded all over it, brown liquid spewing everywhere.

Mir stared at her handiwork, then turned and ran.

After sprinting what felt like a safe distance from the Running Realm, Mir walked toward the park at the edge of Sandford. She couldn't bear the thought of going home. She imagined Stella's arms around her, saying it was okay, she would find another job. And even if she didn't, it would still be okay. There were ways to pay for university. There were student loans and lines of credit and scholarships. Mir felt crushed under the weight of so many options.

What's the right decision? she thought. *Should I leave Sandford? What if it all goes wrong, the way it did for my grandfather? If I don't leave, then what? Why can't someone just tell me what I should do?*

Mir wandered through the park, reaching the mouth of the river where it joined the ocean. She sat on the edge of the riverbank and stared at a cargo ship slowly chugging its way out of the Sandford harbor. There were large shipping containers stacked on the ship, the names of various countries painted on the side. China. Argentina. Chile. *Is that where they're going or where they're from?* Mir wondered.

Her chest felt hollow. Mir leaned forward and dug her fingers into the grass in front of her, trying to think. She still had a year between now and graduation. She could get a new job. Who was hiring? Evan's dad, maybe. She could haul sod and cringe when she saw him coming, towering over the landscaping site, swearing at anyone who wasn't doing their job to his satisfaction. Evan hardly ever swore. How did someone like Evan, who thought making people laugh at his jokes was the ultimate achievement, have such an angry father?

Mir plucked at the grass, tossing bits of it to the side. She could ask Ms. Archer for help with scholarship applications. She could apply for student loans. Wade through paperwork and tax returns, not understanding any of it, except for the mounting debt to pay for something she wasn't even sure she wanted.

What's wrong with me that I don't know what I want? Mir thought.

The hollowness in her chest worked its way upward and burst out of her in an awful, gross sob. She bawled angrily for a long time, face turned to the grass under her hands, her body ridged with frustration over the unfairness of it all. It wasn't fair that Berg was better suited to growing carrots than running a business, it wasn't fair that tourists wanted to buy yoga pants instead of books or comics, it wasn't fair that things couldn't remain exactly how they were for one more measly year. Mir ripped up a few more strands of grass, flinging them futilely out in front of her.

When she was done crying, Mir wiped the snot off her face with her work-shirt sleeve and walked toward the park entrance. There were several joggers slowly running down the path, sneakered feet beating a soft rhythm against the ground. Mir paused, recognizing Weldon as he jogged easily ahead of her.

Mir watched him run, the way his feet struck the ground emphatically in the arc of each stride, his dark hair bouncing in rhythm, the inward-turned expression on his face. She thought about putting her hand on his shoulder, her palm catching on the bunched muscle, then sliding down his back.

"Weldon Warrick," Mir said. Weldon jogged on, oblivious. Mir took a deep breath and yelled his name.

"WELDON WARRICK!"

He missed a step, recovered, and turned toward her, pulling white earbuds out of his ears.

"Why are you here?" Mir said.

"What?"

"Why are you here?" Mir said again, the last word coming out in a dry croak. Her throat was raw from crying. She hoped she'd wiped all the snot off her face.

Weldon started walking toward her, then stopped and stood several yards away.

"Why am I here in Sandford? Or why am I here in the cosmic sense?"

Mir stared at the ground, feeling stupid and wondering what she actually meant by the question. There had been some logic behind it, but now she couldn't remember what it was.

"I'm here because I screwed up," Weldon said. "I pushed my dad too far. I thought he'd put up with me acting like an idiot, but he proved me wrong. He's making that movie and he can't have me distracting him." Weldon wrapped the white earbuds around his iPod, tucking it into the pocket of his shorts. "I guess I'm also here because years ago my grandfather and your grandfather made comics together, and those comics are still really important to some people."

"I lost my job," Miriam said.

"The job in the . . . um, the bookstore?" said Weldon. "I'm really sorry to hear that."

"It's stupid," Miriam whispered, her face pointed downward. The emptiness in her chest had faded, leaving behind dull embarrassment. *It was a stupid job. I was stupid to care about it.*

Weldon didn't say anything. Mir could still feel him

standing in front of her. She couldn't look up. *Why did I say his name? Can I tell him to go away?* Mir continued staring at her boots, feeling every second tick by.

"I don't think it's stupid," Weldon said. "It meant something to you. If something means something to you, it's never stupid."

Mir looked up. Weldon was standing a few paces away from her, hands on his hips, sweaty and glowing from his run. Mir felt the thing in her chest flutter a little. She liked how Weldon's hair was pushed back from his forehead. It made him look a bit younger. A bit more like a boy.

"Even if that thing is a comic book?" Mir said.

Weldon blinked at her.

"Comic books mean a lot to some people," he said. "That friend of yours I met at the store the other day, I could tell he loved comics. Don't they mean anything to you?"

"No," said Mir, her throat raw. "I think they're pretty awful. I think they destroy the people who love them the most."

Weldon looked down at his hands, his palms turned up. He seemed to be gathering himself, preparing to say something he'd been thinking for a while.

"I think your family is really cool. I don't know the whole story, but I'm sorry for what my family did to yours. You should—your family should have some part in this movie, in what the TomorrowMen became. I'm just—I would've liked to get to know you better. I guess that'll never happen because, y'know, all that shitty history we have, but—" He spread his hands wide, gesturing helplessly. "I don't know. You just seem cool, that's all."

Mir stared dumbly at him. She remembered Weldon Warrick peering intently at Stella's painting, hung on the wall of the Emporium of Wonders, his hands in his jacket pockets. Weldon Warrick sprawled on the ground in the parking lot, looking up at her with a crooked grin, his eye already swelling shut. Weldon Warrick at her family's table, laughing at Henry's stories, listening to Nate tell him about his favorite cartoon show.

And now Weldon Warrick was telling her she was cool, telling her he was sorry. Something tore in Mir's chest, a heavy web that had wrapped itself around her the day she had first looked up her grandfather on the internet. When she'd first realized that there were so many things that could have been different. If Micah Kendrick hadn't signed away the rights to his characters, if he hadn't gotten sick, if Stella had been willing to carry on the copyright fight for him. So many small things, building up to one giant truth: the TomorrowMen and all their riches were lost to her family forever. It was a relief to feel that heavy, angry web bend and rip. She felt strange and light.

"I think I've been kinda mean to you," Mir blurted out.

Weldon grinned. He ducked his head and his hair fell across his forehead. Mir wanted to reach out and push it back, to see him look young again.

"Nah," he said.

"Yeah, I have," Mir said. "I wanted someone to be angry at. I'm sorry."

"God," Weldon said, still grinning. "Canadians."

"It's all we know how to do: apologize, apologize, and then apologize some more. Oh——" Mir suddenly cringed, putting her hands over her face.

"What?"

"I threw a coffee—I threw it at the yoga pants store downtown. It splattered all over their window. I can't believe I did that. I'm always the one making responsible decisions, and that was not a responsible decision at all."

"Did anyone see you?" Weldon said. "Anyone who knew who you were?"

Mir thought for a moment.

"I guess not? But what if they have cameras in the store? What if they have video of me throwing the coffee at the window? Did I totally just screw everything up?"

"Probably not," Weldon said. "I mean, to the camera thing. Maybe just stay low for the next few days. You're not going back to work, are you?"

"No, not since I'm not getting paid," Mir said. "But I should call Berg. I kind of . . . I kind of ran out of the store when he said I was fired. He's a terrible businessman, but he's still a friend. I've known him for ages." She pushed a hand across her face, rubbing at her eyes. She felt exhausted.

"Give him a call, but maybe steer clear of the Starbucks for a bit, yeah?"

Mir squinted at Weldon from behind her hand.

"Is that your professional advice, as a career criminal?"

"Absolutely," he said with a solemn nod. "I gotta warn you, though, I charge an arm and a leg for my criminal consulting skills. It takes years of hard work to reach my level of criminal expertise."

"Ha-ha," said Mir. Behind Weldon, a pair of joggers ran by, glancing at them curiously. Mir hoped she didn't still look like she'd been crying.

"Want to walk a bit?" said Weldon, waving his hand in the direction of the running path. "I get horrible muscle cramps if I don't cool down properly after a run."

Mir hesitated. It was close to 5:00 p.m. already. Her work shift normally ended at five, and her mom was expecting her home soon after that. Sunday nights were casual, Stella throwing together a dinner of leftovers or sometimes making a batch of pancakes. She would wonder where Mir was if she didn't show up soon.

"Maybe for a few minutes. Can we walk toward my house? My parents are expecting me home pretty soon."

"You're honest and you defend people's lives armed only with a garden hose and you worry about being home when you told your parents you would be," said Weldon, falling into step with Mir. "You are literally the coolest person I've ever met, Miriam Kendrick."

"Stop making fun of me, Weldon Warrick," said Mir, smiling.

CHAPTER FIFTEEN

Weldon walked beside Miriam. It felt good to look to his right and see her profile against the blue of the slow-moving river by the park. He listened to her talk, their conversation rolling forward easily. They went in the opposite direction from the waterfront, toward the back of the park. The road that led away from the park was rougher than the waterfront road, the houses lining it a little more run-down. Mir walked at a leisurely pace, slower than Weldon was used to, and he paced his steps to keep in time with her.

"I know, I'm a slow walker," Mir said, glancing down at Weldon's deliberate steps. "I can't help it. It's genetic; I have my mom's short legs."

"I come from a family of giants," Weldon said. "I'm the shortest of all of them, actually."

Mir eyed him.

"You're pretty tall."

"My dad's six two. My mom swears she's five ten, but she's

probably six foot one. I'm the one everyone looks down on. A towering five eleven."

"Why doesn't your mom want to be six feet tall?"

"I dunno," Weldon said, raising a hand to brush at a low-hanging branch. Trees lined the road, jutting haphazardly out of front yards. "She used to be an actress, and she has all kinds of . . . weirdness . . . because of that."

"An actress?" Mir said, glancing curiously at Weldon. "Is she famous? Would I know her?"

"Maybe," said Weldon. "She made a lot of science fiction and fantasy movies in the eighties and nineties. And she was a recurring villain on that one . . . space show. Not *Star Trek*. One of the other ones."

"*Stargate*?"

"No, another one——"

"*Battlestar Galactica*?"

"No."

"*Babylon 5*?"

"Nope. Wow, I feel awful. I can't remember the name. I kind of liked that show too. Anyway, she was an evil android."

"*Farscape*."

"Noooo," said Weldon, shaking his head, half in disbelief over his own ignorance. "How do you know so many science fiction shows?"

"I named, like, four. That's hardly 'many.' You're the one who can't remember his mother's TV show."

Weldon laughed.

"I am the worst son," he said.

"I hope this isn't mean, but actors scare me," Mir said, pulling the neck of her work shirt up to her chin. She looked kind of like an embarrassed turtle retreating into its shell.

"Because they tend to be ridiculously attractive and put together? They're like next-level human beings, which can be scary. I get that."

"No," Mir said, glancing over at Weldon. She was smiling, but there was a slight crease between her eyebrows that made Weldon think she might be worried about offending him. "They can do all these different accents, they can put on wigs and makeup and look like a completely different person. Don't tell me you don't find that scary? Actors can pretend to be anyone."

"That is literally the most insane theory about actors I've ever heard," Weldon said, grinning. "They're just people."

"How do you know?" Miriam said, waving her hands dramatically at him. "They could be . . . acting!"

"My mom only acts when she's at work," Weldon said. "She's herself when she's at home." Weldon thought of his mother's icy anger, and wished she'd maybe tried acting at home. She'd once played the captain of a misfit starship crew, marooned on a space mining rig overrun by alien monsters. He'd liked that character. She'd never refused to talk to her crew for days.

They reached a road that Weldon recognized. His uncle had barreled down this road when dropping Weldon off for dinner, heedless of the large potholes in the pavement. Miriam pointed in the direction of her house.

"This is my stop. Thanks for walking me home."

"No problem," Weldon said, disappointed the walk hadn't been longer. He wanted to hear more about her theories on actors.

"I'm sure I'll see you around," Mir said. "It's like someone wants us to run into each other."

"It's a really small town," Weldon said, smiling.

"Even in a small town there are some people I never bump into. But I guess we're magnetized or something, just naturally . . . uh . . ." Miriam paused, her gaze ducking from his, and he realized she was about to say "attracted to each other." Weldon fought the urge to grin at her.

"I guess I'll see you, then," he said, and extended a formal hand toward Mir. She nodded and took his hand, shaking it firmly. She had a good grip.

Weldon walked toward downtown, intent on not looking back at Miriam. He passed a house and glanced up at its darkened windows, hoping he could catch a glimpse of her in the reflection. The windows were angled the wrong way, throwing back a reflection of the house across the street. Weldon sighed and quickened his pace, deciding to jog the rest of the way home.

Twenty minutes later he cruised into his aunt and uncle's yard, feeling euphoric. He rushed through his cool-down stretches, finally walking a lazy circle around the front yard, hands on his hips, head tipped back so he could stare at the sky. It was gray and grouchy-looking, very different from the blue sky of Los Angeles.

Weldon heard the front door slam and looked in the direction of the house. His aunt was walking down the front steps, a red purse swinging from her arm. She smiled when she saw Weldon.

"How was your run?"

"Good," said Weldon. *I saw Miriam Kendrick again*, he thought. *I think we're going to be friends.* A warmth spread across his chest at the thought.

"Your dad called." A bucket of ice water doused the warmth in Weldon's body. He forced himself to keep pacing around the yard.

"He did?"

"He wanted to check in with us, see how you were doing. Get the inside story, apparently. I said you were fine, and you were doing your homework and staying out of trouble."

"Thanks," said Weldon, grateful. His aunt nodded, walking gingerly across the neatly trimmed lawn.

"I remember what it's like to be a teenager, Weldon," she said, still smiling. "You don't need me playing referee between you and your parents."

"I appreciate that," Weldon said.

"But call your dad when you get a chance, okay? He cares about you."

Weldon nodded. The phone in his aunt's bag chirped. She reached for it, and put it to her ear. Weldon wandered a few steps away from her, tipping his head back again. He checked his watch; he'd been walking for eight minutes. Another two minutes would be good enough to avoid any muscle cramps.

"Weldon," said his aunt. He turned to look at her. She was holding the phone out at a right angle from her body, her face pinched.

"What is it?"

"That was my neighbor Mrs. Vos. She's an older lady who lives close to the park by the water."

Weldon waited, not sure what she was trying to say.

"She was walking her dog at the park, and she saw you with Stella Kendrick's daughter. She said you two were talking. You seemed . . . engaged with each other. Then you walked out of the park together."

Weldon continued waiting, baffled by his aunt's behavior. Was she upset? He didn't understand what her expression meant. It seemed halfway between disbelief and anger.

He forced out an awkward "Ye-es?" His aunt's right-angle-extended arm twitched. She seemed to realize she was holding her phone strangely and stuffed it into her bag.

"I don't like the idea of you hanging out with that girl," she said.

Weldon frowned.

"But I already went to dinner at her parents' place . . ." he said, his voice trailing off. *Is she seriously uncomfortable with me hanging out with Mir?* The thought was followed by a flash of anger. *Is she seriously telling me not to hang out with Mir? Because that will be a problem.*

"That's different," said his aunt. "That's Stella being Stella and trying to make friends with everyone. She's always been like that, even back in high school. She had to make up for the fact that the families were fighting by befriending everyone with the last name Warrick. You should have seen her with your uncle."

What the hell? Weldon thought. *Did my uncle and Mir's mom have a thing?* In the back of Weldon's mind, a tiny, eager voice piped up: Does that mean me and Mir can have a thing?

"Stella was the only . . ." His aunt hesitated, her eyes darting away from Weldon. "Well, it was no wonder the boys flocked to her. She was always calling attention to herself. She had pink hair in high school."

"Miriam's nice," said Weldon, bristling. "I don't know anyone in Sandford. She's the one person I've met who I get along with."

"I know, you're stuck in the house all the time and you're away from your friends in California," said his aunt. "But I don't want you to make friends with—with people who aren't good people to know. And then there's the whole history between our families. That man, Stella Kendrick's father, what was his name—"

"Micah Kendrick," Weldon said.

"Micah Kendrick. He tried for years to take everything from your grandfather and father. He dragged out that court case over those comic books for over two decades, demanding he be paid for ideas he legally sold and was well paid for. He was so ungrateful for everything Warrick Comics did for him."

"I thought he sold the rights to the TomorrowMen for nine hundred dollars," said Weldon.

His aunt shook her head vigorously.

"Micah Kendrick made a lot of money off the Tomorrow-Men. He was paid very well to draw the comics for as long as he chose to draw them. Then he threw a fit and sued because he hadn't been made an equal partner, something he didn't deserve in the slightest. It was your grandfather who ran the publishing business that sold the comics, that made them the success they became. Micah Kendrick had nothing to do with that. *Nothing*."

Weldon's aunt spat the final *nothing* out between her teeth.

"All this nonsense about that man being a genius that some cruel company took advantage of. And then after he died Warrick Studios had to pay Stella Kendrick a huge amount of money to end that legal nonsense. That's why she can sit around painting all day, instead of working for a living like the rest of us. She dragged the Warrick name through the mud with that legal case, made us all look like thieves and cheats, and then she took money she wasn't entitled to. Warrick Studios had to pay her to go away."

His aunt's expression went slack, her fury suddenly exhausted. Weldon felt battered by the force of her tirade. Sandford was a very small town. Stella and his aunt must have bumped into each other a few times over the past thirty years. Stella must have sensed his aunt's simmering resentment. She must have known no amount of well-cooked vegetables would fix things between them.

"You can see why I object to you hanging out with Miriam Kendrick," said his aunt. She put her hand to her forehead, brushing back an imaginary stray hair. "Her mother has said some very vicious things about how the Warricks treated Micah Kendrick, things she has yet to apologize for. You are old enough to know how to correctly choose the company you keep, Weldon. I believe you'll make the right choice in this matter."

"You bet," said Weldon lightly. It was unnervingly easy to lie. His aunt smiled.

"Can I get you anything while I'm in town, Weldon?"

"Some bananas, if you're going by the grocery store," said Weldon. "I like to eat them before I run. They're good for energy."

His aunt nodded, still smiling, and left him standing on her neatly trimmed lawn. Weldon went inside and showered, still thinking about Mir. After putting on a pair of shorts and a T-shirt, Weldon lay down on his bed, pulling Stella's painting out from behind the bedside table. Skylark and Skybound stared past him, their elegant hands reaching toward each other. He stared at their hands for a long time, imagining himself reaching for Mir like that.

CHAPTER SIXTEEN

Mir lay facedown on the couch in her parents' living room, rolling the awfulness of the day around in her head. Weldon had distracted her on the walk home, but once she'd opened the door to her house, the reality of losing her job had made her so sad she couldn't bear to do anything but lie face-down on the couch. The house was empty, her dad and Nate off for what Stella called their "weekly father-son bonding," a wilderness club that mostly did hikes through a nearby forest. Nate was good at smuggling home all kinds of weird bugs and slimy things, which he kept in a small terrarium on the front porch. Stella had forbidden him to bring anything alive into the house after an incident with an escaped lizard.

Mir glanced at the clock in the living room: five minutes to five o'clock. She steeled herself. Nate and Henry would come racing through the front door any minute—

Mir heard the clatter of the screen door, but it was Stella

who walked through it, a pile of vegetables in her arms. She looked at Mir in surprise.

"Oh, you're home early. I was in the garden. Didn't see you come in."

Mir sat up, then changed her mind and lay back down on the couch, pressing her face into one of the nearby pillows. The couch was from a local consignment store, but it had been nearly new when Mir's parents had bought it. When Henry and Stella had hauled the couch home, there had been a stern lecture to Mir and Nate that this couch was not like the old one, it was not to be jumped on. This couch needed to last.

Mir heard Stella's footsteps as she walked across the living room. The couch sagged a bit as Stella sat down, putting a hand on Mir's shoulder.

"Are you okay?"

"I got fired," Mir said, her voice muffled by the pillow.

"What?"

"I got fired," Mir said louder, turning her head sideways. "The Emporium of Wonders is going out of business. I lost my job."

Stella put her other hand to her mouth, eyes wide.

"The store's closing? What about Berg? He sank everything he had into that store."

"He did a terrible job running it," Mir muttered, annoyed that Stella's first thought was for Berg and not her. "If he'd been a better manager, I might still have a job."

Stella frowned.

"It might not be his fault, Miriam. Sometimes things fail despite a person's best efforts."

What if I fail? Mir thought. *What if I try my hardest and go to university and graduate and I still don't know what I want to do?* She shrugged, trying to dislodge her mother's hand.

"I should call him," said Stella. "Poor Berg."

"I don't know what to do," Mir muttered. The day had wrung her out, but there was an angry spot simmering in her chest, waiting for the right moment to bubble up. Stella sighed, rubbing her hand sympathetically across Mir's shoulder.

"What do you want to do?"

"I want the hand of God to come down from the sky and tell me exactly what I should do with my life," Mir said. "I want to make a decision that's the right decision."

The span of the summer stretched before Mir. The months used to be comforting, a buffer against the start of the final school year and all the decisions she would have to make. She thought of the university pamphlets Ms. Archer had given her, filled with the faces of students who had taken the plunge and chosen this school or that school. Mir had stared at the faces in the pamphlet photographs, looking for one that seemed doubtful or unsure. Did any of those students regret their decision?

"I had to make a really important decision once," Stella said softly. "I had to decide if I was going to drop my father's legal case against Warrick Comics. All I could think was how every option seemed like the wrong one."

Mir turned her head to look at Stella out of the corner of

her eye. Stella in profile was beautiful, the soft curve of her fore-head matching the curve of the back of her skull, like she was carved from marble.

"I could only make the decision that was right for me at the time. Some people thought I was crazy, that I was throwing away millions of dollars. Your grandfather would have hated me for doing what I did, if he'd still been alive."

Stella smiled distantly, in a way that made Mir's heart ache.

"Sometimes I regret that decision, but most days I know it was the right one. It was right for me at the time."

Stella looked over at Mir, the distant smile still on her lips.

"What do you want to do, Miriam?"

"Leave," said Mir.

The word hung between them. Relief washed over Mir. The lightness she'd felt earlier when talking to Weldon hummed in her chest. There was the thing she wanted, finally. Leave. Leave Sandford, go somewhere that didn't feel so small and cramped. Somewhere with more than one downtown street.

"Okay," said Stella. "Where do you want to leave to?"

Mir thought.

"Toronto. I think I want to go to the University of Toronto. I want to try a bunch of different subjects and find out what I really like doing. I want to live in a city. I want—" She ducked her head, not quite sure how to continue.

"You want to live somewhere that's not confined. You want to walk down streets and not bump into people who have known you your whole life. You want to start fresh in a place that feels like you could explore it for a lifetime and still not discover all its secrets," Stella said.

Mir looked up at her mother, surprised.

"Yeah, exactly. How did you know?"

Stella put her chin in one hand, smiling at Mir.

"This may surprise you, Miriam, but after your father and I graduated from high school, I wanted to leave Sandford. Henry and I talked about it for a long time."

"But you didn't leave," Mir said. "You stayed here."

"We stayed," said Stella. "Together we decided it was best. Your father's family is here, and despite its problems, I like Sandford. Toronto is huge and full of possibilities, but that doesn't mean it would have been a good home for us, or a good place to raise our kids. Besides, the property prices are insane. What we paid for this house wouldn't buy a hole in the ground in Toronto. Here we can afford to live, and I can paint rather than work a day job to pay a mortgage."

Mir wiggled onto her back, folding her hands on her stomach. "So now what? Now I know I want to go to school out of province, but how do I pay for it? You guys don't have any money, and what I have saved from my job isn't enough."

"We'll find a way," said Stella. "I'll set up an appointment with your school guidance counselor and we'll make this work. Somehow. There must be scholarships available to you. Your grades are really good. Or maybe financial aid . . ."

"I'll need to find another job," Mir said. Her chest ached as she remembered how she liked organizing the superhero toys in the Emporium of Wonders, plastic men and women in clear boxes, their incredible physiques replicated in perfect miniature. *I really did love that job*, Mir thought. *It wasn't stupid.*

"You will. Have you asked Evan's dad about work? He's hired you before."

"Ugh," Mir said, putting her hands over her eyes. "Landscaping is so much work. So much sod carrying and raking and digging. Dirt is so heavy. And Evan's dad yells when things aren't perfect."

"It's only for a summer," said Stella. "Think about the money you'll earn, and how it'll pay for your escape from Sandford. It makes awful work so much easier when you have something to look forward to. And"—Stella squeezed Mir's shoulders with both hands—"you have a really big adventure coming up."

"I haven't even been accepted into university yet," Mir said. "It might not happen."

Stella smiled.

"We'll cross that bridge when we come to it."

There was a thump and a clatter on the porch outside, and Nate came charging into the house, his jacket streaked with mud. Stella lunged off the couch and grabbed for him, stripping the jacket off before he could smear the dirt on anything. When Nate was muddy he liked to share that mud with everything around him: walls, couches, beds, people. Henry came into the house at a slower pace, stopping to unlace his boots, which were also caked in mud.

"Looks like you had a good time," said Stella, her hands on her hips. Henry reached for Stella and swept her into a crushing hug.

"Be normal parents!" Mir yelled from the living room, sitting up on the couch. "Stop being so . . . *smoochy*. You've been married for like twenty years or whatever. Act normal, for Pete's sake."

"Twenty years!" Henry gasped, pretending to be shocked. "Has it been that long? 'Pon my word, I swear it was naught more than nineteen years. Good woman, was I wrong?" He held Stella at arm's length, looking her up and down.

Stella put a hand on his arm.

"Stop making jokes. Miriam's had a rough day."

Henry walked over to stand beside Miriam, looking down at her. He was wearing his usual plaid shirt and jeans combination, his blond hair sticking up every which way, like it was straw in need of a pitchfork.

"What happened?"

"I lost my job," Mir said. It felt more real to say it this third time. Maybe next would be Evan or Raleigh. *I should really call Raleigh*, Mir thought. *Enough of this weirdness. I've known her forever and Jamie's only known her for a year. She wouldn't throw me away completely because of him.*

Henry frowned, his blond caterpillar eyebrows drawing downward.

"Really sorry to hear that, Miriam. What happened?"

"The store's going out of business," said Mir. "Guess it'll

become another Starbucks or some tourist trap build-your-own-canoe place."

"Is Berg okay? He's had that store for years."

"Everyone is very concerned about Berg," Mir muttered, then felt guilty for being annoyed. "I mean, I am too. It's terrible for Berg too." Mir dragged a chunk of her hair over her shoulder and picked at the ends of it. "That was kind of jerky of me. Sorry."

"You're upset, you're allowed to be jerky," said Henry.

Stella moved into the living room, sitting on the floor and crossing her legs.

"Miriam's made a decision about next year," said Stella. "Go on, tell him."

Henry's gaze moved from Mir to Stella and back to Mir again, his eyes bright. Sometimes he seemed like a little kid, always overly excited by things, always curious. He and Nate were so similar, collecting weird odds and ends, telling stories that always seemed to evolve into absurd adventures. "It's never too late to have a happy childhood," he would say to Mir when she told him to grow up and be like the other dads. "Stop being so silly!" Mir had yelled at him once, and Henry had marched around the kitchen, an exaggerated frown on his face, lecturing the stove to "stop that, stop being so silly!"

"I want to go to Toronto for university," Mir said. Henry blinked, surprised. "If I get in," Mir finished. Henry's gaze darted toward Stella, then back to Mir, confused. He rubbed a hand through his hair.

"Are you—are you sure? That's so far away."

His voice sounded small and shocked. Sitting cross-legged on the ground, Stella looked up at her husband, frowning.

"Would you prefer she stay here and not go to university?" Stella said. There was an uncharacteristic edge in her voice. Henry looked down at her, still rubbing his head with his hand. His hair looked like a starburst of static.

"No, of course not. I want Miriam to go to university if that's what she wants. But why Toronto? There are universities in this province. I don't know why she'd have to go all the way to Ontario for school. That's a two-day drive away. It's an airplane flight."

"I want to see what living in a big city is like," Mir said. It was strange watching her father and mother disagree on something. They argued occasionally, but never in front of their kids. She couldn't remember ever hearing them yell at each other.

"There are cities here!" Henry said. "There are cities two hours away. There's Halifax, and Fredericton . . ."

"Henry—" said Stella, uncrossing her legs and starting to stand up.

"People leave and they don't come back," said Henry. The lines around his eyes seemed to deepen, dragging his face downward. "My brothers left for Alberta and the oil sands industry when they graduated high school, and they didn't come back. I see them maybe once every five years. This country is too damn large."

"Dad, I don't know if I'm even going, it's just something I

want to apply for. I might not get in," Mir said, feeling small and troublesome for making her parents argue.

"Henry," said Stella, the word a warning. "This is a decision that was very difficult for Miriam. We need to support her in it. Don't be selfish."

"It's selfish to want to see my kid more than once every five years?" Henry said, his voice rising. "I've seen this happen to so many families here. Kid goes away for school or work, promises to come back when debts are paid off or they've got their degree, but they never do. Families are split up, spread all over the country. Everything is breaking apart."

"There's nothing here for young people," Stella said. "There's so little industry, nothing besides what the shipyards and tourist trade provide. Can you blame them for leaving?"

Henry's hand scratched frantically through his hair. Stella reached for him, pulling his hand away from his head and lacing her fingers through his. Mir huddled on the couch, trying to burrow into it. She had finally chosen between staying and going. Her foot was on the path, the first step taken. Behind her was her father, telling her not to go.

"I'm sorry," Mir said. *I'm sorry I don't want to stay. I'm sorry I didn't fall in love with a boy at my high school, the way Mom and Raleigh did.*

"I need a little time to get used to this," Henry said, staring down at his hand laced with Stella's. He gently unwound her hand from his and walked away from them, out of the living room. Mir heard the door to her parents' bedroom close.

Stella turned to Mir, her eyes bright and almost watery.

"I want to make an appointment with your guidance counselor. What about Monday?"

"Sure," said Mir. "Monday's fine. I think she'll be really happy to see you."

Stella reached out and touched Mir lightly on the shoulder, walking past her into the kitchen. Mir lay down on the couch, staring at the ceiling. She felt scraped raw, but also lighter, so much lighter.

I made the decision that was right for me at this moment, she thought. Mir closed her eyes, half smiling.

CHAPTER SEVENTEEN

Summer was trying its best to come to Sandford. A sunny day as clear and warm as a spring day in California was followed by a double-digit plunge in temperature. To Weldon it felt like the weather was deliberately toying with him.

Weldon ran in the park every day, so often that he got to know the other joggers, nodding at them when they passed one another. He surfed the internet, reading all the news about the TomorrowMen movie on comic blogs and movie news sites. He watched a million TV shows about the intricacies of owning a pawn shop. And he tried to accidentally bump into Miriam.

The Emporium of Wonders was gone. Physically the store still stood, the posters in the window slowly curling from the heat as summer crept into Sandford, but the front door was locked, the CLOSED sign turned permanently outward. Weldon had returned to the store the day after running into Miriam at the park, and wandered in conspicuous circles in front of it, hoping someone might venture out. No one had. Not Mir, not her manager with his sad ten-dollar haircut and worn-out khaki pants. For the following three days he walked by the store, pretending to head to the Running Realm, always eyeing the darkened windows of the former Emporium of Wonders.

At the Running Realm, Ellie had frozen him out, taking extreme care to talk to him only when she had to. Weldon felt guilty and bought a new pair of shoes, hoping the commission would ease the tension between them. It didn't.

A week passed with no sign of Miriam. It was as though the magnetic force that had been pushing them together had suddenly expired. In desperation, Weldon considered going to her house. He imagined walking up the porch steps, knocking on the door, and then—what? Weldon tried to picture it in his head.

SCENE 1: Weldon Warrick walks up the stairs of the Kendricks' house. He knocks on their front door. Stella Kendrick answers the door.

WELDON: Hello.

STELLA: Hello, Weldon! Come in, come in! Miriam's been expecting you. She's decided she doesn't hate you anymore and would like to be your friend. She is flattered you decided to show up unannounced at her home. Would you care for a homegrown organic tomato? Or a hug?

Or—

SCENE 2: Weldon Warrick walks up the stairs of the Kendricks' house. He knocks on their front door. Miriam Kendrick answers.
WELDON: Hello.
MIRIAM: Ugh, why are you here? I said I don't hate you, but it doesn't mean I want you hanging around. Explain yourself.
INCREDIBLY LONG SILENCE THAT ENDS WITH THE UNIVERSE COLLAPSING IN ON ITSELF LIKE A DYING STAR.

Weldon shuddered. If he was going to show up at Miriam's house, he'd need a reason. Until that reason occurred to him, he was stuck wandering the streets of Sandford, hoping to run into her.

———

The second Saturday of June was glorious. Fluffy clouds dotted the sky, and the river below the bridge gleamed as Weldon jogged into town. It felt like summer, a real, proper, American summer.

Weldon jogged down Sandford's main street, eyes sweeping the sidewalks and storefronts for Miriam. Summer tourists had started to pour into the town, taking up space in the Starbucks and filling the front window of the make-your-own-pottery store with misshapen mugs. Many of the tourists were doggedly stereotypical, wearing wide floppy hats and T-shirts with the names of the places they'd visited on them. They spilled off the cruise ships that docked at the waterfront and swept into Sandford, eager to spend their American money on an authentic piece of East Coast Canadiana.

Weldon continued jogging, skirting past a couple taking pictures of a tiny maritime museum that had recently popped up, ready to teach the new influx of people about the history of the waterfront. Weldon jogged down to the park and watched a sleek white boat sail away from the harbor, tourists relaxing on its deck. He took the long way out of the park, the way he and Mir had walked together the last time he'd seen her.

Weldon reached the road that led to the Kendricks' house and stopped, looking down it. The road snaked away from him, rising and then falling out of sight. He couldn't see Miriam's house, but he sketched it out in his mind: patchwork yellow paint job, sloping front porch. He took a step down the road, then stopped and turned back.

A grimy truck turned down the road and drove past Weldon. It stopped suddenly and reversed, shooting backward so the cab was level with him. Weldon looked up, surprised. Miriam's father leaned out the driver's side of the cab, a smile already locked in place.

"Weldon!" yelled Henry. "Hello! How are you? It's been a while! About time we got some proper spring weather! I always forget how long it takes for summer to finally get here, even though I've lived in Sandford all my life. You'd think I'd know by now. But it looks like it's finally here!"

Weldon blinked, the torrent of words flying over his head. Henry remained leaning out the cab window, beaming at him.

"Yeah," Weldon finally managed.

"Going for a run?"

Weldon glanced down at his clothes, double-checking that was what he was doing.

"Yeah. Almost done. I ran through the park earlier."

"Did you see the cruise ships?" Henry said. "They're predicting a record number of tourists this year. There's life in the old town after all." He laughed, leaning back in the front seat.

"That's great," said Weldon, not sure how else to respond. Tourists were great, weren't they? They brought money in exchange for misshapen coffee mugs.

"It is!" Henry beamed. He swiveled his attention back to the road, preparing to drive off. "Nice seeing you! Enjoy the weather."

"Um, wait—" Weldon said desperately. "Um, I haven't seen Miriam in a while . . . she told me she lost her job at that store downtown?" He flicked a thumb over his shoulder in the direction of the Emporium of Wonders. "I was just wondering if everything was okay?" Weldon finished with a shrug.

"You know about that?" Henry said.

"Yeah," said Weldon. "I ran into her in the park two weeks ago. She told me."

Henry stared at him, thoughtful.

"You don't have many friends in town, do you?"

Weldon shook his head.

"No, sir."

"Please call me Henry," said Henry. "'Sir' is someone . . . well, someone not me. No one who chased an already castrated bull around a pen for three hours when they were eighteen is called 'sir.'"

"Okay," said Weldon, grinning. Henry reached over to the passenger's side of the truck and unlocked the door.

"Hop in. Miriam's at home and I don't think she's busy. You guys can hang out."

Weldon scrambled into the truck, fishing behind his shoulder for the seat belt. He'd just clicked it into place when Henry took off, hitting a nearby pothole with a heart-stopping thunk. It took barely a minute for them to reach the house at the end of the road, Henry bringing the truck to a screeching halt in the gravel driveway out front.

"It's less damaging for a car to hit a pothole at high speeds than slow speeds," Henry yelled, hopping out of the cab. "Science!"

"I'm not sure that's true . . ." Weldon muttered under his breath, trailing behind Henry. Henry threw open the front door and barreled into the house, shouting that he was home. The kitchen was empty. Henry looked around, a puzzled expression on his face. From the living room beyond came Miriam's voice.

"Mom's in her studio," Miriam said. "Nate's out back. You're so loud, stop yelling."

"Yelling is good for the lungs and heart and probably the kidneys," said Henry. "Science says so! What're you gonna do."

"I would like to see the data on that," Miriam's voice said. Weldon stood in the doorway, Henry blocking his view of the entrance to the living room. He hesitated, not sure if he should walk past Miriam's father.

"I found your friend Weldon," Henry said, stepping to the side. Weldon saw Miriam sitting cross-legged on the floor of the living room, a mass of paper spread out around her. Her hair was tied in a bun on the top of her head, shaped like a lightbulb of inspiration. She looked up at him and smiled.

At the sight of her smile, light filled his chest, pressing his ribs outward. He worried he might float upward to bump against the ceiling, radiating light through his T-shirt. That would be embarrassing.

"Hi," she said.

"Hi," Weldon said. "Your dad ran into me."

"Oh god, I hope not. I was driving the truck." Henry laughed uproariously. Miriam stared at her father, expression deadpan.

Henry thumped through the living room, taking an exaggerated step over Miriam and her pile of papers. He waved, grinning at Weldon and his daughter.

"I'm gonna see what my woman is up to. You kids have fun hanging out." The screen door banged loudly as he walked through the back door. Miriam sighed. She leaned an elbow on one knee, chin on her hand, peering down at the papers next to her.

"He's so loud," Miriam said. "I used to think it was funny when I was a kid, but now I'm kinda over it."

Weldon walked toward her, pausing at the living room entrance to remove his shoes. In the living room he sat in front of Mir, outside the halo of paper strewn around her.

"My dad thinks my mom married him for his sense of humor—she really does think he's hilarious—so if he's not funny all the time she'll, like, leave him for a funnier man," Miriam said, her expression still deadpan.

"That's actually really funny," Weldon said. Miriam nodded, looking down at the papers spread in front of her. They seemed to be printouts of some kind, listings from a database.

"What's this?"

"We don't have decent internet on our computer, so I got our neighbor to print off a bunch of job listings. It's just easier," said Mir. "But she charged me for the paper and ink, if you can believe that."

"You don't have the internet?" Weldon was genuinely shocked.

Miriam glanced up at him, pointing over her shoulder at an ancient beige computer on a desk in the corner of the living room.

"Oh, we have internet, if you think dial-up is internet. Our house is outside of the wired area of Sandford, so we can't actually get fast internet. Unless we want to pay a ton of money for it, and my parents are not those kind of people."

"But the internet's a utility," Weldon said. "I didn't think anyone was still stuck with dial-up. I mean, you're only a half hour walk outside of Sandford."

"Welcome to rural Nova Scotia," Miriam sighed, fiddling with one of the papers in front of her. "You can be a ten-minute drive from a proper town, and the phone companies still won't bring the good stuff to your neighborhood because it's not profitable enough."

"I'm appalled on your behalf," Weldon said. "No one should have to surf the internet on dial-up. You should, I don't know, start a petition."

Miriam looked up at him, the edge of her mouth turning up in amusement. She shrugged.

"I've made my peace with it. No proper internet for me until I live somewhere other than this house."

Weldon gestured at the strewn halo of papers. "So this is job hunting for the internet deficient?"

"Yeah," said Miriam. She reached for one of the printouts and held it up. "It seems like a lot of job openings, but it's pretty slim pickings. Most of the summer jobs in the area are physical, and they want to hire giant dudes with muscles. I am not a giant dude with muscles." She tossed the listing aside and stared at the papers surrounding her.

"There's gotta be something in there," said Weldon. He picked up one of the listings and saw it was for a barista at a coffee shop and required three years' experience. He put the listing down.

"Maybe," said Miriam. "I haven't been looking as hard as I should. Finals are coming up and I've been studying a lot. But I need to find something before the school year ends, or I might be out of luck."

"Why is it important you get a job this summer?"

Miriam looked up at him.

It's important she get a job for the summer because her dad isn't the producer of a two-hundred-million-dollar superhero movie, dummy. Don't ask such stupid questions, Weldon thought, trying to keep the grimace off his face.

"Have you ever been to Toronto?"

"Toronto? Once, when I was a kid, I think," Weldon said, relieved Mir had decided not to be offended by his stupidity. "That's the city with the giant tower, right?"

"The CN Tower, yeah. I want to go there for school. Well, not the actual tower; I want to go to the city it's in for school."

Her tone was casual, but he could hear the eagerness underneath it. Something had happened since he'd last seen her, something she was excited about. He wondered if she'd smiled at him earlier only because she'd been thinking about Toronto. He hoped not.

"Cool," he said. "I've heard it's a great city."

"It's huge," said Miriam, her hands fluttering to her mouth like she was trying to prevent a bubble of joy from bursting outward. "It's the largest city in Canada. It's full of artists and writers and lawyers and . . . so many people. Different kinds of people."

"I always liked that about LA," Weldon said. "Every kind of person there."

"I keep forgetting that's where you're from," said Miriam. "You don't know the simple pleasures of being trapped in a small town."

"Guess not. I mean, San Diego's small in comparison to LA—"

"It's not small compared to Sandford," Mir laughed. "Nothing is as small as Sandford."

"True," Weldon said.

They sat in silence for a few minutes, Miriam shuffling through the printouts strewn on the floor. Weldon thought it would be very nice to keep sitting on the floor for several more hours, as long as he could watch Miriam sift through her papers.

Eventually Miriam sat back from her halo of papers, leaning against the front of the couch and putting her head in her hands.

"This sucks. There's nothing. I'm gonna be stuck working for Evan's dad all summer. He's gonna yell at me, and not the way my dad yells. Not in a fun way."

"Want to hear about my shitty summer job?" Weldon said.

Miriam turned her head toward him, peering between her fingers.

"You had a shitty summer job?"

"Several."

"Aren't you rich?"

"Ha," said Weldon. "I guess compared to most people. But that doesn't mean I didn't have to work. My dad had summer jobs, so of course I had to have them too."

"Let me guess: it builds character."

"So much character," said Weldon.

Miriam pulled one hand from her face and gestured at Weldon. "Tell me about your crappy summer jobs."

"First my dad put me to work in Warrick Studios. None of the artists or writers who make the TomorrowMen comics work in-house. Pretty much everyone works either from their home or their own private studio, but most of the preparing of the comic pages for print is done in-house at Warrick Studios. All the editors work there too. So one summer my dad made me work at the studio. I got paid a tiny amount of money and I got to shred paper, fetch coffee, and run errands for these editors who hated me because I was the boss's kid."

"Nobody likes nepotism," Miriam said.

"I would've worked any other job," Weldon said. "I don't like hanging around Warrick Studios. It'd probably be interesting if you're really into the comic industry, but I'm surrounded by that stuff all the time. I can't escape it."

He shrugged.

"The next summer I told my dad I'd find a job on my own, and went to, like, the worst coffee shop in our neighborhood to see if they were hiring. I got paid minimum wage to work their drive-through. Half the time I got the order wrong because the intercom was so terrible, and people would literally go through the drive-through wearing nothing but their bathrobes. But it was better than getting dirty looks all day at my dad's business."

"People would go through a drive-through in only their bathrobes?" Miriam said, wrinkling her nose.

"Yep."

"Ew."

"You have no idea," said Weldon.

The screen door banged and Miriam and Weldon looked up. Stella came through the door, paint splatters on her arms and clothing. Henry was behind her, a smudge of bright purple paint on his cheek. Stella smiled when she saw Weldon.

"Hello, Weldon."

"Hi," said Weldon. "Miriam's been telling me about her job hunt."

"Oh, yes," said Stella, staring down at the papers strewn on the floor. "Miriam tells me this is something that would be a lot easier if only we had better internet."

"It would be," said Miriam grumpily.

"Probably," Stella agreed. "Maybe someday the internet gods will smile upon us, giving us the high-speed access we so desire, but for the moment we don't have it, and thus we must all make do."

"Sigh," said Miriam.

Stella turned to Weldon.

"Will you be staying for dinner, Weldon?"

Yes, Weldon thought, delighted, then realized he couldn't.

"I'm really gross from jogging," he said, gesturing at his running clothes. "And I gotta get home. My aunt and uncle are expecting me. They're probably wondering where I am now, actually." Weldon glanced at his phone, alarmed at how late it was. It would be a problem if his aunt and uncle got home and he wasn't there. *I'm being good*, he thought. *I'm going to Comic-Con in a month, so I have to be good.* He stood, feeling stiff. Sitting cross-legged on the floor after running had been a terrible idea.

"Miriam, why don't you see Weldon out?" said Stella, nodding at Mir. She scrambled to her feet, pausing to collect the job listings. Stella waved her off, saying she would do it.

Weldon followed Miriam out on the porch. She turned toward him and he saw a shadow had fallen across her face. They stood opposite each other, suddenly awkward.

"Maybe we could hang out again," Weldon said.

"Maybe," Miriam said, but she didn't look at him. Weldon felt his heart lurch in his chest. Had she changed her mind about the smile? One minute she seemed happy to see him, the next she withdrew. He chafed at the unfairness of it. *I said I was sorry for what the Warricks did to her, and she said she was sorry for being mean to me. So can't we just be friends?*

"Well, goodbye," Weldon said. Mir nodded, but her gaze was inward, and she didn't seem to notice when he began walking down the road away from her, toward home.

CHAPTER EIGHTEEN

Miriam sat on a small stone bench outside her high school's front doors, swinging her legs underneath it. Evan was lying on his back beside her, hands folded on his chest, staring up at the sky. He was frowning, and the frown had notched a small divot between his eyebrows. Mir wanted to ask him what he was thinking about, but he'd been quiet that day, and she worried it was something serious. Mir didn't think she could handle any serious conversation at the moment: her stomach was doing cartwheels as she watched the high school entrance for Raleigh and Jamie. Today was the day she was going to tell them about her plans for next year, about school and Toronto and leaving Sandford. Mir had been practicing her speech over and over in her head.

Hey, guys, I have something to tell you. I've decided about next year. I'm going to Toronto—

Hey, guys, I want to tell you something. I'm applying for university next year, out of province—

Hey, guys, I want—um—I need—

Hey, guys, I—

Terrible.

Mir had told Evan about her decision the day after she'd made it. He'd picked her up and swung her around in a circle, shouting congratulations. When he'd put her back on the ground, she'd searched his face for any sign that he wasn't as happy as he seemed to be, but there was nothing. She'd asked him to come with her to tell Jamie and Raleigh, and he'd agreed. It would be the first time in weeks all four of them had been together.

"I don't think I want to give that Warrick guy the Tomorrow-Men comic script," Evan said now.

Miriam looked over at him. His eyebrows had drawn even farther down his forehead, the divot between them deepening alarmingly.

"Why?"

"I dunno," said Evan. "I just changed my mind, I guess."

Mir stared at Evan, concerned.

"Did something happen?"

"No, nothing. I just—" Evan looked toward the front of the school. The doors opened and a trio of ninth graders tumbled out, shouting and pushing one another. "I just feel like maybe it's stupid to give him this script. It's like you said: Warrick Studios isn't going to hire me to write their comics, so what's the point?"

"I shouldn't have said that," Mir said.

"Nah, you're right."

"No," Mir said. "I was wrong. The script is good, and we should finish it. And you should finish it because . . . because getting hired shouldn't be the only reason you write a comic script. You should finish it because you have the chance to make something awesome."

Evan chuckled.

"My dad would say that's damn dirty hippie talk, Mir," he said, folding his hands under his head and looking back toward the school doors. "He's always like, No point in doing something if you're not gonna get paid for your labor."

"Do you agree with that?"

Evan continued looking in the direction of the school doors.

"No. I know your mom doesn't get paid to make those paintings, and they're still worth doing. The way she paints the TomorrowMen is incredible."

Evan looked back at Mir, his hands still behind his head.

"I mean, she should get paid to paint the TomorrowMen. If everything was fair, she would. But it's still awesome that she paints them."

Mir nodded. *It is awesome*, she thought.

"We've got most of the script written down," Mir said. "It won't take much to finish it. Please?"

"I was thinking about the script the other day, trying to think of ways to make it better," Evan said. "I kept thinking about it and suddenly I couldn't remember anything that was good about it. Every word I'd put down on paper felt like the wrong word. And I hate the ending. There's something wrong about the ending."

"Evan—"

"Mir, it's fine." Evan pushed himself into a sitting position, looking over his shoulder at her. The frown line between his eyebrows was gone. His usual smile was back in place, beaming out from underneath his beard. "I think writing the script was worth doing. But I don't think I want anyone to see it. I don't know why I even asked that Warrick guy if I could send it to him."

"The script is really good," Mir said. "You have something to say about Tristan Terrific, and you say it in an interesting way. I really—I want—" Mir looked away from Evan. His smile was starting to fade.

"Why's it important to you I do this?" Evan said.

"I don't want you to give up," she said. *Is that true?* Mir thought. Half of her did want something for Evan, something that wasn't related to his father's business. Something for him alone, because he was kind and sweet and deserved it. The other half of her felt selfish and grasping. She wanted Evan to write a story because it made him a little more like her.

"I feel so weird about it," Evan said. "I just wish I hadn't been all, 'Ooh, lemme send you a TomorrowMen script, David Warrick's son.' Me and my big mouth. I'm always saying stuff before I think about it."

"I like that about you," Mir said. "You say what's on your mind. And most of the time it's something nice."

The school doors swung open and Jamie and Raleigh walked out. Mir's heart leaped at the sight of them. She'd seen them in the halls before class the past week, and had made polite conversation. Today was different. Her stomach did one final cartwheel as she stood up. Evan stood up beside her and started to walk toward Jamie and Raleigh.

Mir snagged his sleeve.

"I want to finish the script. It's your script, you can do what you want with it. You don't have to give it to Weldon Warrick, but I still think you should finish it."

Evan stood opposite Mir for a moment. Finally he nodded.

"I'll finish it. Then we'll see. Is that enough?"

"Yeah," Mir said, "it is."

They walked to meet Jamie and Raleigh. Raleigh's face was turned toward Mir, and the warmth in her expression made Mir's heart ache. She was dressed in a yellow-and-green summer dress, clashing with Jamie's black and gray T-shirt and jeans. They looked so different from each other. And yet they had chosen each other, out of all the teenagers in Sandford. Mir wished it was different, then felt awful for wishing something so cruel.

"Hi," said Raleigh. "You guys going home?"

"Yeah," Mir said. "We were waiting for you, actually. I wanted to talk to you about something. But I can talk while we walk."

"That rhymes," said Raleigh, smiling. "You're a poet."

They fell into step, Mir beside Raleigh, who held hands with Jamie. Evan walked beside Jamie. They had walked home together like this most of last year. The year before that, it had only been Mir, Raleigh, and Evan, with Evan in the middle. When Jamie joined the group, he pushed Evan's orbit outward, as though trying to slingshot him away from Miriam and Raleigh.

"How are things going with your job hunt?" Raleigh said. Mir had told her about the bankruptcy of the Emporium of Wonders the day after it had happened. It was easier to talk about losing a job than choosing to leave home and go to school in Toronto.

"Terrible," said Mir. "I can't find anything that doesn't require barista experience. Why are there so many coffee shops opening up in Sandford?"

"There's a gourmet burger joint opening where the Emporium of Wonders used to be. Maybe they need people," Jamie said. His gaze was straight ahead, not aimed at Mir. He was careful and polite with her whenever they'd bumped into each other the past two weeks, but he rarely made eye contact. Mir had started to feel like she was floating whenever she talked to him, his lack of eye contact untethering her from the conversation.

"Thanks," said Mir. "I'll check them out."

"What did you want to talk to us about?" Raleigh said.

Mir took a breath.

"I'm going to apply for university next year. Out of province. Probably Toronto. Maybe Montreal."

Raleigh turned toward Mir, her expression puzzled.

"Oh," she said. "Didn't you tell me you were doing that already? I thought you did."

"No," Mir said. "I just decided. I—it's been driving me crazy recently, trying to decide if I was going to apply or not next year, don't you remember?"

"No," said Raleigh. "I swear you told me you were going already. Like, months ago. I kinda thought you decided that was what you wanted in grade nine."

Mir stared at Raleigh. Raleigh's hair was pinned back at the sides with two butterfly barrettes. It made her look younger than sixteen. Mir blinked at her stupidly, trying to process Raleigh's words.

"You went into the advanced classes in grade ten," Raleigh said. "I stayed in the general stream. Kids in the advanced stream go to university. Isn't that how it works?"

"No," said Mir. "I mean, yes, but not always. I just—I just decided I wanted to . . ." She stopped, not sure how to continue. Raleigh was still looking at her, waiting.

Jamie laughed.

"Oh, please," he said. "You're acting like this is something you actually had to decide. It's not. You were planning to leave for years."

"No," said Mir. Jamie turned toward her. The look in his eyes was ugly.

"You're not some genius, you know," he said. "I've read your essays. Mine are just as good. But you get this opportunity because your family won some comic book lawsuit—" Evan shoved him, hard. Jamie stumbled away from Raleigh, spinning around to face the three of them.

"What the *fuck* is your problem?" Evan said. The words came out hot, like how his father yelled. Mir had never heard Evan yell before. It was awful.

"The fuck *my* problem is? Don't ever touch me again, asshole—"

"You're always such a dick to her—" Evan was screaming, his face flushed.

Next to Mir, Raleigh started to shake. "Stop it, stop," she whispered.

"I'm a dick? I'm a dick?"

"I'm pointing at you, aren't I? You're the one dropping bullshit about her family, saying they're secretly rich or some shit—"

"You're so in love with her you can't see how far your head's up her ass! Fuck you!"

Their words piled on top of one another. Mir stood rooted to the spot, watching it unfold. She felt strangely removed from the fight, as though she was watching it behind glass. Beside her, Raleigh was crying, her hands held up over her mouth. Jamie's eyes were black with anger, the cords on his neck standing out as he screamed at Evan. They stood opposite each other as they fought, neither boy taking a step forward. Mir was thankful for that, at least. She didn't have a garden hose to separate them.

"She treats the rest of us like we're beneath her! Just because her grandfather wrote some fucking comic books! Who gives a shit—"

"He *drew* the fucking comic books!" Evan roared. "You're so full of shit you don't even know what her grandfather did!" Mir felt a ridiculous urge to laugh. No one screwed up comic book facts when Evan was around.

"Who cares?" said Jamie. He reached up and pushed a hand through his hair, flipping it back from his forehead. He looked over at Mir and Raleigh.

"You're not so special," he snarled at Mir. "You just have parents willing to cosign your student loan."

"Yeah," said Mir softly, "I do." A wave of sympathy swept over her. Her parents were willing to risk themselves financially for her. She knew then Jamie's weren't.

Jamie held out a hand for Raleigh. She went to him, and the four of them stood for a moment, staring at one another. The divide between them felt infinite. Jamie turned and walked away, Raleigh beside him. Mir watched her go, the finality of the moment echoing across the empty street.

Mir and Evan walked home in silence. They usually split up when they reached Sandford's main street, Mir heading away from downtown, Evan going through it to reach the suburbs on the other side. This time Evan continued walking beside Mir. Finally they stopped at the beginning of Mir's road.

"Thanks for defending me," Mir said. Evan shrugged, shaking his head.

"Just saying what's on my mind. Fuck Jamie. Fuck him and the horse he rode in on."

Mir sighed, rubbing tiredly at her eyes. All she wanted was to lie down on her bed and pull the covers over her head.

"I thought if I kept pretending, kept acting like everything was okay, then things would be," Mir said. "Jamie is such a butt."

"Jesus Christ, Mir," Evan said. "Watch your fucking language."

Mir laughed, shaking her head.

"Sure thing, Evan."

He reached out, wrapping his arms around Mir. She closed her eyes and rubbed her cheek into his T-shirt. She felt exhausted, like she'd run a marathon while holding her breath.

"Oh," Evan said, "I remembered what I forgot to tell you." Mir pulled away, looking up at him.

"There's a golf course opening up across the bridge. My dad did some landscaping for them earlier in the year, and I think it'll be open in a couple weeks. They're looking for turf workers for the summer. Y'know, to make the grass look pretty." Evan grinned at Mir. "You could apply. No experience needed."

"Wouldn't I have to get up really early in the morning?" Mir asked. Next to physical labor and Evan's dad yelling at her, getting up early was her least favorite thing.

"Sure," said Evan, "but it's not heavy work. I think they

mostly need people to cut and maintain the grass and those sand traps. You should call them soon if you want a job. They'll probably go fast."

"I hate getting up early," Mir said.

Evan reached out and placed his hands on her shoulders. He bent his face toward her, and Mir had the sudden horrible thought that he was going to try to kiss her.

"Suck it up, kid," Evan said. "You're an adult now, and with great power comes great responsibility."

Mir smirked.

"You read too many comic books, Evan."

"I read just enough." Evan turned and walked down Sandford's only downtown street, waving goodbye to her over his shoulder.

In the kitchen of her parents' house, Mir stared at the phone on the wall. She had already reached for it three times, deciding at the last minute that it was too soon to call Raleigh. *I don't want that fight to be the last time I see her*, Mir thought. *Even if we're not going to be friends anymore, it can't end like that.* A small voice in the back of Mir's mind piped up, eager and pointed: *It could end exactly like that.* Mir pressed the heel of her palm into her eye, willing the small voice into silence.

The house was empty. Mir wasn't sure where the rest of her family was. She longed for Nate or her dad to come thundering through the front door, to fill the silence with noise and distraction. She didn't want to go to her room and lie on her bed and cry. She felt like she'd cried too much lately.

Mir thought of Jamie screaming at Evan and felt sick. *I need someone to talk to. Someone. Anyone.*

The phone book was on the top of the fridge. Mir pulled it down and flipped through the residential numbers, heading for the *W* section. There were five Warricks listed, but only one with the initials *A & K*. Mir hadn't met Alex or Katherine Warrick, but she knew their names from looking them up online. Alex Warrick had a short Wikipedia entry explaining that he was the brother of Warrick Studios' David Warrick and had written one issue of *Ultimate Skybound* in the early 1990s. Wikipedia had an encouraging note under the entry that if anyone wanted to add more to Alex Warrick's page, they should feel free to do so.

Mir dialed the Warricks' number. It rang three times.

"Hello?" said an older male voice.

"Is Weldon there?" Mir said. There was a pause at the other end of the line.

"Yes, he is. Just a minute."

There was the sound of the phone being placed on a hard surface, and whoever Mir was speaking to shouted toward the bowels of their house. "Weldon! You have a phone call." Then there was a second long pause, followed by the sound of footsteps, and Mir heard Weldon say, "A call on the landline? Weird."

"Hello?"

"Hi," said Mir. "It's Miriam."

"Hi," said Weldon. Mir heard his voice suddenly glow with warmth. She put her back to the kitchen wall and slid down so she was sitting on the floor, cradling the old-fashioned receiver to her ear. Mir pressed her phone-free hand to her other ear and tried to ignore the silence of the house.

"Hope I'm not bothering you," Mir said.

"It's kinda funny you called," Weldon said. "I thought maybe you were pissed at me again."

"Why?" said Mir, surprised. She tried to think back over their last conversation. She'd been babbling about Toronto and complaining that her parents didn't have good internet, which was making her job search hard. She thought that conversation had gone kind of well. She couldn't remember anything that would make him think that she was angry with him.

"I dunno," said Weldon, "you seemed kind of upset or something when I left. I thought maybe I'd offended you by not staying for dinner. I was really gross from my jog, so—"

"Oh, no," said Mir, remembering suddenly. "No, I'm sorry, I didn't mean anything by that. I just—I was just thinking about how I had to tell my friends how I was planning to leave Sandford, and how terrible that was going to be. Sorry. It wasn't anything you did."

Weldon laughed. "Nah, I'm the one who's sorry. Stupid of me to assume you were mad at me. Guess I just always think someone is."

"Did you do something bad again?" Mir said, her tone light.

Weldon laughed again. Mir closed her eyes and hugged her knees, listening to the sound of him.

"Nope. I'm being good," he said. He paused, as though waiting for her to say something in response. Mir continued to hug her knees, saying nothing.

"Did you call for any particular reason?" Weldon said finally. Mir hesitated, suddenly nervous. Weldon hadn't grown up in Sandford, where almost every person you passed on the street was familiar. Mir knew whatever she chose to tell him wouldn't get back to Jamie or Raleigh, because Weldon didn't have a small-town connection to them. Compared to her Sandford friends, Weldon was a stranger, and in a way that made him feel safer to talk to.

"I had a terrible day," Mir said. "I wanted to talk to someone. There's no one home at my house right now."

"Why was your day terrible?"

Mir remembered Jamie's eyes going black with anger. She felt Raleigh quiver beside her, heard her friend whispering "Stop it, stop" as though that would make everything go away. She saw the sunlight glance off Raleigh's metal barrettes as she turned away, her hand entangled in Jamie's.

"I told my best friend I was planning to leave Sandford to go to university. Her boyfriend said I thought I was better than everyone else." Mir heard her voice climb a few octaves as she finished talking. *I will not cry*, she told herself. *I have cried once already this month and that is quite enough.*

"Jeez," Weldon said softly. "That's . . . uh, kind of a rude thing to say about someone."

"He wants to leave too," Mir said. "He's smart, really smart. He even won some of the school essay awards. He beat out my essays a couple times. But I guess his parents can't afford to send him to university."

"So he's being a jerk to you because you're getting to do what he wants to do," said Weldon.

Mir shrugged into the phone.

"I guess."

"That's a jerk thing to do."

"He's my best friend's boyfriend," Mir said. "She's probably going to marry him someday, so if I want to stay friends with her, I have to deal with him. I keep wishing she picked someone less ambitious, I guess. If he didn't want to leave Sandford, maybe we wouldn't be fighting like this."

On the other end of the line, Weldon waited. Mir could almost see his head bent forward over his aunt and uncle's old phone. She could almost see the way the front of his hair hung down over his forehead, like he was trying to hide behind it. She wished he were here next to her, so she could reach out to push his hair back and see his face.

"My dad doesn't want me to leave Sandford either," Mir said.

"Why not?"

"Everyone in this town leaves. Everyone young. My dad's brothers left years ago, after they graduated high school. I've met them, like, twice in my entire life. So I'm doing what everyone else does, and my dad doesn't want me to."

"You have to do what's right for you," Weldon said.

Mir nodded into the phone. Her back was getting sore where she was pressing it against the wall, but the wall was so comfortingly solid she didn't want to move away.

"Yeah," she said, "but I feel like crap for doing it."

"I'm sorry," said Weldon.

Mir chuckled.

"Don't apologize, you sound all Canadian," she said.

"I'm half Canadian," Weldon said. "I've never lived here, but my dad's Canadian and I get citizenship through him. So I'm allowed to be a little apologetic. It's in my blood."

"You have the curse," Mir said.

"Guess so."

Mir heard the sound of crunching gravel under tires. A door slammed and running feet thumped toward the house. Nate and her dad were home.

"I gotta go," she said. "My dad and brother are home."

"So you don't need me anymore," said Weldon, but his tone was teasing.

Mir hesitated.

"Hey, you want to come with me to a golf course tomorrow?"

"You're going golfing?" Weldon said.

"No," said Mir, "I'm applying for a job. I'm going down first thing to drop off a résumé. Evan told me a new golf course is hiring turf workers, but I need to apply soon. Want to come?"

"Yeah," said Weldon. "I'll be your reference. I'll tell them that you can defeat great armies with only a garden hose."

There was a loud clatter at the door as Nate came in, his curly hair flying. Mir looked up at him and smiled. Nate looked at her quizzically as he thumped toward his bedroom, probably wondering why she was sitting on the floor.

"Don't tell them that," Mir said. "Those are definitely not job skills required for working at a golf course."

"Too bad," said Weldon. "I mean, most employers would consider it a bonus if they knew they were hiring a superhero."

"If I get this job, it will take a superheroic effort for me to get up every morning at six a.m.," said Mir.

There was further thumping at the door as Henry came into the house. He grinned at Mir and stepped around her with exaggerated care. Mir watched him, trying to be annoyed but mostly feeling sad. Since she'd told him about her plans to leave Sandford, he had refused to discuss the issue, retreating into comedy whenever she tried to talk to him.

"Where do you want to meet?" Weldon said.

"At the bridge, your side of it. The golf course is down there, with the rich folk."

"Of course it is," said Weldon, deadpan.

"Nine a.m. tomorrow, okay?" Mir said.

"Okay," said Weldon.

They said goodbye and hung up. Mir continued sitting on the kitchen floor, listening to the sounds of her dad and brother moving around the house. *We're just meeting up*, she thought firmly to herself. *It's not a date or anything, we're just . . . going to see a golf course about a job.* But something in the air around Mir felt different, the atmosphere charged with a strange but not unpleasant tension. She hugged her knees to her chest, closing her eyes. *We're just meeting up*, Mir told herself again, trying and failing to keep a smile from her face.

CHAPTER NINETEEN

Weldon set the cordless phone down on its cradle with a soft click. He stood in his aunt and uncle's kitchen, staring out the window above the sink. Their backyard was as pristine as their front yard, the shrubs at the edge of the property line impeccably sculpted. Weldon's uncle had a small toolshed at the far right of the backyard, painted the same color as their house. Everything matched. Everything was just so.

Weldon put his hands on the counter in front of him and leaned forward. What had Miriam said? *I had a terrible day. I wanted to talk to someone.* So she had called him. She had reached out to him. They hadn't been brought together by the small-town coincidences of Sandford, or Mir's mother trying to heal some ancient family wound. She had sought him out, of all the people she knew. She didn't even have his phone number, and still she'd called. It might not mean anything, Weldon lectured himself, but still he felt triumphant. She had called him.

He turned away from the window and walked up the stairs

to his temporary bedroom, nearly bumping into his aunt, who was heading downstairs.

"Who was that on the phone?" Aunt Kay said.

"Someone from the running club," Weldon said, the lie as smooth as silk. "Just letting me know about an upcoming meet. I forgot to give them my cell phone number, so they called you."

"Ah," said his aunt, smiling. She glided past him, disappearing into the kitchen. Weldon resumed climbing the stairs. In his bedroom, he flopped on the bed, reaching for his phone and navigating to "contacts." He stared at it, then finally hit the "call" button.

"Hello?" Weldon's mother said.

"Hi, it's—it's Weldon," Weldon said. He always identified himself by name when he called his mother. There was a tiny part of him that was afraid she'd respond "Who?" if he said "It's me."

"Hi, kiddo," Emma said. "You calling for any particular reason?" She sounded a little tired, but not stressed or hostile. Weldon realized he'd been holding his breath and let it out slowly.

"Maybe," he said. "Well, yeah. Comic-Con's in about a month, and Dad said I could go with him."

"Did he?" said Emma.

Weldon paused, feeling his way forward, like he was creeping across thin ice.

"He said it was okay if I came down for the TomorrowMen

trailer premiere. I hope—I hope I can see you when I'm in San Diego?"

There was a pause on the other end of the phone. Weldon waited, not sure what it meant. The ice underneath him shivered, cracks spider-webbing outward.

"I'm not going to be at the con, kiddo," Emma said. "But you can come see me at home, if you want."

"Of course," he said. Of course she wouldn't be there. Of course she wouldn't want to be anywhere near the Tomorrow-Men movie, produced by her ex-husband. Weldon closed his eyes and remembered his parents years ago, still together but just beginning to fight like the end was coming. They were walking down some street in Burbank, the three of them, his parents arm in arm, him trailing behind them. He couldn't remember the street. He couldn't remember why they were walking. No one walked in LA. His father had looked up and seen a billboard for some superhero movie. Which movie Weldon couldn't recall, but he remembered David Warrick looking up at the billboard and saying, "We're so close. Any minute now we'll get the TomorrowMen movie made. It'll be bigger than X-Men, it'll be bigger than any of the Marvel movies." Emma Sanders had laughed. "It'd better be soon. I'll be too old to play Skylark in a few years."

"I won't be at the con the whole time," Weldon said now. "I'll come visit you. Maybe Saturday? The con's always a mess on Saturday. I hate how crowded it gets."

"All the fake nerds, clogging up the con," said Emma, but her voice was teasing. "I know, I'm mean."

"You totally are," said Weldon. He paused, not sure how to continue. At the other end of the phone, Emma waited, listening.

"Hey," he said finally. "Can I ask you about something?"

"I'm your problem-solving lady, kid. Lay it on me."

"It's not really a problem . . ." Weldon hesitated, then plunged forward. "I kind of met someone? Here in Sandford."

"Really!" said Emma.

Weldon warmed at the sound of interest in her voice.

"But things are kind of . . . I don't know, complicated."

Emma chuckled. "You've got the beginnings of a great romantic comedy there. Why are things complicated between you and this girl?"

"Because her name is Miriam Kendrick."

"Kendrick, why does that sound familiar?" Emma said. There was a sharp intake of breath on the other end of the phone. "Weldon, did you get mixed up with someone from Micah Kendrick's family? I thought David sent you to Sandford to keep you out of trouble."

"I'm not in trouble," Weldon said. "I've just hung out with her a few times. Her family had me over for dinner. They're—they're really interesting."

"Jesus, small towns," sighed Emma. "I don't think I could stand it, always running into people whose dirty secrets you know. I think I'd suffocate." She paused. "Well, tell me about this girl, kiddo."

She saved my life with a garden hose. She wears terrible sweaters that swallow her whole body. She hated me at first, but then she apologized for being mean. And she just now called me to talk about her terrible day. She has a face like the face Micah Kendrick drew on Skylark forty years ago. She's the coolest girl I've ever met.

"I don't know, I just like her," he said, fumbling for words. "I like being around her. I like having conversations with her. She's very—she's very honest."

"Weldon," said Emma, "please don't tell me you have a thing for this girl because she doesn't like you."

"What? No," said Weldon, a little offended.

"You're very good with people. You're very good at making someone feel like the universe revolves around them. I've seen you do it. And I've seen you lose interest in people because they like you back, and you think that makes them too easy."

Weldon put his hand to his head, digging his fingers into his hair. He tried to explain.

"Her parents invited me over for dinner. They live in this run-down house that looks like it was painted by a kid. She has a younger brother named Nate. They have a garden next to their house where they grow vegetables." Weldon ticked all the facts he knew about Miriam off in his mind: where she lived, what her home was like. He'd peeked into her life and seen something messy and wonderful. He'd eaten at her family's dinner table.

They seemed whole and perfect. Nothing like his family, smashed to pieces.

"Sandford salt of the earth, huh?" said Emma. Her tone bit a little.

"They seem so normal," Weldon said.

"In relation to us."

"Yeah."

He heard his mother moving around in her kitchen in San Diego. A thumping noise, probably her opening the sliding glass door at the back of the room. Maybe she was standing and staring out over the patio. The Kendricks' garden was three times the size of his mother's small, paving-stone-filled yard. Hardy, bristling desert plants lined Emma's tiny patio, a defiant attempt to bring green to an inhospitable environment. Emma was good at tending the little desert plants, but they'd never match Stella's lush tomato vines.

"They're probably as messed up as we are, kiddo. Just better at hiding it."

Weldon bowed his head, pulling the phone from his ear. The ice was breaking around him, but he didn't care.

"I like them, Mom. I like her."

"And what's this thing going to be? Some summer fling? Be careful with this girl. The Warricks have done enough to the Kendricks."

"I wouldn't—" he started, indignant, then stopped.

"I don't want to hurt her," he finished.

"Good," said his mother. "I'm glad to hear the Kendricks seem like they're doing all right. I always felt a little uneasy about how Micah Kendrick was treated by Warrick Comics. Twenty years ago all I wanted was a TomorrowMen movie, and the legal case over the character rights was preventing that from happening. Now, I don't know . . . I guess I feel more sympathetic toward the man."

"I heard Micah Kendrick sold the rights to the TomorrowMen for nine hundred dollars when he was in his twenties," Weldon said. "But then Aunt Kay said that wasn't the whole story, and he made a lot of money drawing the comics. So which is it?"

"Both," said Emma. "He did sell the rights to the TomorrowMen to Warrick Comics, and for years everything was fine. Joseph Warrick wrote the TomorrowMen and handled the business end of things, and Micah Kendrick drew the comics. All he wanted to do was draw. But then the comics started selling like crazy, and Joseph Warrick wanted to capitalize. He'd struck it rich with the TomorrowMen; why not try to milk it for all it was worth? So then came the spin-off shows and merchandise. And because Micah Kendrick had signed away his rights to his part of the TomorrowMen empire, he wasn't included in any of these new ventures."

"Jeez," Weldon breathed, feeling sick.

"Your father and I first tried to get the TomorrowMen movie going back in . . . oh, much too long ago. The movie was so close to going into production . . ."

"I'm not sure I remember that," Weldon said.

"You weren't born yet," Emma said. "But it doesn't matter. Micah Kendrick swooped in with one last lawsuit and that was the end of Emma Sanders as Skylark. He fought that final legal battle like his life depended on it. Spent years crawling through the court system, and your father was right there with him, determined to come out on top."

Emma chuckled sadly.

"I loved Skylark. I felt it was the role I was destined to play. And for years I hated the artist who created her."

Weldon remembered the face of Micah Kendrick, young and smiling, on his laptop screen. He hadn't seen any pictures of Miriam's grandfather in her house.

"Did you ever meet him?" said Weldon.

"Once," Weldon's mother said. He waited, the phone pressed to his ear. "At the very end of the legal fight. Well, the part that was the end for him, because he got sick. His daughter, what's her name—"

"Stella," said Weldon.

"Stella, yeah. She kept fighting for him for a few years after, but I think she was—I don't know if the comics meant to her what they meant to him. She took the buyout the studio offered her, much to your father's surprise. She was married and had a kid, and it seemed like she just wanted the lawsuit to be done with."

Weldon looked over at his painting of Skylark and Skybound, still leaning against his nightstand. Only the lower half of

Skybound's body was visible from Weldon's angle, the superhero's legs jutting out from behind the bed. Weldon remembered the painting of Tristan Terrific in Stella's studio, the dozens of other paintings of the TomorrowMen pinned to the walls. It was as though Stella was still fighting to reclaim what she'd given up years ago.

"Maybe," he said softly.

"Anyway, I didn't even talk to him. Micah Kendrick, I mean. It was at the old Warrick Comics building, the one here in San Diego. I don't know why he was there. He just walked right by me, didn't even know who I was. I remember seeing him and thinking, *There's the reason I didn't get to play Skylark.* This single person, standing in the way of all my ambition."

Weldon heard his mother sigh, and his hand tightened on the phone, worried she might go to pieces over the memory. But she continued, her voice only wavering for a second.

"It was cruel of me to think that about him."

"Why was he at Warrick Comics?" Weldon said.

"I think he came to see your father. I don't know, maybe Micah Kendrick thought David might be more open to discussing things." Emma laughed, the sound like a raw nerve. "But you know your father."

"Yeah," said Weldon. He pressed his cheek into the bed. He pictured his father in all his righteous fury. He didn't want to imagine Micah Kendrick in front of his father, trying to regain something that had been so completely lost to him.

"It sounds ridiculous, but comics are everything to some

people," said Emma. "This sad little pulp art form that only became important once it got profitable to chew them up and turn them into movies. The money's ruined comics."

"Yeah," said Weldon. *Money ruined things for Micah Kendrick and Joseph Warrick*, he thought. *Money ruined things for my parents.* But he knew that wasn't the whole truth. His parents had begun to fight years before the TomorrowMen movie went into production. And when it became obvious that Emma Sanders was too old and not famous enough to play Skylark in a two-hundred-million-dollar superhero movie, the final string connecting his parents had snapped.

"Why am I dumping this on you?" Emma said. "I'm an awful mother. I wish I could do something good for you, Weldon. Something that wasn't me venting my crap all over you. You're the kid; I'm the adult."

"It's okay," he said. "I like you the way you are."

"You're a good kid."

"Not really," he said.

"Well, I like you mostly the way you are," Emma said, "but you need to stop with the theft and vandalism. Legally, I'm not allowed to like that."

"Okay," said Weldon, meaning it.

They talked for a few more minutes, about things that weren't comics or Comic-Con, and then said their goodbyes.

"Keep me updated on how things go with Miriam. Just . . . be careful, will you?" Emma said with a sigh.

"I will," Weldon promised. He tried to ignore the twinge

of resentment in his stomach over his mother's concern for Miriam. *I'm not my father*, he thought. *I'd never hurt Mir the way he hurt Micah Kendrick.*

He hung up and continued lying on the bed for another forty minutes, until his aunt called him down for dinner.

CHAPTER TWENTY

Mir's alarm went off with a screech and she flailed for it, nearly rolling off the bed. She hit the snooze button and stared blearily at the clock, wondering why she'd set it for 8:00 a.m. on a Saturday. Slowly the events of the previous day came back to her: the horrible fight with Jamie, calling Weldon, the plan to meet him at the bridge at 9:00 a.m. so she could apply for a job at the new golf course. Mir rubbed a hand across her face, hit the off button on her alarm, and propped herself into a sitting position. *If I get this job I'll be up every morning at the crack of dawn, so suck it up. Eight a.m. is nothing*, Mir thought, grumpily pulling at the sheets.

In the bathroom, Mir pushed open the shower curtain and stood under a hail of hot water, hating how tired she felt, and how the memories from yesterday kept poking unbidden into her brain. The way Jamie had looked at her when he'd told her she wasn't so special. Like she was nothing but the thing she had, the opportunity he wanted. Under the cascade of water, Mir closed her eyes, forcing the thoughts of Jamie and Raleigh from her mind, thinking about Weldon instead.

She remembered Weldon standing in her mother's studio the night he'd come over for dinner, his face shining as he bent over Stella's paintings. At first, Mir had wanted to grab Weldon by the shoulder and drag him out of the studio. But instead she had watched him and waited, and at last he had turned his face from Stella's paintings, his expression filled with wonder.

I think I like him, Mir thought. *I think I more than like him.* It felt strange to hear the words in her head. It was something Mir thought she'd known for a little while, but hadn't been able to acknowledge until now.

Hair tied up in a towel, Mir padded back to her bedroom and got dressed. She had one nice outfit for most occasions, a dull black dress that managed to look both matronly and like something a six-year-old would wear. Stella had bought it for Mir a year ago, after a fight over one of Mir's sweaters and whether it was appropriate to wear to a cousin's wedding. Mir had worn the dress to the wedding and maybe twice since then.

Mir piled her hair on top of her head, carefully winding it into a bun, and inspected her reflection. The face that stared out of the mirror seemed alien to her. She could see nothing of Stella in her reflection. Mir tilted her head up, then down, but the familiar resemblance to her mother eluded her.

"You look so grown-up," said Henry from the doorway. Mir looked up at him. He was wearing a T-shirt and long pajama pants and his old bathrobe, the one with permanent coffee stains on the front.

"Gonna see the new golf course about a job," Mir said. She turned away from the mirror and scooped up her résumé, printed off last night from her parents' ancient computer. It was very meager. The Emporium of Wonders had been her only real job.

"You're right to want to leave Sandford," said Mir's dad. Mir hesitated. The clock read 8:27. It would take at least thirty minutes for her to walk to the bridge to meet Weldon. But Henry had chosen this moment to talk to her.

"I'm sorry I want to leave," Mir said. Henry shook his head, smiling.

"Your mom wanted to, when we first talked about getting married," he said.

"I know," Mir said. "She told me the day I lost my job. It was kind of strange to find that out."

"Yeah," said Henry. "She wanted to leave for the same reasons you do. To see if we could find someplace with more opportunity. Someplace . . ." Henry shrugged, looking down. "Well, you know."

"Yeah," said Mir, knowing. *Someplace that's not so small and cramped. Someplace where you can walk down the street and not bump into people who've known you your whole life.*

"I wanted to stay here. My parents are here. All my cousins and their kids. This is where I grew up, working on my parents' farm. It's so much a part of me, and I didn't want to let it go."

Mir stood in the middle of her room, watching her father.

He absently dragged one toe across the worn carpet, still look-ing down.

"Your mother stayed in Sandford for me. She's never re-sented me for it. I don't think she does." Henry looked up at Mir, and for the first time she saw how she resembled him, at least a little.

"I shouldn't ask the same thing of you," Henry said. "I just got scared when you said you wanted to go out of province for school. It brought up stuff I didn't know was still there. I felt like you might leave forever."

"I won't," said Mir.

"I know," said Henry. "You'll always be my kid. Here, in On-tario, or wherever else you choose to go. I want—" Henry paused. "I want you to do what you want to do next year."

"Thank you," Mir whispered, grateful. Henry turned away from the doorway and shuffled down the hallway. Mir heard the sound of her parents' bedroom door closing softly.

Mir made it to the bridge at seven minutes past nine. Wel-don was already waiting there, leaning against one of the bridge's iron supports. He was wearing the same well-cut jacket he'd worn the first time Mir had seen him, and the thing in her chest fluttered excitedly.

"Hi," Mir said.

Weldon turned and grinned at her.

"Hey!"

He tilted his head as he noticed her dress.

"Oh, you look—"

"Don't," said Mir. "This is the best I can do at this point in time. Someday I'll learn to dress like a proper grown-up lady, but I've got better things to do now."

"You look nice. Like you're going to hang out with the Addams Family. They had style."

Mir peered down at her dress.

"My mom bought this for a wedding."

"Oh," said Weldon, looking so chagrined Mir couldn't help but laugh. She waved a hand at him.

"Hopefully whoever does the hiring at this golf course will look past my outfit and see the hardworking person who really wants a job."

They walked beside the road leading away from the bridge. The houses were nicer here than on the other side of the river. They didn't have chunks of paint missing from their walls, or sagging porches. The lawns were neatly cut and the gardens looked like they'd been meticulously planned.

"How much more school do you have?" said Weldon.

"Next week's the last week," Mir said. "Thank god. I have one paper due and two exams and that's it."

"Studying like crazy?"

"Kinda," Mir said. "One exam is geography, which is all memorization, so I'm studying hard for that. The other is English. Not a lot of studying for that. It's usually two essay questions, so you're fine as long as you've read whatever book you were assigned and are good at explaining, I don't know, the role of fate in *Macbeth* or whatever."

"I haven't gotten to that play yet," Weldon said. "I did *Romeo and Juliet*—"

"The worst play," sighed Mir. "A couple of thirteen-year-old kids killing themselves over love. So stupid."

"I thought it was kind of sad," Weldon said. "I thought it was more about the stupidity of adults, two families clinging to an ancient feud while their kids died around them. The adults started the fight and when Romeo and Juliet die because of it, then they decide that maybe hating each other for something that happened ages ago might be a ridiculous way to live your life."

"Sometimes when you're hurt it's hard to let things go," Mir said. She looked at a house on the other side of the street, an inky black SUV parked in the driveway. "Sometimes you look at other people and all you can see is what they have and what you don't have."

"Are we still talking about *Romeo and Juliet*?" Weldon said.

Mir laughed, shaking her head.

"Maybe. Maybe not."

"Let it remain a mystery," said Weldon, smiling.

The rolling greens of the golf course appeared before them. Large riding mowers were already sweeping across the grass, drivers guiding them precisely. Mir felt her stomach quake nervously. *Please give me a job*, she thought. *Give me a job so I won't be so dependent on Evan. So I don't have to walk on eggshells around his father for the rest of the summer.*

"Can I walk in with you?" said Weldon.

"Yeah. I'd like that."

They walked down the golf course driveway toward a long metal shed, where half a dozen people in hard hats and dusty T-shirts were milling around. A blond woman with a tanned face bounded enthusiastically out of the metal building, shouting orders at the group. The milling people trotted into the building, some emerging driving groundskeeper carts, flatbeds piled high with dirt or rakes.

Mir tried to catch the eye of the blond woman, but she was a human tornado of organizational leadership, trotting from one section of the metal building to the other. Finally the woman tore back the way she'd come, nearly running into Mir. Mir mutely held out her résumé, not sure what to say.

"Hi," said the woman, "anything I can help you with?"

"I heard you were hiring?" Mir said, her voice squeaking. "I was hoping for a summer job."

"I *am* hiring," said the woman, and her smile flashed blindingly white teeth at Mir. "I'm Holly. What's your name?"

"Miriam Kendrick," said Mir. Holly took her résumé and stared at it for several seconds.

"Miriam, can you be here six days a week at six a.m. sharp?" said Holly. Mir felt her stomach drop. The start time was even earlier than she'd expected. She'd have to get up at 5:00 a.m. to make it to the golf course in time.

"Yes," said Mir. "Yes, I can do that."

"And you're okay with driving one of these things?" Holly pointed at one of the carts driving by.

Mir nodded, holding her breath.

"Okay, you're hired. Start a week from Monday. We pay twelve bucks an hour to work turf, and we need people for the entire summer, right up until Labor Day. I assume you'll have school in September, but we've got plenty of stuff to keep you busy until then. Hey——" Holly's gaze flickered toward Weldon. "You want a job too?"

"I'm American," said Weldon. "I don't have one of those . . . whatever a Canadian social security number is."

"Too bad," said Holly. "We're short-staffed and behind schedule. Anyway, you——" She pointed at Mir.

"Miriam."

"Okay, Miriam. Sorry. I'll learn your name in a few weeks. Maybe. Anyway, be here at six a.m. a week from Monday. We'll give you a shirt to wear that'll identify you as staff. Wear steel-toed boots and pack a decent lunch. The shift goes from six a.m. to two p.m., with half an hour break for lunch, and we all work Saturdays. You good with that?"

"Yes," said Mir. The word came out louder than she'd intended, almost a shout.

Holly eyed her, then smiled.

"Don't let me down. The course opens in a week and we gotta keep this place looking shiny. See you a week from Monday." She walked away, already shouting instructions at a trio of workers.

Mir let out her breath in a long sigh.

"That was so—"

"Anticlimactic," Weldon chuckled. "I could've gotten a job too."

"I probably didn't even need to wear this dress," Mir said, staring down at her matronly ensemble. "You wore jeans and a T-shirt and she wanted to hire you too."

"But then I wouldn't have seen you in that dress, which was a very important moment for me," Weldon said.

"And now you'll never see me wear it again," Mir said. She turned and marched back up the driveway toward the suburbs. Weldon fell into step beside her, his hands in his jacket pockets. Mir glanced at him and saw that he was smiling.

"Let me buy you a coffee to celebrate," said Weldon.

"Shouldn't I buy you one as well?" said Mir. "You almost got a job too."

"I did," said Weldon. "And I bet it would have been a much better job than running errands for the editors at Warrick Comics. How about you buy me a coffee and I'll buy you a coffee."

"I'd prefer tea," said Mir. She looked up at the sky. It was very blue, almost too clear and bright for Sandford. *Summer is so short here*, she thought. Things all of a sudden seemed a little easier. She had decided what she was going to do after high school, her father had forgiven her for wanting to leave, and she had a job. A job that was not working for Evan's father. All the pieces were there, everything falling into place—

Mir remembered the fight yesterday. Jamie's cold fury, the way he'd told her she wasn't so special, Evan yelling at him. The sound of it was horrible. Her stomach churned, and the familiar heaviness settled over her shoulders. Something was still broken. She didn't know if she could fix it. She didn't know if she wanted to.

"You okay?" said Weldon.

"Yeah," said Mir.

They reached the Starbucks twenty minutes later. Mir tried not to look at the window of the Running Realm. There was no sign of her assault on the store, the window wiped clean of thrown coffee. She looked guiltily toward the Starbucks counter, but to her relief, there was no sign of the barista with spiked hair. *I hope she didn't see me throw that coffee the last time I was here*, Mir thought.

"What do you want?" said Weldon, staring up at the menu hung behind the Starbucks counter.

Mir thought, then settled on a cup of green tea.

"I know, I'm boring."

"Hey, like what you like," said Weldon, ordering a coffee for himself. They sat opposite each other at a knee-high corner table by the window. She and Raleigh had spent hours there last summer, when the Starbucks was brand new and seemed like a rare, exotic addition to Sandford. Mir held her cup close to her face, breathing in the comforting smell of green tea. Weldon propped one ankle on his knee, leaning his head back to look out the window. Mir glanced up at him, liking the way the line of his throat curved into his jawline.

"So how are you going to spend the rest of today?" Weldon said, still looking out the window.

"Sleeping," Mir said, blowing on her tea.

Weldon grinned.

"That's a waste of a Saturday, Kendrick," he said.

"I like sleep," said Mir. "Normally on weekends I sleep until eleven. Or twelve. Or later."

"The next two months are gonna be rough for you."

"I can do it," said Mir.

"I believe in you," said Weldon, still smiling. He took a sip of his coffee, his hair falling over his forehead. He brushed it back.

"I need a haircut."

"I could give you one," Mir said. "I cut my mom's hair. I'm really good at it." Weldon looked up at her, his face guileless. It took a minute for him to remember Stella's lack of hair. He laughed.

"Good one."

"What, you don't think I could do it?"

"Oh, I totally believe you could," said Weldon. "I just think—"

He stopped. He was looking at someone out the window, a tall female form walking past them. It was a girl, a little older than Mir. Mir knew her name, Ellie. She was related to Raleigh, a sort-of-distant relation, something like her mom was second cousins with Raleigh's mom. Mir had seen her working at the yoga pants store, and at the time had felt unfairly hostile toward her, an employee of the enemy.

Ellie turned her head slightly as she walked by the window, and Mir saw her gaze catch on Weldon. Her step faltered. Ellie's eyes were hooded slightly, and Mir saw them narrow as they darted toward her. Then with a toss of her ponytail, Ellie was gone, stomping out of sight.

Mir looked over at Weldon. He was smiling as he stared out the window, in Ellie's direction. She recognized that smile, the one he'd beamed at her while sprawled on the ground in front of the Emporium of Wonders. She hadn't realized how plastic it looked, something calculated to snap into place over Weldon's real face. The fluttery feeling soured in her stomach, and she dropped her gaze to her cooling tea. *For someone I think I more than like, I don't know you at all*, Mir thought. She suddenly felt very small and foolish, stupid for thinking *I more than like you* things about Weldon Warrick.

Weldon turned away from the window and rubbed a hand across his face, the smile deepening into a grimace.

"Well, that was awkward," he said. Mir said nothing, staring at her hands. Weldon looked over at her, his gaze anxious.

"Mir, I—"

"I don't really know you," said Mir. "Our families have this weird history, but it's not like you know me or I know you, not really."

"I'd like to get to know you," Weldon said. "And I feel like maybe you did too? But right now I think you're angry with me."

They sat silently for a moment, Mir half listening to the sounds of the other customers in the Starbucks. Someone was ordering a coffee that had about fifteen words in its name. Latte, foam, whipped, cinnamon, chocolate sprinkles. The list went on and on.

"I'm not angry with you," Mir said. "I just . . . realized there's a lot I don't know about you."

Weldon stared out the window, his eyebrows drawn down. A small knot of tourists were ambling down the street, peering in the window of the make-your-own-pottery store. The tourists gathered in a group to discuss something, then pushed open the door to the store and went inside.

"What happened with you and Ellie?"

Weldon's mouth twitched, and he shoved a hand through his too-long hair.

"You know her?"

"She's related to one of my friends," said Mir.

"Jeez, small towns," Weldon said. "Everyone knows everyone. Must be like living in a fishbowl."

Mir waited, watching him. She was very aware of the feeling of the cup in her hands, her fingers wrapped around it tighter than necessary. Weldon hesitated, glancing out the window one last time, then continued.

"I think she's a little like you. Wants to leave Sandford, isn't sure how to do that. I got—I was kind of dismissive with her. I acted like living in Los Angeles, being the son of David Warrick and all the opportunities that provided me, wasn't a big deal."

He shrugged.

"I still don't want anything to do with my dad's business, but I shouldn't have been so casual about it. I know—" And he looked up at Mir. "I know it would mean a lot to you if your grandfather had stayed at Warrick Comics, and you had the chance to be involved with that world."

"Yeah," said Mir. "It would mean a lot."

Her fingers reached for him. They slid across the knee-high table between them and brushed the back of his hand. She felt her skin against his, the tips of the first two fingers on her hand gliding across Weldon's wrist. Mir's stomach felt like it was trying to flutter out of her throat, Weldon's hand still and warm beneath her fingers. She forced herself to breathe in, a quick, shuddery sigh.

"I like you," said Mir. "Even though it kinda scares me."

Weldon took her hand between his and turned it palm up, brushing his thumb across her palm. The feeling of his touch was strangely soothing, and the thrumming in her stomach settled to a gentle hum. Weldon's gaze was open and hopeful, vulnerability sketched around his eyes. *He could really hurt me*, Mir thought, *but I think I could smash him to pieces if I wanted to.* It was a frightening and exhilarating thought.

"I like you too," Weldon said.

He smiled, real and warm.

"I want to get to know you better, if that's okay."

"It's okay," said Mir.

They sat at the Starbucks corner table until their drinks went completely cold, their heads bent together over their clasped hands.

CHAPTER TWENTY-ONE

Mir sat half sprawled on the couch in her parents' living room, willing herself not to fall asleep. *Gotta get used to getting up early*, she thought grimly. *Can't take naps, gotta adjust to this new sleep schedule. I can do it.* A blanket of exhausted numbness washed over her. All she wanted was to roll sideways, press her cheek into the couch cushion, and sleep forever. Mir leaned to her right, then heard her mother's voice, calling from the kitchen.

"Miriam," said Stella, "why is Raleigh standing in our front yard? Did she forget how doorknobs work?"

Mir sat upright abruptly, her stomach lurching. The fight flooded back into her mind, the finality of Raleigh turning away from her, hand entangled in Jamie's. It had seemed so much like an ending she and Raleigh had been racing toward for the past year.

Stella's head poked into the living room, peering at Mir.

"Are you going to go ask her to come inside? When was the

last time she even came over here? You two usually hang out at her place."

"She has the good internet." Mir stood up, trying to ignore the nervous feeling jangling in the pit of her stomach. "She has Netflix."

"Ah, yes, we are so bereft, here in the land of dial-up," Stella said, eyeing Mir as she walked through the kitchen to stare out the front window. Raleigh's familiar form was a few steps away from the porch, her hands stuffed into jean pockets, looking up at the house.

"Is everything okay with you two?" Stella said from behind Mir.

"No," Mir said.

"Can you work it out?"

Mir shrugged, thinking of the fight. Evan yelling, Jamie yelling, Raleigh turning away from her.

"I don't know." She walked to the door and pushed it open, stepping out onto the porch. Raleigh was looking to her left, toward Stella's vegetable garden. At the sound of Mir's feet on the porch, Raleigh's gaze jerked back toward the front of the house. Mir stood opposite her, waiting. Raleigh looked down, took a deep breath, then looked back up at Mir.

"My boyfriend has consistently been a total asshole to you for . . . well, a really long time," Raleigh said. "I kept . . . I kept not seeing it. I guess I didn't want to see it. But I should have, and I'm really sorry."

Raleigh ducked her head, as though keeping eye contact with Mir was painful.

"I should have told him to stop, that what he was doing was garbage," Raleigh said, and Mir caught the fracture in her voice. "I should have defended you. You're my best friend. I mean . . . you were. If I hadn't . . . y'know, ruined everything."

"It wasn't okay," Mir said softly. "I know I kept telling you everything was okay, but it wasn't and I was afraid to say something. I mean, you're in love with him. I thought you'd choose him over me."

Raleigh nodded grimly.

"Yeah," she said. "I am in love with him. My boyfriend treats my best friend like dirt and I'm still in love with him. I'm the worst."

Mir stood on the porch, waiting. In front of her the sun was slanting downward, brightly painting the edges of the Sandford skyline. Raleigh had her back to the sun, shadows gathering across her face.

"I told Jamie he has to apologize to you," Raleigh said. "I wanted to come and talk to you first, to see if it was okay for him to apologize. If you don't want to see him or me again ever, I understand. But I wanted . . ." The fracture spread through Raleigh's voice, splintering it. She took another breath and continued.

"You've been the best friend I could've ever asked for. You deserve all the cool things, and I hope you get to run the world someday."

"I don't think I want to run the world," Mir said. "That seems like way too much responsibility."

Raleigh laughed, wiping at her nose with the sleeve of her shirt.

"Yeah, it does," she said, shrugging. "But I believe you could do it. Anyway, I should go—"

"You don't have to go," Mir said. She sat down on the porch steps, wrapping her arms around her legs. Raleigh turned away, but only to sit on the step beside Mir. She rested her elbows on her knees, looking out over the yard in front of her. A small part of Mir ached to reach out, to touch Raleigh's shoulder, anything to prove that things would be fine. But she still felt the presence of the fight, the heaviness hanging over her shoulders, pressing her downward.

"I don't think it's ever going to be the same between us," Mir said. "I don't think it can be." Images flickered into Mir's mind, all the little moments with Jamie over the past year. His words that pushed her deliberately away from Raleigh, all his sharp edges that caught on Mir.

"Yeah," Raleigh said softly. "I know." She pushed a hand through her hair, shoving brown curls away from her lightly tanned face. "Can I tell you a story?"

"Sure," said Mir.

"Do you remember that summer when you and your parents took that monthlong vacation?"

Mir rubbed a hand across her knee, looking at Raleigh out of the corner of her eye.

"Yeah. We drove down to New Brunswick and Maine. We camped a bit. It rained a lot. I think I was twelve?"

"Thirteen. It was the summer before we went into high school," said Raleigh. "It was the longest we'd ever been apart. I saw you every day at school. On weekends you'd come to my house or I'd come to your house and your mom would make us eat all those horrible vegetables."

"Yeah," said Mir, remembering Raleigh's face scrunching up in horror as Stella piled homegrown green beans on her plate.

"I swear I hate squash so much because in seventh grade your mom served it to us for dinner for, like, two weeks straight. I have squash PTSD. I'm never going to be able to eat squash again." Raleigh looked down, picking at an invisible thread on her jeans. She was smiling a little.

"Yeah," said Mir again.

"I remember when you told me you were going to be away for that month in the summer. You were really mad. You didn't want to go. Stuck in a car with your parents and your brother for weeks. You tried to convince your parents to let you stay with me, but of course they said no. I remember being so upset because I couldn't imagine going so long without you. A month without seeing you, without telling you something that was important to me."

Mir stared at the tops of her knees. Raleigh's words seemed to be coming from far away.

"For the first few days you were gone, it was horrible. I had this ache in the pit of my stomach. I didn't know who to talk to when I had something to say. You know my mom, she's kinda—she's kinda hard to talk to."

Mir remembered coming home from the vacation, her family piling out of the car, exhausted from the long hours spent crammed together. Nate was cranky and Henry snapped at him when he grumbled about bringing the luggage inside. Mir couldn't wait to see Raleigh. She had thought of Raleigh constantly for the final few hours of the drive home, feeling a fierce tugging sensation the closer they got to Sandford. She dragged her duffel bag into the house and dumped it on her bed. Stella was already in the kitchen, tiredly putting together a dinner of boxed mac and cheese. Mir had stood behind her, swaying back and forth, hurting for Raleigh. Stella had turned around and seen the anxious look on Mir's face.

She'd sighed and made a shooing motion with her hands, and Mir tore off down the road. She ran the entire way to Raleigh's house, arriving sweaty and out of breath. Raleigh had been watching TV. When she looked up at Mir, her face seemed different, as though she'd grown a year in the month Mir had been away.

"Oh," Raleigh had said, "I thought you weren't back until next week."

Now, sitting on the porch of her parents' house, Mir hugged her knees.

"I remember that," she said.

"I knew you were going to leave Sandford, even then," Raleigh said. "I knew it in my tiny tween lizard brain. You were so much better than me at school, and you were always looking forward, always thinking about stuff that you wanted in the future. We were thirteen years old, and you had a savings account to pay for university tuition. You were already collecting pamphlets from different schools. I mean, who does that when they're a kid?"

"I did," Mir said, half to herself. The memory warmed her. She remembered opening up her first savings account at the bank, feeling safe and happy whenever she deposited the money she got from her parents for babysitting Nate.

Raleigh continued.

"I didn't—I don't really want you to go. It would be nice if you stayed here in Sandford with me and Evan, but I know better. And I knew I had to figure out a way to be okay with you leaving. I guess that summer trip was me taking that first step. But I didn't want"—Raleigh dragged in a ragged breath—"I never wanted it to happen like this. Where I screwed things up because I couldn't see that my boyfriend is jealous of you. I always thought that . . . I don't know, you'd leave, and I'd have this friend in Toronto or Montreal or wherever. And I'd get to visit."

They sat in silence, watching the sun slip downward, toward the Sandford skyline.

"Do you want to leave too?" Mir said. It was something she'd never thought about, that Raleigh, who always seemed so grounded and content, might want to escape Sandford too.

"No," said Raleigh. "This is my home. It's where I'm

supposed to be, I think. But it still sucks getting left behind, you know?" Raleigh stared down at her hands, her fingers spread over her knees. "I'd go back and change everything about this past year if I could. If I had the power of . . . who's the Tomorrow-Man who can travel through time?"

"The Mage of Ages," Mir said. "He time travels using the power of Excalibur, which never really made sense to me."

"None of those superheroes make sense," Raleigh said. "But I still loved their TV shows." She stood up, brushing off the butt of her jeans. She turned toward Mir, her face falling deeper into shadow. "You're going to do such amazing things, Mir," Raleigh said softly.

"I'm going to try," Mir said. "Raleigh, it might . . ." She paused. Raleigh stood in front of her, waiting. Mir still felt that heavy weight on her shoulders, all the hurt that had culminated over the past year. But just now the pressure had eased ever so slightly. "It might be okay if you visited me in Toronto."

Raleigh blinked, her eyes suddenly bright.

"Really?"

"Maybe. I don't know how I'll feel after we graduate, but I think it might be okay." Raleigh smiled, and the fondness in her expression made Mir's heart ache.

Mir watched Raleigh walk away, feeling like a cloth that had been wrung dry. She stood and walked back inside her house, to where her mother was waiting in the kitchen. Stella opened up her arms to her daughter, and Mir slipped into the embrace, wordlessly.

The first Monday of Mir's new job came swiftly. Her alarm buzzed at 5:00 a.m., and it took every ounce of strength not to slap it silent and go back to sleep. The night before, she'd prepared a lunch and left it in a paper bag in the fridge, a pink *don't touch, miriam's* sticky note stuck to the outside of the bag. Nate had a habit of consuming everything in the fridge that wasn't claimed by sticky notes. Mir had gone to bed early but had lain awake staring at the ceiling, growing more and more frantic as the hours ticked by. The grit in her eyes was a testament to how little she'd slept.

Mir staggered out the front door of her house. It was still dark outside, but a line of sunlight was creeping along the rim of the horizon. Mir couldn't remember the last time she'd seen the sun rise.

She woke up as she walked toward the golf course, feeling almost alert as she approached the bridge. To her surprise, Weldon was leaning against the supporting column of the bridge. His face brightened when he saw her.

"Hi," he said.

"Hi," said Mir, remembering the feeling of his fingers brushing against the palm of her hand.

"I wanted to wish you good luck on your first day of work," said Weldon. "And maybe I can walk you home afterward? We could get coffee, if you're still awake. If you don't want to take a nap immediately."

"No naps," said Mir. "Gotta try to get a proper early morning sleep schedule going, may God have mercy on my soul."

"Getting up at five a.m. is extremely awful," Weldon said. "Don't expect me to be here every day."

"Of course not," said Mir, the thing in her chest fluttering happily at the thought of Weldon crawling out of bed far too early to meet her.

Weldon hesitated, then shyly reached out his hand. Mir slid her hand into his, and they walked toward the golf course. The glowing seam at the base of the horizon was cracking open, spilling colors across the sky. Mir tipped her head back and stared at a line of brilliant red arcing above her. She wanted to say something, to point out to Weldon the strangeness of this moment, the two of them walking hand in hand to her brand-new job. But she stayed quiet, enjoying the silence.

The golf course sprawled before them, awake and buzzing. Red-shirted employees flocked around the long metal shed, green turf carts barreling in and out, flatbeds piled with dirt and turf-care paraphernalia. Mir felt her stomach lurch, nervous at the thought of new co-workers, new skills to learn. But she also felt eager. This would be her job for the summer. She mentally calculated the number of work hours per day times her hourly rate of pay, then multiplied it again against the number of days left in the summer. She could already feel the money safe in her bank account, slowly growing, counted against the cost of university tuition. It would never be enough. But it was a start.

"Good luck," said Weldon, turning toward her. Her hand

was still wrapped in his. Mir tugged her hand free and walked down the golf course's long driveway, throwing a wave back over her shoulder toward Weldon.

"I'll see you this afternoon."

———

After eight hours of raking bunker sand and filling divot holes, Mir said goodbye to her new co-workers and staggered toward home. She saw Weldon was waiting for her at the top of the golf course driveway. He grinned and fell into step beside her. Mir was relieved he didn't try to hold her hand; she felt like she was caked head to toe with dirt.

"How did it go?"

"My legs hurt," Mir said.

"Seriously? It can't have been that bad."

"It was fine," said Mir, and it had been. Holly had intercepted Mir on her way to the turf shed, handing her a red T-shirt with the golf course's logo embroidered on the chest. "So you look all official-like," Holly had said, apparently unaffected by the early morning hour. After pulling the T-shirt over her head, Mir had been assigned to a group of other turf workers, and sent out to rake the sand bunkers. The turf workers started an hour before the golf course opened to players, so that hour was when they hurried to rake the starting holes. At 7:00 a.m. on the dot, golfers in peaked hats and ridiculous pants were already lined up, eager to tee off.

Mir had raked bunkers until her arms felt ready to fall off, then had been sent out onto the green to fill in divots, dropping clumps of seeded dirt into notches carved in the grass. By the time lunch rolled around, Mir's stomach was growling fiercely.

But it had felt good. The other members of her crew seemed nice, mostly college students home for the summer or high school students looking to save money for university. There was one girl with brightly dyed red hair who worked at the golf course "so I can finally buy a motorcycle that isn't a hand-me-down piece of crap from my cousin." Mir had liked the girl, who had arms already tanned and toned from raking bunkers.

"Just fine?" Weldon said.

"Okay, better than fine," Mir said, smiling down at her work boots. "Pretty okay, actually. Just wish it wasn't so early."

"You'll get used to it," Weldon said. "Maybe it'll even turn you into a morning person."

"That is extremely unlikely," said Mir. "You underestimate my devotion to sleep."

They stopped at the Starbucks on the way back to Mir's house. Weldon got coffee, and insisted on buying Mir a tea.

"It's going to be too hot for tea soon," Mir said, carefully sipping a cup of orange pekoe. "Guess I'll have to start buying the frozen coffee drinks, and die of sugar overdose."

"Kendrick, you put four teaspoons of sugar in that tea," said Weldon, pointing at her cup. "I think you've built up a resistance to large quantities of sugar intake."

"There are advanced levels of sugar consumption that even I haven't mastered," Mir said.

They sat in silence for several minutes. Weldon turned his head to glance out the Starbucks window, and Mir took the opportunity to admire his profile. He caught her looking when he turned back toward her, and raised his eyebrows. Mir shook her head, smiling.

"Who do you look the most like, your mom or your dad?" Mir said.

"My dad."

"I guess," said Mir critically, peering at him. She had looked at photos of David Warrick online, but didn't think the resemblance between him and Weldon was strong. There was a little of David Warrick in Weldon's eyes and jawline, but they didn't have the same nose.

"I really don't look like my mom. She looks kinda like . . . like an elf queen from *Lord of the Rings*. I don't look like that." Weldon grinned and gestured at his face, his crooked nose, the acne scars on his jaw. "Clearly."

"Like Galadriel?" Mir asked. "I saw those movies. They were good. Kinda long, though."

"If you wanted to find the largest per capita population of elf queens, you'd find them in Los Angeles," said Weldon, leaning back in his chair and lacing his hands behind his head. "So many Galadriels, just walking around like they're nothing special. Put them anywhere else in the world and they're goddesses. But in Hollywood, they're just one of dozens."

"That's kinda sad," Mir said. She felt a sudden surge of sympathy for Weldon and his strange, dysfunctional family. She reminded herself to google photos of his mother the next time she had access to a computer with good internet. *Is that weird?* Mir thought. *Looking up photos of the parents of this guy I like?*

"You remember a while back when I came by your old job, and we talked about comics?" Weldon said.

"Sure."

"Remember how you described your mom's painting? Like painting was a practical need, a necessity?"

"Yeah," said Mir.

"My mom was like that about acting," Weldon said. "She was never famous, not above-the-movie-title famous, but she worked regularly. And I think she really loved what she did. She was good at stepping into a different character's skin and becoming that person. And, well . . ." Weldon stopped. He stared out the window, his face turned away from Mir.

"I think it really hurt when she stopped getting work," Weldon said. "I mean, can you imagine your mom not painting?"

"No," said Mir. She tried to picture Stella without her brushes, without smudges of paint on her cheeks and hands. She tried to imagine Stella closing the door to her studio forever. The thought horrified her.

"It's hard for actors," Weldon said. "They depend on other people for their craft. They need writers; they usually need other actors. Sometimes a stage or a camera and people to work that camera. And they need an audience. I think that's the most important thing, an audience. Maybe that's something you don't need if you're a painter."

"Sometimes you do," said Mir, thinking of her grandfather. Micah Kendrick had longed for people to read his comics. He had wanted it so badly he had signed away the rights to his creations.

"Of course," said Weldon. Emotion lined the skin under his eyes.

"My mom was supposed to be Skylark in the TomorrowMen movie," he continued. "My parents met at San Diego Comic-Con years ago, when it was just this weird little get-together in a hotel, not the massive thing it is now. My mom was dressed as Skylark, and my dad . . . I guess he thought that was a sign they should be together. He said she looked like she stepped out of the pages of the TomorrowMen comics."

Mir held her breath, waiting. She had the feeling that Weldon had never spoken these words aloud before. It was like he was peeling back the shining outer layer of himself, letting her see the vulnerabilities under that beautiful shell. It thrilled and frightened her a little.

"They wanted to make the TomorrowMen movie together. My dad would produce it, my mom would play Skylark. But the movie didn't get made when it was originally supposed to, because of the legal case over the rights to the characters. And while the court stuff was happening, comic book movies became these massive, massively expensive things. The budget for the TomorrowMen movie went from forty million to two hundred million. And suddenly my mom was too old and not famous enough to play Skylark in a two-hundred-million-dollar movie."

Weldon smiled distantly.

"My mom says money ruined comics. I don't think so. I think it just ruined my dad and her."

Weldon's gaze flickered up to Mir, and he abruptly leaned back, pushing his hair from his forehead.

"Why am I rambling on about my family?" he said.

"I like hearing about them," said Mir.

"Why?" Weldon laughed, embarrassed, eyes darting away from Mir.

"Because they're a part of where you came from, and I want to know you better," Mir said.

Weldon reached out and took Mir's mug of tea from her hands. He placed the mug carefully on the table in front of him, and took one of Mir's hands between his own. Mir's chest fluttered happily at his touch.

"Right," said Weldon. "Can you tell me something super personal now, so things are even?"

Mir thought, trying to temper the thrumming in her chest. It was distracting. What was even more distracting was Weldon's thumb lightly skimming across her palm.

"When I was eight I got so mad at my dad about something, I can't even remember what, I dunked his toothbrush in the toilet and then put it back in the toothbrush holder."

"Nooooo," Weldon said, his eyes wide.

"Yes," said Mir. "He used that toothbrush for about a week, and then I felt so bad about it, I went and bought the exact same toothbrush with my allowance and replaced it. I've never told him what I did."

Strangled laughter burst out of Weldon.

Mir watched him, glad for his amusement.

"Was that personal enough for you?"

"It was amazing," sighed Weldon, still chuckling. "I can't believe you did that. I mean, I'm an actual criminal and I've never done anything that bad."

His fingers slid between hers, their hands intertwined and locked. Mir stared at their laced-together fingers, feeling strange and thrilled all at the same time.

"Stick around," she said softly. "Maybe I'll tell you more personal things."

"I'd like that," said Weldon, and smiled in a very real way.

CHAPTER TWENTY-TWO

In the week that followed, Weldon thought about Miriam every moment he was awake. He thought about her in the spaces between his strides when he jogged. He thought about her while eating dinner with his aunt and uncle. He thought about her as he finished his last school essay and emailed it to his mysterious internet teacher. He woke up every morning at 5:00 a.m. and walked to meet her by the bridge. Her face was always closed and sleepy that early in the morning, and he loved the way it brightened when she saw him.

"Hi," she would say.

"Hi," he'd say back, and then he'd reach out his hand for hers.

They went out for coffee every afternoon after she got off work, sitting opposite each other in the tiny nook at the back of the Starbucks. Mir always had tea. The kinds of teas changed from day to day, but it was always tea.

When they sat down at their table in the corner, Mir

would reach her open hand across the shellacked wood surface, toward Weldon. She wouldn't quite look at him when she did it, but the corners of her mouth were always turned up a little bit, as though she was nervous and amused by her nervousness. Weldon would slide his hand into hers, confident that a super-hero could burst through the Starbucks and he wouldn't even notice.

"I think I'm getting used to getting up at five a.m.," Mir said, staring down at her cup of honey blossom herbal tea. "I still want to die when I hear my alarm go off, but I think I want to die slightly less than I did last week."

"I told you you'd become a morning person," Weldon said, and Mir squeezed his hand, just a little.

Weldon longed to touch more than her hand, but he decided he would wait for her to touch him, as she'd done when she first reached across the table. *That way I hopefully won't screw it up*, Weldon thought. But he wished he didn't have to wait between now and whenever Mir chose to reach across the distance between them.

When Weldon went back to dinner at Mir's house, he told his aunt that he was going for an evening run with the Running Realm group. The look Stella gave him that night made him suspect she knew he and her daughter had been holding hands in the Starbucks every afternoon that week. But she didn't say anything, and the serving of vegetables she piled on his plate was as generous as ever.

After dinner, he and Mir sat on the floor of the living room and played a game of Monopoly with Nate and Henry.

"Why are all the player pieces colored rocks?" Weldon asked, staring at the pile of brightly painted stones Mir was sorting through.

"Because sometimes certain parents are too cheap to buy a new copy of Monopoly and their children have to play with a game with all the pieces missing that they bought at a yard sale like ten years ago," Mir said, shooting a pointed look at Henry.

"Hey, we still have the hat," Henry said, picking up the small pewter top hat. Nate snatched it out of his hand.

"I'm always the hat," said Nate.

"I'm always the green rock," said Mir.

"I'll be the red rock, I guess," said Weldon, but Henry's hand snagged the rock first.

"I'm always the red rock," said Henry. "You can be purple."

By the end of the game, Henry and Nate were so wound up they were yelling at each other over the advantages of owning all four railroads or Boardwalk. Weldon won the game over Henry by a very narrow margin. When his defeat became inevitable, Henry reached solemnly across the board to shake Weldon's hand.

When it was time for Weldon to leave, Mir walked with him out to the front porch. They stood in the near-darkness for a moment and pretended to be very interested in staring at the horizon. Because he was looking away from her, Weldon didn't realize Mir was reaching for him until he felt her hand on his arm. Then she was next to him, very close. Weldon tried not to breathe. He felt the warmth of her cheek pressing against his chest as she slid her arms around him. She fit almost perfectly under his chin. If he leaned forward, he could rest his chin on the top of her head. Before he could move, she pulled away from him, muttered a flustered "Good night!" and tore back inside the house. Weldon was left standing alone on the porch in the darkness, feeling the imprint of her body seared against him.

When he got home, Weldon's aunt was waiting for him.

"Where were you? You said you were going for a group run, but when I checked the Running Realm schedule, there wasn't one this evening."

"Having dinner at Miriam Kendrick's house," Weldon said. His aunt blinked, a hurt look crossing her face. Weldon stared her down, feeling stubbornly defiant. He couldn't remember ever fighting with her, even when he was a kid. But right now felt like a good time to start.

"You lied about your whereabouts so you could sneak off to Stella Kendrick's house?" his aunt said, sounding almost plaintive.

"I just wanted to see Mir," he said. "You don't like her family, and I thought you'd tell me I couldn't see them."

"I don't *dislike* the Kendricks," Weldon's aunt said sharply. "I dislike what they did to us. I told you about all that legal nonsense Stella Kendrick's father dragged us through, and you still think it's okay seeing her daughter? I don't understand."

"They didn't do anything to us," Weldon said. "But I think we did plenty to them." He felt angry, but it was a different kind of anger from the one that urged him to steal cars. This anger was hot in his chest, fueled by the feeling of Mir pressing up against him as they said goodbye on the sloping porch of her falling-down house. "Stella Kendrick would be standing on the red carpet at the TomorrowMen movie premiere if it wasn't for us."

"That's ridiculous," said Weldon's aunt. "There wouldn't even *be* a movie if it wasn't for the work your grandfather and father did. They built Warrick Studios."

"You're right," said Weldon. "All Micah Kendrick did was draw the comics Warrick Studios was built on."

Weldon's aunt recoiled. She hesitated, then shook her head, as though to remind herself of something.

"Legally we did nothing wrong," she said, but she sounded doubtful. "I know—I know the buyout given to Stella was generous. It was more than what she deserved."

Weldon said nothing, staring at his aunt. *She deserves so much more*, he thought. He remembered Stella's studio, filled with paintings of the TomorrowMen. He wondered if she painted them because she felt she had to, if it was like she was reclaiming her father's characters for him.

"Do you know what people say about our family online?"

Weldon's aunt said. "They say we robbed a man of his legacy. They say we used the court system to steal ownership of those comic book characters. But we won the court case over those comics, so how can that be? How can people say that we exploited someone, if everything Warrick Studios did was legal? How is it fair that people get to say things like that?"

"Katherine," said Weldon's uncle. Alex Warrick's frame nearly filled the kitchen entrance. He didn't look angry, but his expression was darker than normal, as though a passing thought had troubled him. Weldon's aunt turned toward him.

"You know what they'll say about us when the movie comes out," she said to her husband.

Alex Warrick sighed.

"Maybe Warrick Studios deserves some of those criticisms," he said.

Weldon turned toward his uncle, surprised at the admission. It was something he didn't think his father would ever admit.

"You can't believe that," said Weldon's aunt, staring aghast at her husband.

Alex Warrick shrugged.

"I don't know," he said. "Maybe everything in the Kendrick case was handled legally, but some of it didn't sit right with me. I love my brother, but sometimes he is much too harsh with people he thinks are in his way."

Weldon watched his aunt and uncle, the anger ebbing from him. Alex Warrick had firmly rejected the world of the TomorrowMen. He'd written one issue of the comic years ago, then stepped away from the empire David Warrick had built, never to return. *I guess he didn't like how my dad built that empire*, Weldon thought.

"Anyway, none of this matters," Weldon's uncle said.

"It does!" insisted Weldon's aunt.

"Hardly anyone knows who Micah Kendrick or Joseph Warrick are. The comic books don't matter," said Alex Warrick. "Millions of people will see the TomorrowMen movie that David is making, but they won't read the comics the movie's based on. Most people don't care who created the TomorrowMen, they're just looking for a movie to watch on Friday night."

Weldon's aunt drew in a shuddering breath.

"I don't like people saying things about us," she said. "It isn't fair."

"No, it isn't," said Alex Warrick with a quick shake of his head. Weldon didn't think he was talking about the Warricks being unfairly maligned online.

"If Weldon wants to hang out with Stella's family, that's fine with me. Stella's a good person," said Uncle Alex. He looked over at Weldon, who felt small and exposed under the intensity of his uncle's gaze. It was somehow more intimidating than all the times his father had yelled at him.

"What isn't fine with me is you lying to us about it. I don't want you to do that anymore, Weldon. Am I clear?"

"Yes, sir," Weldon said, feeling like he was about to melt into a guilty puddle at his uncle's feet.

"Okay. You're welcome in our home anytime. You're part

of our family and we love you, but if you want to live here, you don't get to lie to us." He looked over at his wife, who was watching the conversation with a startled expression. Weldon suspected she'd never seen this side of her husband either. "Is that all right with you, Kay?"

Weldon's aunt sighed, folding her arms across her chest.

"I suppose."

Alex Warrick reached out and patted his wife's shoulder in a way that was both formal and fond. A moment of unspoken communication seemed to pass between them, and she looked over at Weldon, nodding firmly. Then she walked from the kitchen, leaving Weldon alone with his uncle.

"Does your dad know you're seeing Stella's daughter?" Alex said.

"No," said Weldon. "I mean, it's really early, we're just—" He remembered the feeling of Mir pressed against him, and felt his face start to get warm. "We're just hanging out, seeing where things go," he finished lamely.

Alex chuckled.

"Well," he said, "isn't that too damn perfect."

"Are you going to tell my dad?" Weldon asked.

His uncle shook his head.

"No, you tell him when you're ready."

Alex walked out of the kitchen and up the stairs after his wife. Weldon stayed standing where he was for several more minutes, looking out of the kitchen window at his aunt and uncle's perfectly neat lawn.

The weather had turned unusually hot for Sandford.

"Is there anywhere to swim around here?" Weldon asked Mir as they walked toward the Starbucks. He was getting used to the 5:00 a.m. wake-up time, filling the hours Miriam was working with jogging and practicing his pool shot on the table in the basement. He was getting pretty good at spinning the pool ball into whatever pocket he was aiming for.

"There are a couple beaches outside of town," said Mir, "but they get crowded on nice days. I like the lake better, although it's got a squishy bottom."

"Can we go to the lake?"

"Why?" asked Mir, eyeing him.

"Because swimming is fun and it's hot out. That was literally my entire thought process."

"You sure there isn't an additional 'I'd like to see Mir in a bathing suit' part to your thought process?" said Mir, smiling.

"I would never!" said Weldon, faux outraged. *Yes, absolutely, I would love to see you in a bathing suit, preferably a bikini*, he thought. Mir had abandoned her oversized sweaters since the weather turned warm, but her work uniform of a golf course T-shirt and shorts barely an inch above her knee was hardly more revealing. *This golf course is run by damn puritans*, Weldon had thought the first time he'd seen her uniform. He had started inspecting whichever of Mir's knees was closest to him during their hand-holding sessions at Starbucks. He was startled to see both of her knees were speckled, freckles dotting constellations across her skin.

"Swimming would be nice," Mir mused. They had reached the Starbucks, and she paused in front of it. "Do you want to go now? Do you have a swimsuit?"

"Mine's back in California. I'll buy a new one," said Weldon, flicking a thumb in the direction of the Running Realm. "They sell bathing suits in there."

"I gotta go home and get my stuff too," Mir said. "Want to meet at the lake in half an hour?"

Weldon pulled out his phone.

"Show me how to get there and I'll be there."

Five minutes of Google Maps later, Weldon walked into the Running Realm, his brain already working in overdrive at the thought of Mir in a bathing suit. He made a beeline for the swimwear section of the store, and stood in front of a mannequin for several minutes, staring blankly. A vision of Miriam in a pink bikini floated behind his eyelids.

"Can I help you?"

Weldon turned and saw Ellie, her honey-colored hair hanging long and straight in a frame around her face. Weldon's toes curled a little.

"I'm looking for swim shorts," he said.

Ellie gestured with an uninterested wave of her hand toward a nearby clothing rack.

"All of our swimwear is on that rack," she said.

Weldon turned and began shuffling through the hanging

shorts. He could feel Ellie's gaze hot on the back of his neck. He inspected a pair of green shorts, making a show of being interested in the lining.

"So is that other girl giving you what you want?" said Ellie.

Despite the air-conditioning in the store, Weldon felt a bead of icy sweat roll down his neck.

"What does that mean?"

Ellie's eyes glittered beneath her hooded eyelids. She smirked.

"I mean, you just wanted a summer distraction, right? Someone to fool around with before you skipped back to LA."

She was standing with her arms folded, leaning against one of the store displays. Weldon felt like his entire body was melting under her gaze. He forced himself to stare back.

"Sure," he said, and his voice had a snarl in it that he'd never heard before. "That's all I wanted. From you, at least." He pointedly held out the green shorts to her.

"I'll take these. I'm paying with a credit card."

Nearly an hour later, Weldon trudged along the gravelly back road toward where he and Mir had planned to meet. The walk from downtown to the lake should have only taken him twenty minutes, but he'd taken a wrong turn on one of the dirt roads that crisscrossed Sandford and had gotten lost.

There was a scattering of people gathered around a thin slice of sandy beach at the lake. Two kids splashed in the shallows, pulling up clumps of mud from the lake's bottom and flinging them at each other, shrieking. A couple was sprawled under a giant beach umbrella, skin already tan and shining from the sun. On the far side of the water, massive evergreens jutted from the shoreline, casting long shadows. Weldon held a hand up to shade his eyes, looking for Mir. He saw her standing on the edge of the beach, her back to him. She was wearing a tattered straw hat, boy-cut swim shorts, and a bikini top. Weldon's heart did a happy little lurch at the sight of her bare back. *Totally wearing a bikini. Yessss.*

Weldon walked toward Mir.

"Hi."

Mir turned, and it took every ounce of Weldon's self-control not to allow his eyes to dip below her collarbone.

Mir grinned, her face shaded by the hat.

"You made it!"

"I got lost," admitted Weldon.

"Google Maps, defeated by Sandford's terrible back roads. Tell that to . . . um, Bill Gates? Who runs Google?"

"Some nerds," said Weldon. "Nerds with more money than we'll ever see in our lifetime. Nerds with solid gold pocket protectors."

"Yeah, okay, nerds," Mir said. She waved her hand at the tiny beach. "This is it! Nice, huh?"

"It is," said Weldon, turning to look at the lake. Mir turned to look as well, and Weldon slid his eyes toward her, his face still aimed at the lake. Her bikini top was red-and-white checkered, not pink, but that didn't matter. What mattered was the curve of her waist above the belt line of her blue swim shorts, the way the skin on her lower back looked so pale, like parts of her hadn't seen the sun in a very long time. He remembered the feeling of her body pressed against his the night she had hugged him. He almost felt light-headed.

Mir's head started to swivel back toward him, and Weldon shifted his eyes frontward, making a show of looking out over the treetops on the other side of the lake.

Mir pointed at his Running Realm bag.

"You want to change?"

"Sure," said Weldon.

Mir pointed at a small wooden structure at the tree line behind them.

"That's the public washroom, only place to change around here. It smells kinda bad, but it's not so horrible if you can change quickly."

"I'll be super fast," said Weldon, and trotted toward the washroom. It was a small, two-door structure, one bathroom for women, one for men. Weldon walked into the men's side and dressed quickly, holding his breath as he stripped off his T-shirt. He stuffed his clothes into the Running Realm bag, and paused as he caught a glimpse of himself in the cracked mirror above the bathroom's lone sink.

You just wanted a summer distraction, right? Ellie's words rang in his mind.

"It's not like that," Weldon said out loud. He leaned his

forehead against the door frame of the bathroom, feeling queasy. *But what is it like? I like her, I think she likes me. Am I going to screw this up and hurt her? My family's already taken her inheritance.*

He pushed back from the bathroom door frame and walked out into the summer sunshine. Mir turned to look at him as he walked toward her. She smiled, her face shadowed by the floppy brim of her hat. Weldon pushed the last echoes of Ellie's voice from his mind, and smiled back.

Mir swam for a grand total of fifteen minutes, then climbed out of the lake and fell asleep on her towel on the sliver of a beach. Weldon considered lying down as well, but instead decided to swim across the lake. It took ten minutes of an easy front crawl to reach the other side, and fifteen minutes of back-stroking to reach the beach again. Mir was still sleeping, white smudges of sunblock covering every inch of exposed skin. Weldon sat next to her for a while, feeling foolishly happy, then wandered back into the lake, practicing underwater handstands. After his twelfth handstand attempt, he noticed Mir was awake.

"Sorry," she said, looking embarrassed as he trudged out of the lake. "I've been trying not to take naps because they mess up my sleep schedule, but I'm tired all the time. Getting up at five every morning will always be the worst."

"No worries," said Weldon, plopping down beside her. She'd brought a towel for him, a tattered white-and-red beach towel with a Canadian maple leaf emblazoned on it. It seemed both patriotic and a little disrespectful to put his wet butt on it.

"It is so nice out," Mir sighed, sitting up. "I could stay here forever. Nice days are like unicorns in Sandford."

"Every day's like this in Los Angeles," Weldon said. "Always sunny, always gorgeous out."

"And I bet no one appreciates it," said Mir, smiling at Weldon from under her giant hat. "Would you appreciate a unicorn if they were as common as horses?"

"That's a very strange analogy to make," Weldon said.

"I like seeing the seasons change," Mir said. "It'd be unnatural to have this kind of weather in January."

"You like all the snow? What is it with Canadians and snow?"

"No," said Mir, "it's not that we like it. I mean, some people do. People who ski or play hockey and stuff. But it just feels wrong not to have it. It's a renewing process we go through every winter. We hibernate, waiting out the cold, and when spring comes, it's like we're reborn into the world."

"Amazing," said Weldon, meaning it.

Mir laughed.

"No, it's silly. Canadians are just stubborn. This is where we've decided to live, so we've convinced ourselves that we're okay with our terrible winters. We're good, really, we are! Look, we're playing hockey in backyard rinks. Everything's cool! Get out of here with your good weather, Californians."

Mir leaned back on her towel, stretching her arms above her head. Weldon hoped he was doing a good job of not being obvious that he was staring at her.

"Hey," he said, "can I ask you something?"

"Sure."

"It's something kinda personal. I don't want to pry, really."

Mir looked up at him, curious.

"Okay."

"I mean, if you don't want me to know——"

"Weldon, just ask," Mir said.

"Okay," said Weldon, "your last name is Kendrick, right?"

"Yeah," said Mir.

"So . . . um, isn't that your mom's last name?"

Mir peered at Weldon, confusion on her face. Suddenly she got it.

"You want to know why we're the Kendricks and not the Joudrys."

"Joudrys?"

"It's my dad's last name," said Mir. "When they got married, he took my mom's name."

"Oh," said Weldon, feeling relieved at the simplicity of the answer. Why hadn't he thought of that? Mir's parents seemed pretty nontraditional; it made sense they might use Stella's last name instead of Henry's.

"I don't know why, though," Mir said, her tone thoughtful. "Maybe it had to do with . . ." She paused, frowning. "My dad told me recently that my mom didn't want to stay in Sandford when they started talking about getting married. Maybe him taking her name was, I don't know, a trade. Something he could give her in exchange for staying here for him."

Mir rubbed her arm, looking pensively down at the sand.

"I didn't know she wanted to leave," she said. "She never told me. Even when I was, y'know, freaking out about what I wanted to do next year. Whether I wanted to stay or go."

"She probably didn't want to influence your decision," Weldon said.

Mir nodded absently, sifting her fingers through the sand.

"Yeah," she said, "probably."

Mir looked up at the lake. Afternoon sun was reflecting off the water, blindingly bright.

"This time next year, everything will be different," she said.

Weldon reached out to brush his fingers across the back of her hand.

"Different is good," he said. "Scary, but good."

"Yeah," said Mir, and leaned toward him, resting her chin on his bare shoulder.

"Whatever happens, I think it will be okay. I'll be okay. I think." And she turned her head toward Weldon's, bumping the tip of her nose against his cheek. He felt her lips lightly brush against his jawline and froze, not sure if he should turn his head to meet her. But she pulled back, tucking her chin against his shoulder again.

They stayed like that a long time, until the sun dipped below the tree line beyond the lake and the evening turned cool and crisp.

CHAPTER TWENTY-THREE

Mir kept wanting to reach out and touch Weldon. The safest option seemed to be to keep her hands by her sides. It was easiest when they were at Starbucks, because then her hands were occupied by his, and there were people around to spoil the mood. When Weldon had suggested they go swimming, she had almost turned him down, nervous at the thought of him only in swim trunks and equally nervous about him seeing her in a bathing suit. But she'd agreed, because the weather was scorching and the thought of diving into a cool lake was appealing. And maybe a tiny part of her wanted to see Weldon with his shirt off.

At home she'd stripped off her clothes, changed into her swim shorts and bikini top, and stared at herself in the mirror in her room. The parts of her that had been exposed to the sun by the golf course uniform had freckled a bit, and she peered at her knees and elbows, feeling almost giddy. She put her hand on her stomach, then imagined Weldon's hand on her bare skin and had to quickly leave her bedroom in a flurry of activity. Sunblock, a towel, an extra towel for Weldon, and sunglasses went in her canvas beach bag. She tried to shove all thoughts of Weldon and his hands touching her out of her head.

Mir was relieved when she'd gotten to the beach ahead of Weldon. It allowed her time to spread out her towel, smoothing out the pebbly sand so it was comfortable to sit on. And then he'd appeared, sweaty and annoyed over getting lost. He'd changed into his swim trunks and it had been fine. She hadn't exploded in a confetti burst of hormones, although she'd very much wanted to reach out and slide her hand up Weldon's neck from his shoulders to where his hairline began on the back of his head. That whole area of Weldon looked like it would be very nice to touch. She kept her hands firmly by her sides, in case they might mistakenly wander toward him.

Mir wasn't sure if Weldon was looking at her while they sat by the lake. Sometimes she thought she saw his eyes slide in her direction, but whenever she turned toward him, he seemed to be looking some other way. Feeling bold, she lay down on her beach towel and reached her arms over her head. She saw Weldon's head turn toward her, his eyes flickering downward. Then he seemed to freeze, staring straight ahead at the lake in front of them. The thing in Mir's chest gave a happy little jump, and she tucked her arms behind her head, trying not to smile too much. He wanted to look at her and he was trying his best not to.

After they'd talked for a bit, about Mir's family, about how things might change next year, Mir felt Weldon's fingers brush against the back of her hand. She leaned toward him and rested her chin on his shoulder. His skin was warm from the sun and he smelled like sunblock. Mir felt the fluttering in her chest start up again, and she wished she could slide her hands forward, wrap them around Weldon's bare torso and bury her face in the back of his neck. At one point she'd turned her head toward him, awkwardly knocking her nose against his cheek. She'd quickly turned away, embarrassed over her clumsy attempt to kiss him, worried she'd spoiled the mood. But Weldon hadn't reacted, so she remained where she was, her chin tucked carefully against his shoulder. Like touching him was the most normal thing in the world.

It was nearly dinner time when Mir got home from the beach. She flopped facedown on her parents' couch, feeling exhausted and exhilarated all at once. Stella, who had been doing dishes in the kitchen, stuck her head into the living room.

"Long day?"

"When you get up at five a.m., every day is long," Mir said grimly.

Stella leaned on the living room door frame, drying her hands with a dish towel.

"You getting up that early is a great hardship," she said, deadpan. "So you remind us every day."

"No fair," Mir muttered into the couch pillow. "Stop picking on me."

Stella laughed. "I know, I am very mean. So, tell me how Weldon's doing."

Mir pushed off the couch, rolling onto her side to look at her mother.

"Um, he's fine."

"And you two are, what? Hanging out?"

"Yes," said Mir, feeling her stomach twist. She remembered the feeling of Weldon's shoulder as she leaned her cheek on it, how thrilling it felt to be so close to him. In the living room doorway, Stella looked down at the dish towel in her hands.

"I didn't expect this when I invited him over for dinner."

"Are you going to tell me not to see him?" Mir said.

Stella looked up at her, surprised.

"Oh, Miriam, no. Of course not. It's just . . ." Stella hesitated.

"Things are complicated," Mir finished for her.

Stella nodded.

"I like Alex Warrick," she said. "David, Weldon's father, was always a little nuts. Desperate to leave Sandford, like he thought he was above this town. Alex wasn't like that. He was sweet." Stella folded the dish towel, pressing it against her body. "I see a little of both of them in Weldon."

Mir got up from the couch and went to her mother. She slid her arms around Stella, wrapping her in a hug. Stella pressed her face into the hollow of Mir's shoulder.

"If he doesn't treat you right, you dump his ass, okay?"

"Okay," said Mir.

After dinner that evening, Mir called Evan.

"How's early-morning Miriam holding up? You actually making it into work?"

"I'm a very responsible human being," Mir said, "so yes."

"Good to hear."

"Other than the early start time, the job's pretty cool. I'm getting muscles from raking the bunkers."

"You'll be Hulked out by the end of the summer," Evan said. "Super buff Miriam. That can be your superhero name."

"What would my superpower be? The ability to wield a plastic rake and make sand look freshly groomed?" Mir said.

She missed Evan. She'd seen him only twice since school let out. The combination of her new job plus hanging out with Weldon had made finding time for socializing difficult.

"What if there was a supervillain who made all the sand traps in all the golf courses of the world super mucked-up, and the—um, what's the Stanley Cup of golf?"

"The Masters?" Mir said. "I think that's the big one. I don't really know anything about golf."

"And you work at a *golf course*! You're a fake golf girl."

"They'll find me out any day." Mir wound the phone cord around her hand. "Evan, I want to talk about the TomorrowMen comic script."

There was a pause on the other end of the phone. Mir waited, hoping Evan would speak first. When he didn't, she said helpfully: "Y'know, the Tristan Terrific story that we were writing?"

"Yeah, I know," Evan said. Mir thought she heard tension in his voice. "The one I said I didn't want to give to Weldon Warrick, even though I was the one opening my dumb mouth and being like, 'Oh, hey, let me be a total fanboy and slip you this script.' Ugh. I'm so embarrassed."

"It's a good script, Evan," Mir said. "I think we should give it to him."

"It doesn't have a good ending," Evan said. "It's a day in Tristan Terrific's life. We wrote all this stuff about how he's tempted to use his superpower on people and force them to do things, and the ending is him fighting bad guys and using his power on them anyway? It doesn't feel right."

"I think I have a better ending," said Mir. The ending had come to her as she'd lain on the couch, thinking about saying goodbye to Weldon a few hours earlier. He'd walked away from her toward his aunt and uncle's house, still in his damp swim shorts. His walk and the way his hair was spiked every which way from his swim in the lake had sparked something in her mind.

"We keep the climax. Tristan Terrific is confronting the bad guys on the roof."

Mir could see it in her head, the drawings on the comic page laid out before her. The drawings looked like the artwork in the comic book Evan had been reading that day by the lake, months ago. What was the artist's name? Stuart Sams? No, Samuel. His drawings were abstract but powerful, black brushstrokes indicating the curve of a cheekbone, the knuckles on a man's hand. There was something in the artwork that reminded Mir of her grandfather's drawings, the ghost of Micah Kendrick still haunting the TomorrowMen. Mir closed her eyes.

Tristan Terrific, former villain turned TomorrowMan, was standing on a rooftop, surrounded by men worse than him. He'd always struggled with morality, but on this particular day he had done good. He'd saved the city from the plans of these men, and now they'd cornered him.

"He's totally thwarted them. Their evil plan to harm the city has been defeated because of the heroic things Tristan has done over the course of the day. The bad guys know they've lost, but they're going to get revenge and kill him."

Tristan pushed his hair back from his eyes. He had a shock of white through his hair, like a lightning bolt. He looked at the men in front of him. He could make them do anything. With a word. With a smile.

Mir paused, giving Evan a chance to absorb the story. He waited. She plunged on.

"Originally we had it that he controls their minds and just walks away, but we know that's wrong. Tristan Terrific can't do that to people, because he's not a villain anymore. He's a hero."

Every day was agony for Tristan Terrific. His power simmering in his mind, his fingers itching to reach out toward the men in front of him, to command them to do what he wanted. It would be so easy. And these were evil men. Men worse than him. Men who would hurt innocent people unless they were stopped. Tristan Terrific had the power to stop them forever. All he had to do was reach within himself and choose.

"Yeah, okay," said Evan. "So then what?"

"He jumps off the building."

Tristan Terrific fell backward, without making a sound.

"And as he falls, he's triumphant. Because he is a hero. He saved the city, and even more than that, he had a chance to use his powers and violate the mind of another person. Even though it was a bad person and his life was at stake, he chose not to use his powers for evil."

Tristan Terrific counted the floors as he plunged down the side of the building. He was laughing, but it was from disbelief. Skybound always believed in him. Not Skylark, not the rest of the TomorrowMen. There was always suspicion in their eyes when they looked at him. Even when he proved himself to them over and over. This would be the ultimate proof. He chose not to use his evil power, not even to save himself. That would show all the TomorrowMen that at the very bottom of his black heart, Tristan Terrific was a hero.

Mir realized she was smiling. The phone was quivering in her hand. She felt a warmth in her chest, so similar to what she felt when Weldon touched her.

"It's a cathartic moment for him, because throughout the story he's always tempted to use his powers. He's always terrified that he will, that he'll cave completely and become a villain again."

"So does he die?" Evan asked. "I don't think we can kill him—"

"No; at the very last second Skybound flies in and saves his ass," Mir said. It was a short story, only twenty-two pages long, but it had a beginning, a middle, and an end, and they had made it. Together, her and Evan.

It was an undignified rescue, Skybound snagging Tristan by his ankle. Tristan hung upside down, frowning at the flying man in the cape. "You ruined my heroic sacrifice," he said. Skybound smiled, looking off into the horizon. "You're not allowed to die," he said. "The world needs heroes." Tristan Terrific rolled his eyes. Skybound was a lot to take sometimes. He was so good, so perfect. He believed in other people. Tristan had seen so much darkness in others, it was hard not to be swallowed up in it. But whenever he felt like giving in to his villainous side, there was Skybound, showing him the way. "Thanks, buddy," said Tristan Terrific. "Anytime," said Skybound.

"Okay," said Evan.

Mir hesitated. "Okay what?"

"It's a good ending; let's do it. Let's give this sucker to Weldon Warrick and have our asses rejected by the fine editors at Warrick Studios."

"Yay!" said Mir.

"You gonna type it up?"

"Um," said Mir, "I already did. I mean, if you didn't like the ending, I would've changed it . . ." She trailed off, realizing how it might sound to Evan, her trampling all over his story without his permission.

"Put your name on it too," Evan said.

"Evan, it's your story——"

"No," he said, "it's our story. We made it together."

Mir closed her eyes, imagining Evan, his head bent over his

278

phone, sitting on the bed under the watchful gaze of his *Anchor-man* poster. His room was so full of stuff. Comic books of all kinds, TomorrowMen toys, a pile of video games in the corner. He loved it all.

"You're the best, Evan," Mir said. She hoped he wouldn't hear the way her voice quivered when she said his name.

"I know," said Evan.

The phone pressed to her ear, Mir put her back to the kitchen wall and slid down it. She sat on the floor and wrapped her arms around her knees.

"Things are going to—I mean, no matter what, even if I leave—I mean . . . you and me—" She couldn't get the words out. They tangled on the tip of her tongue, tripping over one another.

"Absolutely," Evan said. "You and me, Mir, bros for life. That cool?"

"Yeah," said Mir. She closed her eyes, smiling. "That's cool."

———

Mir trudged down the golf course driveway, feeling as though she had been punched in the face by the sun. Some days the sun seemed to be closer to the Earth, hanging right behind her shoulder like a fiery eavesdropper. Mir thought about the lake and longed to be there already, submerged in cool water. At the end of the driveway she saw Weldon's familiar shape, a backpack thrown over his shoulder. She'd suggested they meet at the lake, but he'd insisted on meeting her at the usual spot on the golf course driveway. *We can walk to the lake together*, he'd said. *You can make sure I don't get lost.* And he had grinned sheepishly, because the excuse was so thin.

"Hi," Weldon said, smiling.

"Hi," Mir said, and her heart did its happy little lurch at the sight of his smile. It was such a different smile than the one he'd first beamed up at her from the ground of the Emporium of Wonders' parking lot. It was real and beautiful, and made Mir want to slide her arms over his shoulders and place her hands on the back of his head and—

"I brought my own towel this time," Weldon said. "It's slightly less patriotic than the one you lent me, but I figure that's a good thing since I'm not fully Canadian. I feel like Farley Mowat's ghost is going to haunt me for the sacrilege of putting my wet American butt on a Canadian flag towel."

"Farley Mowat is known for being a particularly patriotic and vengeful ghost," Mir said. "Wait, you've heard of Farley Mowat?"

"Sure," said Weldon, glancing at Mir in surprise. "My dad's Canadian, remember? He left Sandford really young, but he's still from here. He gave me a bunch of old Farley Mowat books when I was a kid. I liked *The Dog Who Wouldn't Be*."

"I've never actually read any Farley Mowat books," Mir said.

"Oh my god. Will they kick you out of Canada for that?"

"Fortunately, I have read the complete works of Lucy Maud Montgomery, so I think they'll let me stay."

"Who's that?"

"She wrote *Anne of Green Gables*," Mir said. "A classic of Canadian literature, possibly the greatest Canadian book of them all. A breathless ode to bosom friends, the magic of imagination, and the joy of wearing a dress with puffy sleeves."

"There's so much about Canada I don't know," sighed Weldon.

"We *are* very mysterious," Mir said. "But don't worry. I can teach you to be so Canadian that even the vengeful ghost of Farley Mowat will be fooled."

Weldon reached for her hand, and Mir laced her fingers in his.

"I'd like that," Weldon said, and smiled his beautiful, very real smile.

They spent the whole afternoon at the lake. Mir stayed in the water longer than usual, paddling around in circles while Weldon lazily back-stroked beside her, his eyes turned upward to the blue dome of the sky. After several loops around the lake, Mir reached for Weldon and he dove under the water, pulling her down with him. She wrapped her arms around his shoulders, her hair trailing behind her as he dove down. At the bottom of the lake the water was cool and dark, and Mir kept her eyes closed, her face close to the back of Weldon's neck. Weldon's legs kicked and propelled them forward, and they shot across the bottom of the lake. When he brought them to the surface, Mir gasped for air, determined to hang on to him until the last possible second.

"You okay?" Weldon asked as Mir spluttered and coughed.

She nodded.

"Sorry, I stayed down kinda long."

Mir reached for him.

"Let's go again."

By the time Mir and Weldon reached her house, the sky was shot through with purple. Mir's stomach did a little flip-flop as the familiar shape of her home peered over the horizon. The Tristan Terrific script, neatly folded into a manila envelope, weighed heavily in her backpack. She kept remembering it over the course of the day, her hand reaching in the direction of her backpack, then pulling away when she decided it wasn't the right moment. But now the day was over, and she was out of time. It was now or never.

Mir stopped. Weldon walked on a couple more steps, then realized she wasn't beside him. He stopped and turned toward her, his face quizzical. The sun was setting in front of him, a splash of light turning the hair across Weldon's forehead pale blond. Mir realized she very much wanted to kiss him.

Instead she bent down and fumbled with her backpack. The script felt heavy as she pulled it out. Weldon looked at the envelope curiously as she handed it to him.

"We finished the script."

Weldon stared at the envelope in his hand, then looked up at Mir.

"The what?"

"Open it," Mir said. "Open it and see."

Weldon opened the envelope, unfolding the script. He peered at the title, at Mir and Evan's names under it, confused.

"We finished it," Mir said, suddenly feeling anxious. He wasn't reacting the way she thought he would. She had expected recognition and excitement, not confusion. Weldon was looking at her like she'd told him a joke that he wasn't getting.

"What is this?" he said.

"It's the Tristan Terrific script my friend Evan wrote," Mir said. "Well, he wrote and I helped. I came up with the ending. Sorry it took so long to finish. We were—well, I was kind of distracted with finishing up school and then losing my old job and then my new job and then you . . ." She trailed off. Weldon was staring at her blankly.

"Don't you remember?" she asked weakly. "That day you came by the Emporium of Wonders, when I was still working there. And Evan was there and he asked you—"

"The guy with the beard," Weldon said, his expression jolting with the memory. "The one who was a huge TomorrowMen fan. He said something about pitching a TomorrowMen script."

"Yeah," said Mir. "And now we've finished it." She pointed at the paper in Weldon's hands. "That's it. We wrote a story about Tristan Terrific. Evan mostly wrote it, but I helped a little. You said you could show it to your father. You said . . . you said you'd do that." Mir heard the anxiety creeping into her voice.

Weldon looked down at the script.

"Shit," he whispered. Mir felt ice water trickle down her back. *Please don't let me have screwed things up for Evan*, she thought. *He didn't want to give the script to Weldon, I made him do it.*

Weldon extended his hand, gesturing for Mir to take the script back.

"Mir, I can't," he said.

"Why?" said Mir. "That day in the store, you said you could give Evan's script to your dad . . ."

"I know," Weldon said. "But I can't. For legal reasons Warrick Studios doesn't take unsolicited submissions for Tomorrow-Men comics. They won't look at anything by a writer they don't know, somebody they haven't asked to pitch. It's just how it works."

The script hung in the space between them. Mir saw Weldon's outstretched arm waver a little from the weight of it.

"So you lied? I mean, why?" Mir saw black close in around Weldon, like she was looking at him from the wrong end of a telescope.

"I was trying to impress you," Weldon sighed.

"By lying to me?"

"I knew who you were, okay?" Weldon said. "I knew your grandfather had created the TomorrowMen with my grandfather. I knew there'd been a legal fight over the rights. I thought . . . I don't know what I thought. Maybe that I could prove to you that I wasn't like the rest of the Warricks."

He looked up at her, his hair streaked with light from the

setting sun. Behind Weldon was nothing but a vast expanse of darkness. Mir took a step backward.

"What am I doing with you?" she said. It came out wet and hurt.

Weldon blinked. He let his hand, still holding the script, fall to his side.

"I screwed up. It was a shitty thing to do. I didn't mean—"

"I pressured Evan to give you the script," Mir said. "I made him do it. He didn't want to. But I made him, because him writing a story, him wanting to do something different, made him a little like me. So I wouldn't feel so alone in this town full of content people who are so frigging *okay* with being here." Mir bowed her head, squeezing her eyes shut. "I'm such a selfish jerk."

"You're not," Weldon said, his tone alarmed. "He's your friend, I'm sure he'll forgive you. Blame me. It's my fault anyway."

"You lied to me."

Weldon nodded. His mouth was pressed into a grim line.

"I did. I'm sorry."

"*You don't get to be sorry!*" Mir howled. Her voice broke on the last word. Weldon took a step back, as though she had pushed him.

"I mean, seriously, what am I doing with you?" Mir said. Her hand was pressed to her mouth. Pieces of the last month tumbled in her head. Weldon and Evan in the Emporium of Wonders,

Evan glowing with excitement. Stella screaming that her father was too proud to compromise, and that was why the TomorrowMen were no longer his.

"I'm not like this," Mir whispered. "I'm so practical. I've had a savings account since I was ten. I shouldn't be *dating* someone whose family wrecked mine."

"That's not fair," Weldon said. "This has nothing to do with anything that happened forty years ago."

"It has everything to do with that," Mir said. "It's about the Warricks screwing over the Kendricks. It's how this will always play out. Forever and ever."

"So that's how this is going to be?" Weldon said. "We fight, and you're going to bring up what my grandfather did to your grandfather? You're going to throw something I wasn't even alive for in my face?"

Mir's head snapped up. Weldon met her glare, and the anger on his face softened a little.

"Oh," said Weldon. "That's why you wanted my dad to buy the script. You want the TomorrowMen back."

"No," lied Mir.

She started to walk past him and he reached for her, his fingers brushing her shoulder. Weldon's face was smooth and calm and smiling. The mask had slid down over his real face, snapping into place.

"Miriam," he said. "C'mon. Let the TomorrowMen go." Mir saw the last bit of sunlight reflect off the hair hanging over Weldon's forehead, a lightning bolt of white shooting through his dark hair. For a moment, Tristan Terrific, not Weldon Warrick, stood in front of her. She recoiled.

"Don't try to make me feel something I know isn't real," she said. "You don't have that superpower."

She turned and ran toward her parents' house. The sound of the slamming door echoed into the black night.

CHAPTER TWENTY-FOUR

Weldon leaned his head against the airplane window and watched San Diego unfurl underneath him. He'd seen the city from the air dozens of times and usually loved the way it looked: palm trees and stucco-roofed houses, mountains jutting up in the distance. In the crowded marina, boats were tied to every available dock, bobbing in the harbor like toys that belonged to some monster child. Weldon closed his eyes and felt the plane dip downward. He was home.

It had been two weeks since the fight with Mir. He'd left her alone afterward, although he hadn't wanted to. His fingers itched to call her. He still woke up at 5:00 every morning, fumbling around in the dark for the alarm clock before realizing it hadn't gone off. The first few mornings he'd lain there in the dark, listening to birds chirp and watching the black line between his curtains slowly turn brighter. He'd waited until he heard his aunt and uncle leave for their jobs, then had pulled himself out of bed and eaten a breakfast of cold cereal. He hadn't felt like running.

His aunt and uncle knew something had happened. His aunt was bustling and concerned. She didn't say anything, but there were extra servings of his favorite foods at dinner, helpful notes she left him in the kitchen, suggesting things he might like to do in Sandford that week. Things like fun runs, haunted tours of nearby landmarks, and rock climbing at a small outcropping twenty minutes outside town. Weldon drove to the rock-climbing spot but changed his mind at the last minute, spending the next few hours driving aimlessly down country roads. When he'd gotten home, Aunt Kay had asked how he'd enjoyed himself, and he'd lied, feeling guilty for reneging on his promise not to. "It was so much fun, Aunt Kay. I really liked it. I might have to go down there more often." His aunt had beamed, looking delighted and a little relieved. From the living room, Weldon's uncle eyed him from behind his iPad.

"Is there something going on with you?" Alex Warrick had asked, cornering Weldon after dinner.

Weldon shrugged.

"I screwed things up with Mir."

Alex looked sympathetic.

"There's a lot of history between our families," he said. "Maybe too much to put on you kids."

"Yeah," Weldon said. "I guess so."

Weldon opened his eyes. In the clogged heat of San Diego, the plane touched down. Weldon ignored the waiting driver with a WARRICK placard and hopped in a cab outside the airport, giving the driver his mother's address.

"You here for Comic-Con?" the driver asked.

"Yeah," said Weldon. "But I used to live here."

"Not anymore, though, huh?" the driver asked.

"No," said Weldon. "Now I live in Canada. On the East Coast."

"Canada? Bummer, man."

"Yeah. It's a pit," said Weldon, thinking of the feeling of Mir's chin resting on his shoulder.

They sped along the waterfront, banners for Comic-Con hung from every streetlight. The air was heavy with humidity, and it smelled like a storm was coming. Ahead Weldon saw the massive shape of the convention center, crouched patiently beside the waterfront. Then the cab turned toward the city center, and Weldon lost sight of it.

Emma's house looked the same as it had always looked, small and tidy. Weldon stood outside it for a moment, staring up at the stucco roof, the off-white exterior. His room had been at the very top of the house, one wall slanting with the shape of the roof. There was a small round window at one end of his room, and during the weeks his mother was home, Weldon liked to stare out that round window and watch her as she puttered around in the backyard, fussing with her collection of hardy desert plants. She had gone to a galaxy far away, ruled it as a blue-skinned alien queen, and returned home to him and his father. Because she loved them more than she loved her vast alien empire, her millions of warriors, her thousands of alien starships.

The door was open.

"Mom?" Weldon called as he stepped through. Silence. There was a soft meow from the kitchen and his mother's very ugly cat, Charlie, wandered toward him. Weldon stared at the cat.

"How are you still alive?" he said wonderingly, bending to stroke the cat's back as it rubbed against his legs. "She's had you longer than I've been around. Are you secretly immortal?" Charlie hissed crankily in reply.

There was the sound of someone thumping down stairs, and Emma Sanders walked into the kitchen, arms full of dusty papers. She started when she saw Weldon, the papers spilling and scattering across the kitchen floor.

"Weldon!"

"Sorry," Weldon said sheepishly. "I should've called ahead."

"No, it's okay," said Emma, smiling. She held out hands covered in grime, then realized how filthy they were and laughed, rubbing her palms against her jeans. "Wait, wait, let me clean up a bit and then I'll hug you." She went to the kitchen sink and vigorously began scrubbing at her arms and hands with a wet dishcloth.

"When did you get in?"

"Just now," Weldon said, looking around the kitchen. It

looked the same as it always did. Checkered black-and-white tile on the floor, olive-green stripes painted on the walls. Yellow-and-orange cabinets. An explosion of carefully chosen colors. Emma loved color.

"Didn't your father send a car for you?"

"Yeah," said Weldon. "But I felt like seeing you first."

"You're sweet," said Emma, and leaned back against the sink, drying her hands with a towel. She reached her now-clean hands out to him. Weldon remembered her wrapping her arms around him when he was small. He would squirm and complain that he didn't want to be hugged, he wasn't a baby anymore. Her hugs had all but vanished as he grew older, and he looked back on his younger self with jealousy. *You didn't know how great you had it, kid*, he thought, as his mother slipped her arms around him. For the briefest of moments her cheek was next to his ear, and then she was gone.

"So," said Emma, "have you seen the convention center yet?"

"No," said Weldon. "What's it like this year?"

"Same old. The big thing this year is an HBO show based on a Japanese comic about a serial killer. Prime HBO grimdark stuff is what I've heard, very brutal, very bloody. They've wrapped the Hyatt next to the con center with fairly inappropriate advertising. There is literally what looks like a giant knife sticking out of the hotel. That'll be a wonderful thing for the kids to see."

"Jeez, who brings kids to Comic-Con?"

"We brought you," Emma said, reaching over to ruffle Weldon's hair. She was still taller than him, and at this point he knew it would always be this way.

"Yeah, but the con was different back then. It wasn't a hundred and thirty thousand people crammed into a convention center four blocks long. There weren't knife fights over seats in Hall H."

"I think it's nice," Emma said, smiling. "I like that parents still bring their kids to the con. They're trying to raise their wee nerds right."

Emma bent and began picking up the papers she'd spilled on the kitchen floor. The papers were thick, old and dusty, with unfamiliar drawings on one side.

Weldon crouched next to her.

"What are these?"

"Old stuff from the attic," his mother said. "I was looking for something. Haven't found it yet."

Weldon held up one of the sketches. Thick pencil strokes sketched vague human outlines, men and women jumping, running, fighting. Men and women with bodies sculpted to near perfection, capes trailing behind them as they battled each other effortlessly.

Weldon frowned.

"These are TomorrowMen sketches."

"Yeah," said Emma. "From the seventies, I think. They aren't signed, but I think they're John Buscema. He did a run on the TomorrowMen at the end of that decade."

She straightened and piled the drawings on the kitchen table. Weldon gave the paper in his hands one last look before adding it to the pile. Emma waved a hand at him.

"Come help me look. I wanted to find them before you came, but you got here early. I know they're around here somewhere."

They climbed the stairs to his old room. Unlike everything else in the house, it wasn't the way he remembered it. The paint on the walls had faded from primary blue to a pasty baby blue. Boxes were piled everywhere. The small round window Weldon loved to look out of when he was a kid was covered by boxes, stacked to the slant the roof on one side of the room. There were dates on all the boxes, out of order: 1979, 1983, 1971.

"What a mess," Emma sighed.

"What is all of this?" Weldon asked, staring.

"The archive," said Emma. "What I could save over the years."

Emma went to a box dated 1967 and opened it. Weldon peered over her shoulder and saw the box was full of paper. There were drawings on the paper, men and women in capes and helmets, striking superheroic poses.

"Is . . . is this all comics? It's original artwork from the TomorrowMen comics, isn't it?"

Emma nodded and knelt on the floor, folding her legs beneath her. She pulled the 1967 box toward her and began riffling through the papers. She sifted through them methodically, pulling out sheets and staring at them critically, before tucking them away. Her hands were gentle as she examined the artwork. Sometimes the corner of her mouth turned up and her eyes went distant and amused, as though the drawing she was looking at had sparked some fond memory.

"Why do you have all of this?"

"Because someone has to remember them," Emma said. She frowned and moved the box to the side, still searching. "Most of this stuff is unclaimed and unsigned. Some of it is drawn by artists who died. Some of it, I have no idea. But I didn't want it to go in the trash. Someone has to remember the people who drew all of this. They deserve better. All artists do."

Emma pushed a hand through her pale hair and stared at the box in front of her. Weldon was suddenly afraid she was going to go to pieces right there as she had done so often during the last years his parents were together. David Warrick yelled when he was angry, but Emma said nothing, the coldness of her fury freezing them all in a wretched tableau.

"Mom, what is this about?" Weldon said. His mother looked up at him, and he was surprised to see determination on her face.

"I have to move on," she said. "I feel like I'm living in these boxes, mourning some alternate history where I was a super-hero in a movie that never existed. I've wasted so much of my-self on that movie."

Weldon crouched beside her, hoping the movement would hide his expression. He felt the familiar slipperiness of the ice around him, but something was different. The cracks were still there, but no longer spider-webbing around him, threatening to splinter the ground he was standing on.

"I started seeing a counselor," Emma said. "I never thought that would be something I needed, but this summer has been so hard. I suppose it was the TomorrowMen movie finally starting up, all the casting news. That other actress playing Skylark. It was . . . difficult." She reached out and lightly touched Weldon's shoulder, then pulled her hand away.

"And then you needed a place to stay for the summer, and I couldn't even give you that. I'm your mother. I'm supposed to be able to be there for my kid."

"You—you were doing the best you could," Weldon said. It was almost frightening to hear her acknowledge she'd let him down. It was easier to continue to see her as she'd been on the movie screen: untouchable and mysterious, a woman who never admitted to making a mistake.

"I could've done better," Emma said, smiling wryly. "So I'm trying to do better now. Letting all of this go is part of it." She reached for another box and resumed digging through the artwork inside.

She found what she was looking for in a box dated 1979. A pile of sheets of paper, wrapped carefully in plastic.

"No wonder I couldn't find them," she said. "It's the wrong box. Weldon, here. Be careful."

She handed him the papers and Weldon unwrapped them gingerly. They were covered in dust, the plastic stiff and brittle. He slid the paper from the plastic, a thin stack of bristol board. He stared at the comic pages. Skylark and Skybound flew across a page, hand in hand. They were laughing, their capes streaming out behind them as they flew. The brushstrokes across the page were thick and black, applied quickly and with great skill. Weldon put the page on the floor and stared at the next page. Skylark and Skybound, still together, talking in a café. Skybound was showing Skylark his city, his world. Everything was new to her, the world of men so full of marvels. There were twenty-two pages in the plastic-wrapped packet, all drawn with the same careful pencil line, inked with a skilled brush. Weldon knew immediately the pages were drawn by Micah Kendrick.

"It's original artwork from the issue when they met," Weldon said.

Emma nodded.

"*Spectacular Space Stories #3*," she said. "Before the Tomor-rowMen were even a thing. Skylark came from her planet a million light-years away, and everyone on Earth was afraid she meant us harm. But Skybound showed her around his neighbor-hood, and she saw humans weren't such a bad lot after all. So she decided to stay and help us. Awfully nice of her."

Weldon nodded, still staring at the pages.

Emma gestured at the artwork.

"Years ago people didn't care about original comic book art. It was pulp nonsense. So much of that old art was thrown away. I saved what I could from Warrick Comics, stuff they didn't want, stuff they didn't think they could sell. I'm going to donate it. There are a few museums that preserve original comic art, and I think they'll take most of what I have in these boxes. But these pages—" She tapped the artwork in front of Weldon again. "I want you to have them. I know they're worth a decent amount of money, especially with the movie coming out next year."

Weldon looked up at his mother, confused.

"You're giving them to me? Why not donate them too?"

"I wanted to do something good for you, kiddo," Emma said. "This is something I can give you, something that's worth something. You can sell the pages and have a nice little nest egg. Maybe money for a car, or rent on an apartment." Emma's eyes flickered downward. "I know you and your dad don't get along. This might give you some breathing space."

"Where did you get these?" Weldon asked.

Emma looked down at the pages, her finger gently traced a line of ink.

"From your father. An engagement gift. He knew I loved that particular comic." She smiled at Weldon, a real smile, warm and engaging. The tightness in Weldon's chest eased a little. Maybe the counselor was helping, and she was getting better. Maybe. Just a little.

"They were a gift to me. Now I'm giving them to you."

Weldon sat back on his heels, staring at the pages. He liked the way Micah Kendrick drew Skylark's mouth, the way the brush traced the outline of her lips. The way she always seemed to be smiling, just a little bit, as though thinking of some private joke. It reminded him so much of Mir. The way she'd looked at him in the Starbucks, before sliding her hand across the table toward him. The way she looked when she reached for him at the beach, and he dove with her under the cool, dark water. Weldon sucked in a breath.

"I want to give these to Mir," he said.

Emma tilted her head, curious.

"Mir? Who's—oh."

Weldon looked up at his mother, suddenly worried he'd hurt her.

"Is that okay?"

Emma smiled. "They're yours to do with as you please. But—are you sure? Original comic art, the really old stuff, can sell for a lot of money to collectors. Are you sure you want to give that up?"

Weldon nodded, staring at the pages.

"She can't know they're from me," he said. "Can you send them to her? I don't—we, um, had a fight." Weldon tried to imagine Mir's face as she took the pages from him, hating that he had this power over her. Weldon Warrick, descending from on high to give Miriam Kendrick something taken from her grandfather years ago.

Weldon kept his head down, still staring at the pages. He felt Emma's gaze boring into the top of his head.

"What happened?"

The story came out of him in fits and starts. Stealing the car on his second day in Sandford, meeting Mir at the Emporium of Wonders. Running into her family at the waterfront, the invitation to dinner. Mir's family. Stella and Henry and Nate and their weird house and Henry's crazy stories and Stella's studio where she painted the TomorrowMen. Mir being angry with him, and then that anger ebbing, just a little. Mir calling him out of the blue, telling him about her terrible day. Mir and him holding hands, him waking up every morning at 5:00 a.m. to walk with her to her golf course job, their days at the lake, the lie about the TomorrowMen script coming back to haunt him, and then the fight that ruined everything. When he finished talking, Weldon realized how tired he was. The trip from Sandford to San Diego had been nearly nine hours of flying.

"I'm sorry, kiddo," said Emma. There were soft lines on her forehead, creasing her pale, nearly perfect skin. Weldon liked the lines. It made his mother look a little more human. A little less like an alien queen with the power to launch ten thousand starships.

"Yeah," he said, looking down at the comic pages drawn by Miriam's grandfather. "Me too."

CHAPTER TWENTY-FIVE

Mir walked down the long golf course drive-way toward Sandford, the heat from the day pressing her downward. The muggy July air felt like soup. Incredibly hot, heavy soup, coating her lungs with heat, covering her with sweat. All Mir wanted was to dive in the cool lake water and stay there for the rest of the summer.

She also wanted Weldon. Her left hand felt empty without his. The walk to and from work was so lonely she felt like she was sleepwalking, zombie Mir putting one foot in front of the other, never sure where she'd end up. She got to work on time, but waking up was so much harder now she knew he was no longer waiting for her.

She'd almost called him. She'd stood in the kitchen and stared at the phone, three days after the fight. Her hand had twitched and she'd reached for the receiver, but then she'd walked away and returned to the couch, where she'd been lying facedown for most of those three days. She hadn't tried to call again. She couldn't make her brain form words that seemed adequate. So the three days had turned into a week, and then another week. And she still couldn't make herself pick up the phone.

What could I say? she thought, staring at her feet as she walked home from work. Ahead of her was their usual meeting place. No Weldon. Of course not.

I'm sorry I blamed you for something that's not your fault. I screwed everything up because I can't let things go. Mir let her breath out slowly. *I want to let it go. But I don't know how.*

Mir wanted so badly to touch him again. She wanted to lean her cheek against his shoulder. She wanted to slide her hands over his shoulders and clasp them behind his head. She wanted to stand on her toes and press her forehead against his, to—

A car horn honked. Mir looked up. An orange pickup truck pulled up beside her, Evan leaning out of the driver's side. At the sight of Evan, a hand grabbed Mir's heart and squeezed hard.

"Hey," Evan said. He was smiling and tan, not dirty and sweaty like Mir. "Are you avoiding me?"

Mir adjusted her backpack strap so she wouldn't have to look at him as she walked toward the truck. When she reached the driver's-side door, she continued staring at the ground. She could feel Evan's gaze on the top of her head. She couldn't bear looking up.

"Kinda," she said.

"I figured. Where have you been?"

"Hiding," Mir said, still staring at the pebbles between her steel-toed boots. "And then feeling more awful because avoiding someone is something only a crummy person would do, so clearly it's not just my brain telling me I'm crummy, it's actual scientific fact."

"Hop in," said Evan, leaning over to unlock the passenger's-side door. "I'll take you home and we'll talk this out."

Mir clambered into the truck, stowing her backpack at her feet. She leaned toward the air-conditioning vents and closed her eyes, enjoying the feeling of cold air across her skin.

"This is because of the script, isn't it?"

Mir looked at Evan. He was leaning against the driver's-side door, chin propped in his hand. For the first time Mir noticed how grown-up he looked. His body didn't seem so unwieldy, like he'd grown into it over the course of the summer. His hair was cut a little shorter than normal, which looked nice on him. The beard was the same, though, a little bit too long, a little unkempt. It was his signature.

Mir nodded.

"What happened? Weldon Warrick thought it was crap?"

"No," Mir said. "He wouldn't even look at it. Some legal thing about not being able to read unsolicited TomorrowMen scripts. Apparently it's a policy Warrick Studios has."

"Huh," said Evan, looking out over the truck's steering wheel. "That's the first I've heard of that, but I guess it makes sense. So why'd he say that stuff in the Emporium of Wonders, about how he could pass the script off to his dad?"

"He lied," said Mir. "He was trying to impress me."

"Huh," said Evan again.

"Are you mad at me?" Mir said. "I—I'm the one who wanted to give Weldon the script. You didn't. I know you love TomorrowMen comics, and this maybe screws that up for you—"

"Nah," Evan said. "I'm not mad at you. It's fine."

Mir stared at her hands. Silence hung between them in the truck cab.

"So are you and Weldon . . ."

"Yeah," Mir said. "We were. But maybe not anymore. I don't know."

"I *knew* he liked you. The minute I saw him come into the Emporium of Wonders that day, giving me that 'Oh, crap, she has a boyfriend' look. I knew he had a thing for you."

Mir's hands twitched. They itched to pick up the phone and call Weldon. They itched to reach across the space between her and Evan and fix things. Mir dug her hands into her knees and they stopped twitching.

"I really liked writing that script," Evan said, still staring out over the steering wheel. "I think I want to write another one."

Mir looked away from her hands and up at Evan.

"I think I want to write something original," Evan said. "Something with characters we completely made up. Not someone else's characters. Not the TomorrowMen or the X-Men or Batman, something new. Something we made all ourselves."

He turned toward Mir.

"You're good at writing too. You made that Tristan Terrific script a lot better than it was originally."

Mir shrugged.

"I was just refining what you wrote. The story was yours."

"So maybe I'm good at story stuff. You can take a story and make it better. You make it something people actually want to read. And you came up with the ending. It was a good ending."

"Thanks," Mir said. "I thought it was too."

"Did you like writing the script?"

"Yeah," Mir said, surprising herself. "Yeah, I really did. It was fun."

It *had* been fun. It had been like assembling a giant puzzle made of story pieces. Little pieces of dialogue and character moments sitting next to larger pieces of action and adventure. She had felt the thing in her chest flutter with excitement as she collected the pieces Evan had created and put them in a more orderly fashion. It had been beautiful watching it take shape on the page, a tapestry of a million tiny story pieces, twining together to make a shining, glorious whole.

"Will you write another script with me?"

Mir turned and looked at Evan, still leaning his elbow against the driver's-side door. He looked mostly the same, but also like parts of him were drawn more sharply into focus.

"Yes," she said. "But I don't want to do a superhero comic. I want to make something different. Is that okay?"

"Absolutely," Evan said. "No superheroes. No tights, no flights, no capes." Solemnly he extended his hand. "Shake, writing partner."

Mir grinned and shook his hand. Evan reached for the

gearshift and threw the truck into first. They drove away from the side of the road, kicking a cloud of dust into the muggy air.

"At some point we'll need an artist," Evan said thoughtfully. "Do you know of any artists who might want to draw a comic by two unpublished writers for little to no money?"

"Actually," said Mir, "I think I might be related to one."

"You think your mom would want to draw a comic?"

"I don't know," Mir said. "But it's worth asking."

———

Mir stood in her parents' kitchen and stared at the phone hanging on the wall. In a single motion she reached for it, and slammed the seven numbers for Alex and Kay Warrick's home phone into the keypad. The phone rang.

Once.

Weldon, I'm still angry about what happened to my grandfather and I took it out on you and that wasn't fair—

Twice.

Weldon, there's all this stuff between our families and I'm trying my best to get over it but—

Three times.

Weldon, I didn't even know my grandfather. He and my grandmother died before I was born and I guess the TomorrowMen is all I have of them—

Four times.

Weldon, I'm sorry.

"Hello?" Alex Warrick said. Mir's heart leaped into her throat and she nearly choked on it.

"Hrk—Hello, um, is Weldon there?"

"No," said Alex, "he's gone to San Diego. He left yesterday."

"Oh," Mir said, stunned. She had not anticipated Weldon being gone, and managed to sputter out an "Um . . . okay" before trailing off. On the other end of the line, Alex waited.

"Um, it's Miriam," Mir said finally. "Miriam Kendrick. I just . . . I needed to talk to Weldon about something."

"He has his cell phone. Do you want his number?"

"Um," Mir said again, brilliantly. "Yes. No. Yes, please."

Alex chuckled.

"How're your mom and dad doing, Miriam?"

"Um," Mir said a fourth time. "They're good, I think? Maybe? Yeah, they're okay."

"That's great to hear. Please tell them I say hi. Here's Weldon's number. You have a pen handy?"

Mir grabbed a pen from a basket of odds and ends on the kitchen counter, and scribbled the number on the back of an electricity bill.

"It's a four-hour time difference between us and San Diego," Alex warned, "so try not to call him too early in the morning. Okay?"

"Okay, thanks," Mir said.

"Good luck."

"Thanks," Mir said again, and hung up, realizing a split second too late she'd forgotten to say goodbye. She stared at the numbers she'd scribbled down on the back of the bill. Her hand fumbled for the phone on the wall, and she punched them into the keypad. She listened to the tinny sound of the phone ringing, practicing what she was going to say in her head.

Weldon, I—

"Hello?"

Not Weldon. A woman's voice. Mir yanked the phone away from her ear and slammed it back on the receiver. She darted away from the phone and ran down the hallway toward her room.

Behind her, the phone rang. Mir froze.

It rang again.

Mir walked back in the kitchen and stared at the phone on the wall.

It rang again.

Mir picked up the receiver, held it to her ear.

"Hello?"

"Nine-oh-two, that's the Sandford area code, isn't it?" the woman's voice said.

"Yes," said Mir.

"Oh," said the woman. "Well, you're not Alex or Kay, since I don't think they'd hang up on me like that. Are you a friend of Weldon's?"

"Kind of?" Mir said.

The woman on the other end hesitated.

"Are you Miriam Kendrick?"

"Yeah," Mir said, surprised. "How did you know?"

The woman chuckled, and Mir heard an eerie resemblance to Weldon in the laugh.

"Just a guess. Listen, Miriam, I'm so glad you called. I wanted to get in touch with you, and here you are. Kismet, fate, whatever. It's perfect."

"Okay," Mir said.

"Miriam, how would you like to come to San Diego? For the weekend, to Comic-Con. I have something here I want to give you, and I don't trust the postal service to get it all the way to Nova Scotia. I think it would be much better if you picked up this item in person and took it home with you. Does that sound okay?"

"Um," said Mir. "I can't fly to San Diego."

"Why not?"

"Because that would be very expensive!" Mir sputtered, outraged. Who was this strange woman, suggesting she just hop on an airplane as though it were the easiest thing in the world?

"Oh, that's no problem. I can pay for your ticket. I'll call a travel agency and get them to set something up. You can fly down on a Friday red-eye flight and I'll send you home on Sunday. You have a summer job, don't you? Weldon said you did. This way you won't miss a day of work."

"I work on Saturdays," Mir said.

The woman on the phone sighed.

"Damn, that's no good. Are you sure you can't get that day off?"

"I don't know," Mir said, thinking of Holly and her devotion to a six-day work week. Maybe she could beg. Maybe she could offer to work every Sunday for the remainder of the summer. It was worth a try. "Maybe. I could ask."

"Great. Miriam, why don't you see if you can get Saturday off, and then call me, and we'll arrange something. Does that sound good?"

"Um," said Mir. "Who are you?"

There was a pause on the other end of the line.

"Oh god," said the woman. "I'm so sorry. I'm Emma Warr— um, Sanders. I'm Weldon's mother."

The elf queen, Mir thought. *Galadriel.* The woman whose beauty in any other city would have no equal, and in Los Angeles was just one of dozens.

"He's asleep on the couch," Emma Sanders continued. "That's why I answered his phone. I think the travel caught up with him. He flew out of Sandford at six in the morning. Poor thing." Mir caught the note of fondness in Emma's voice.

"Why didn't you let him stay with you this summer?" Mir asked. She wasn't sure where the question came from.

"Things are complicated in our family," Emma said. She let out a sad, awkward little laugh. "We're trying to make them less complicated and a little more functional, but it's a long road."

Mir waited, listening.

"Weldon talked about you and your family a lot. He told me about your mom. You seem . . . really good for him."

"The first day we met, he bought a painting of my mom's," Mir said. On the other end of the line, Emma was silent.

Mir closed her eyes, thinking of Weldon.

"I'll try to get Saturday off."

———

"You want what?" said Holly, a carrot stick hanging out of the corner of her mouth like a cigarette. Mir cringed and repeated what she'd just said.

"I—I was hoping I could get this Saturday off. I'll work all the rest of the Saturdays this summer. I'll work longer hours. I'll work all the Sundays too. Whatever you want. I just need—I just—"

"You need this Saturday off more than you need this job?" Holly said. She eyed Mir narrowly. She was sitting in her office in the turf shed, steel-toed boots propped on the desk in front of her. She held a bag of baby carrots in her lap, and was methodically pulling one after another out of the bag, crunching them noisily between her teeth.

"No," Mir said. Her stomach turned over and sweat started rolling down her back. "No, I need this job more than I need Saturday off. But I—I really need Saturday off. So I'll do anything."

"You could quit," said Holly. "Then you'd have every Saturday off for the rest of the summer."

"Please," said Mir.

Holly stuck another carrot in the corner of her mouth and chewed thoughtfully.

"When I hired you, I said this was a six-day schedule. No exceptions."

"I know."

"You've been a great little worker up until this point. What's this about?"

Mir took a deep breath. The whole story hovered on the tip of her tongue, ready to spill out. She bit it back.

"Comics," she said weakly.

Holly looked curious.

"How's this about comics?"

"I need to go to San Diego," Mir said. "To, um, San Diego Comic-Con. There's something there waiting for me. A gift, I think. But I don't know what it is."

"This is all very mysterious," Holly said, deadpan. Mir shrugged helplessly.

"I know. It's all—all I know is I have to go."

Holly stared at Mir for what felt like an eternity, eyes half closed, a carrot held up to her lips. Mir stared back, heart thudding between her ribs. After what to Mir seemed like several hours, Holly reached behind her and fumbled in a backpack, searching for something. She pulled out a bagged and boarded comic book, and slapped it on the desk in front of Mir. It was *New TomorrowMen #68*. Holly tapped the comic.

"You can have Saturday off if you get this signed by Stuart Samuel. I know he's a special guest at Comic-Con this year. I really like his art."

Mir stared at Holly, astonished.

"I didn't know you read comics."

"Yeah, well," said Holly, waving a dismissive hand. "I'm a closet geek. When I was a teenager, girls made fun of me for reading comics and boys thought I was weird for liking the same stuff they did." She looked at Mir, a measuring, slightly approving look. "I'm glad things are changing. Comics should be for everyone."

"They should be," said Mir softly.

Holly made a shooing gesture.

"You have Saturday off. Get going to San Diego before I change my mind."

Mir snatched the TomorrowMen comic from the desk, and ran from Holly's office.

CHAPTER TWENTY-SIX

Standing at the crosswalk in front of the San Diego Convention Center, Weldon glowered at the towering hulk in front of him. Sunlight winked off the domed windows at the front of the building, seeming to glare back. A mass of humanity milled around outside the center, people in T-shirts and jeans, backpacks already bursting with spoils from the convention. Adults in finely crafted costumes, pausing to pose for photographs or respond to delighted shouts with an imperious wave. Wide-eyed kids trailing after parents already frustrated by the crowd and heat, a torrent of people pushing through the glass doors to the convention entrance, desperate to reach the promised land inside.

Weldon sighed, already sick of it all. At the other side of the street, the crosswalk sign blinked on, and he walked toward the building, a swell of people bobbing along beside him. He waved his badge at a security guard and wove through the crowds at the front entrance, into the massive exhibition hall. It was briskly cool inside, air conditioners working overtime. Weldon glanced around, trying to get his bearings. The hall was already packed, eager attendees wandering from booth to booth, hands on their wallets. The booths stretched as far as Weldon could see, massive advertisements for television shows or movies dwarfing smaller booths selling anime cells and embroidered cat pillows. A towering red-and-white Marvel sign hung from the rafters to Weldon's left, opposite the familiar Warrick Studios logo. Dodging a squealing group of Teen Titan cosplayers, Weldon headed toward the Warrick Studios booth.

Weldon slowed as he saw his father, standing with a group of men in a roped-off area inside the Warrick booth. The booth was massive, two arcing displays encircling a bright blue carpet. Banners with art from the TomorrowMen comics were hung from the convention ceiling, Skylark and Skybound flying across the fabric, arms outstretched. An illustration of Tristan Terrific smiled slyly from a nearby banner, his hand gesturing toward Weldon. Other heroes fought and punched their way across the booth, men with blue hair, with indecipherable designs on their chests, women in pigtails wearing sexy, thigh-high boots. Weldon didn't recognize most of the characters.

"Hi, Dad."

David Warrick turned toward Weldon. They'd texted twice since Weldon had landed in San Diego. Once for Weldon to let his dad know that he had arrived and it was not the fault of the poor airport driver that he hadn't gotten to the hotel as planned, and the second time to ask when he should be at the convention to see the TomorrowMen movie trailer. Both texts had elicited brief, workmanlike replies from his father.

"Weldon, finally!" David Warrick said, laughing. His dark hair was combed back from his forehead and the tension lines around his eyes had faded. He looked like he'd been sleeping well, a man who had everything under control. Weldon barely recognized him.

David Warrick waved a hand at the man standing next to him.

"Stuart, you remember my son, Weldon, don't you?"

The man next to David Warrick looked vaguely familiar. Tall and thin, with gray shoulder-length hair and a closely trimmed beard, he had the coiled energy of someone who hated spending time sitting down.

"Stuart Samuel," said Weldon, surprised he'd remembered the name so quickly. Stuart Samuel, artist on New Tomorrow-Men for the past twenty-two issues, grinned, looking Weldon up and down. He extended a hand and Weldon shook it.

"I think it's been about seven years since I last saw you, Weldon," he said. "Good job coming out the other side of puberty."

"Uh, thanks," Weldon said.

"Seriously, I think you were about this big when I saw you last." Stuart held his hand a scant three feet from the floor.

"Maybe a little bigger," Weldon said, amused and a little insulted. "Are you still living in Portland?"

"Yeah, the boss here"—Stuart pointed a thumb in David

Warrick's direction—"keeps bugging me to move to LA, but I like the rain."

"The TomorrowMen comics you've been drawing look amazing," Weldon said. "I mean, your art's always been amazing. I still love the Tristan Terrific spin-off you did. But now it's like, I dunno, next-level amazing."

"Thanks," said Stuart with a dry chuckle. He looked over at Weldon's father. "See? Some people like how I draw those comics."

"Everyone loves how you draw the TomorrowMen," David Warrick said. "The last twenty-two issues have been incredible, an artistic master class. These comics will stand the test of time."

Weldon remembered wandering through the halls of Warrick Studios, pausing outside his father's office door. David Warrick had been yelling at someone on the phone, and from the way the conversation was going, Weldon thought the person on the other end of the call was yelling back. On the drive home from the studio, Weldon's father had muttered: "Stuart Samuel is such a pain in the ass. He's giving me crap because he doesn't think the summer TomorrowMen crossover is any good. He's threatening not to draw it if the writer doesn't get his act together, can you believe that?" David Warrick shook his head in disbelief. "If it was any other artist, I'd fire him on the spot. But he's not just any other artist." Weldon's father laughed, staring over the steering wheel as he drove. "Damn, the man can draw. That's why I put up with his winning personality." He looked toward Weldon, sitting in the passenger seat. "Sales for the *New TomorrowMen* are the best they've been in the past ten years. Who knew comic book readers cared about quality?"

"What've you been up to these past few years?" Stuart asked now. "Besides growing, that is."

"Mostly growing," Weldon said. "And running. And school. And—" He thought of Mir, then pushed her away. "Yeah, mostly school. Pretty boring. But you—you did the design for the TomorrowMen movie costumes. That's really cool. So many people are going to see the movie."

"Yeah," said Stuart, glancing grimly toward Weldon's father. "That was an opportunity."

David Warrick seemed not to notice the look, and beamed happily at them.

"The movie's going to be wonderful," Weldon's father said. He was all but vibrating with excitement. Weldon watched him nervously, wondering how many energy drinks his father had consumed at breakfast. "The first trailer for the movie will premiere in Hall H this afternoon. All the lead actors are here, as well as the director. They'll be doing a Q and A after the trailer and I'll be moderating the panel. Stuart will be there too. He's an important contributor."

"That I am," Stuart muttered.

"It's going to be amazing," David Warrick said, practically glowing with enthusiasm. Beside him, Stuart let out a tiny sigh.

"I'm really excited to see it, Dad," Weldon said. His father reached out and patted his shoulder, almost fondly.

"Excuse me, I see someone I need to have a word with," David Warrick said, his gaze catching on something. He waved a hand at Weldon. "You know where to meet us for the panel? You're coming backstage to watch, right?"

"Sure," said Weldon, pulling a careful smile over his face. He had wanted this so badly. He had ached to join his father at Comic-Con, to listen to the screams of thousands of frenzied TomorrowMen fans, all howling for a glimpse of the movie, the TomorrowMen finally made real. Then everything he and his father had fought about would be wiped clean and forgiven. He was inches from everything he'd ever wanted. But all Weldon felt like doing was going back to his hotel room and crawling into bed. He missed Mir so much.

David Warrick turned away from his son and walked toward a group of men (and one woman) in impeccably tailored suits. They smiled at him, five perfect, identical smiles.

"I hate Comic-Con," Stuart said.

Weldon glanced at him. Stuart was staring after Weldon's father, his expression defeated.

"I know it's been this way for a decade, but comics don't matter here. It's all movies and actors and goddamn celebrities. Comics don't matter to any of these people." He waved his hand at the Warrick Studios banner.

"I can't do it anymore. I'm tired of fighting with everyone at this company, tired of hearing people say 'It doesn't matter, it's just comics.' What does that mean? Of course it matters. Comics matter." He laughed bitterly, shrugging. "They matter to me."

"Me too," said Weldon.

"I just want to draw and tell stories," Stuart sighed. "My contract's up after *New TomorrowMen #30*, and I'm gonna go do my own thing for a bit. I don't know, I'll self-publish something, maybe. Maybe comics about birds. I like bird-watching."

Weldon laughed.

"I'd read that."

Stuart looked at him, appraising.

"You would?"

"Sure," said Weldon. "I love your art. I'd watch you draw the phone book."

Stuart shook his head.

"Thanks, I appreciate that," he said. "At least someone at Warrick Comics gets me."

———

Mir stumbled out of the airplane walkway and into the fluorescent glare of the San Diego International Airport. She blinked her eyes, squinting at the airport and the vague shapes of people hurrying past her. Her eyelids felt like there was grit coating their underside. She rubbed them with the back of her hand. It didn't help.

Towing her carry-on bag, Mir walked toward the nearest washroom and splashed cold water on her face. She stared at her reflection in the mirror: her hair was exploding out from her head in a mushroom cloud of curls, and there were dark smudges under her eyes. She looked like she'd flown overnight from one coast to the other, which was exactly what she'd just done.

Mir looked at her reflection grimly. She reminded herself that she had wanted to make this trip. *Because—because I want to see Weldon*, she thought. *And I don't know why, but if I wait until after Comic-Con, I think it might be too late. He might not come back to Sandford.* Everything about this trip was Weldon's mother's idea. Emma Sanders had organized every detail, all expenses paid. She'd gotten Mir a pass for the convention, something supposedly as rare as diamonds. *I know people*, Emma had laughed when Mir had told her that passes for the con had sold out the minute they'd gone up for sale. Emma even had a guest room for Mir to stay in overnight.

Stella hadn't said a word when Mir had told her about the trip. She had watched Mir pack, hovering in the doorway to Mir's bedroom.

"Do you not want me to go?" Mir had asked.

"I don't know," Stella said. Her perfectly shaped eyebrows were creased, sharp worry lines jutting up between them. "You'll be alone there, with all the Warricks. Why does that bring out my overprotective mom complex?" She looked down at her hands, twisting worriedly in front of her.

"I like Weldon," Stella said softly. "I've always liked Alex. They're Warricks."

She looked up at Mir, still anxious.

321

"I've forgiven them. I've made my peace. But it's a big step to go beyond that and really trust them. I don't like that they bring out this side of me."

Mir nodded, understanding.

"We all have work to do," Stella said. Then she drove Mir to the airport and hugged her tightly, hands pressed to Mir's back.

"Mom," said Mir, "do you want to make a comic book?"

Stella had pulled away from Mir, surprised.

Mir grinned, shrugging helplessly.

"Evan and I want to make an original comic. Want to draw it?"

Stella smiled, cupping her hands around Mir's face.

"I suppose it would only be natural," she said. She stood on tiptoe, kissing Mir on the forehead. "Let's talk about it when you get back."

Mir waved at her mother as she walked through security. Stella waved back until Mir rounded a corner in the security line and couldn't see her anymore.

Mir had slept a little on the airplane. She hadn't thought she would; her stomach was turning too many cartwheels. But eventually exhaustion caught up with her. She leaned her head down on the tray table in front of her and slept. When she woke up, the plane was landing and she was in California.

Shaking droplets of water out of her still-messy hair, Mir rode an escalator down to the ground level of the airport. Ahead of her, wide automatic doors opened on a row of taxis waiting for passengers. Mir walked toward the door, towing her luggage behind her.

"Miriam?"

Mir turned. The most beautiful woman she'd ever seen was standing next to her, silver-blond hair shining in the airport's fluorescent light. The woman stared at Mir, and her slender hand went to her mouth, lines appearing on her smooth, perfect forehead.

"You look like Micah Kendrick drew you," said the woman. "You look so much like Skylark."

Mir stared at the woman, baffled. The woman shook her silvery head, smiling sadly.

"I'm sorry, that was—I'm Emma Sanders. Weldon's mom."

"Hi," said Mir, feeling exhausted and overwhelmed, unsure how to process anything. "I'm Miriam Kendrick."

"Of course you are," said Emma, and smiled at Mir. "Let's go to Comic-Con."

To Mir's relief, they didn't go directly to Comic-Con.

"Overnight flights aren't fun," said Emma, guiding her little Toyota through the San Diego streets. "Let's get you home and showered, and then we'll head over to the convention center. Plus, I want to show you the thing I brought you all the way out here for."

As they drove, Mir peeked at Emma out of the corner of her eye. Weldon looked a lot like her. The nose was different. There was nothing crooked about Emma Sanders's perfect nose, but Mir saw a lot of Weldon in the shape of her chin and mouth.

Emma talked incessantly as she drove, pointing out San Diego landmarks and commenting on the behavior of other drivers. She laughed a little too often, not seeming to notice when Mir didn't respond. It was far beyond ordinary nervousness. She gave Mir the impression she was stretched very thin, her skin holding together a woman made of many broken pieces. Mir thought of her own mother: Stella painting, Stella gathering vegetables from the garden, Stella hugging her husband, her face turned up to his, bright and whole and content. Mir remembered Weldon standing in the dark with her after that first family dinner. He had seemed stunned by what he had just witnessed.

Your family is amazing, he'd said. And she'd responded so glibly. *Yeah, I guess. They work really hard at it.* She hadn't understood why he'd said what he did. She thought she understood better now.

Mir showered at Emma's tiny, perfect house, washing the grit from the flight from her hair and eyes. There was a small pink guest room with a twin bed, its headboard made of looping metal. Mir dumped her carry-on suitcase on the bed and opened it, sifting through the shirts and pants she'd brought. A bolt of nervousness hit her, and it took a good fifteen minutes to decide on an outfit: red button-up shirt, skinny dark jeans. Mir piled her hair on top of her head in a loose bun and stared critically at her reflection. It would do.

In the kitchen, Emma was bending over a stack of papers piled on the table. Mir approached her cautiously. Emma glanced up, and smiled. She waved a hand at the papers in front of her.

"These are what I wanted to give you. Original comic book pages drawn by your grandfather years ago. They're from a very old comic, *Spectacular Space Stories #3*, the issue where Skybound shows Skylark that the Earth is worth saving."

Mir reached out a hand and touched the dusty paper in front of her. The paper was dry and coarse, and a bit of grit rubbed off onto her fingers. She recognized the ink strokes on the page, the way the lines formed to make a face or a hand. They were as familiar to her as the sound of her parents' voices.

"Weldon wanted you to have them," Emma said. Mir heard her voice, but it sounded far away, like Emma was calling to her from a great distance.

"They're probably worth a lot of money," Emma said. "Especially now that the movie's coming out. Weldon said you're going to university after you graduate high school, so maybe you could sell them for tuition. Or keep them forever. It's up to you." Emma smiled, and the smile was a little sad.

"I really love these pages," she said. "The way your grandfather drew Skylark and Skybound, it was like he was drawing people he knew and loved, not characters he made up."

They were people he knew and loved, Mir thought. *They were his creations. They were a part of him.* Mir reached out her hand, her fingers tracing the inky upward swirl of Skylark's perfectly coiffed hair. *You gave me back the TomorrowMen*, Mir thought to Weldon. She had the sudden urge to burst out laughing.

"They're beautiful," Mir said. "I've never seen original comic pages before."

Emma smiled, her gaze still on the artwork in front of her. Finally she turned toward Mir.

"Okay. Now let's go to Comic-Con."

———

Weldon sat backstage at Hall H, watching the TomorrowMen movie actors through narrowed eyes. Beside him, Stuart was slumped in a chair, his arms folded across his chest. Weldon thought he might be asleep. David Warrick was talking animatedly with the actor playing Skybound, a man so stunningly handsome Weldon suspected he had been grown in a lab. Weldon had shaken the man's hand a few minutes earlier and had noticed his skin seemed to have no pores.

"So you're the boss's son!" the actor had said jovially, staring at a spot slightly above Weldon's head. Weldon had nodded, said nothing, and the actor moved on, going over to stand beside the tiny blond woman who was playing Skylark. Weldon had watched as he looped an arm effortlessly over the woman's shoulders, beaming down at her like a benevolent god.

"Actors," Stuart muttered from the chair next to Weldon.

"I don't know why I'm here. They didn't even really let me design the outfits for the movie. It was just, 'Stuart, this character's costume needs a boob window. How do we know she's a superhero if she doesn't have a boob window? The audience demands boob windows!'" Stuart put his hands over his face, muttering a drawn-out "Fuuuuuck." Weldon stifled a laugh.

In the background, the crowd howled. Weldon glanced in the direction of the stage, glad he didn't have to face them. Six thousand geeks, most of whom had slept overnight on the pavement outside the convention center, determined to get a seat in Hall H. All the biggest panels were in Hall H. The biggest superhero movies, the most famous actors. To get a peek at the glamour, one had to be prepared to sacrifice.

"I'm glad you're here," David Warrick said. Weldon glanced up. His father's face was shining. Weldon knew this moment was the culmination of years of planning, a new beginning for Warrick Studios. David crouched next to Weldon.

"I spoke with your aunt and uncle a few weeks ago. They said you've been doing really well this summer. I'm proud of you." David Warrick reached out, tapping Weldon's forearm approvingly.

"I know how difficult everything has been for you in the last few years. I want you to know, you have a place here. With me, with Warrick Studios. If you want, you can come home to Los Angeles now. You don't have to wait until the end of the summer."

"Thank you," whispered Weldon. His father smiled and stood up, walking back toward the knot of actors. Weldon watched him go. His chest felt hollow.

Weldon's phone chirped. He glanced at it. A text appeared on-screen.

MIRIAM'S HERE. WHERE ARE YOU? WE'RE OUTSIDE THE EXHIBIT HALL.

Weldon bolted out of his chair. Beside him, Stuart started with surprise.

"Dad," Weldon said. David Warrick turned toward him. Behind his father, the actors glanced toward Weldon, curious. The man playing Skybound now had one arm looped around the actor playing Tristan Terrific, standing so closely they looked like a couple.

"I have to go."

"What?" David Warrick said, puzzled. "But we're just about to go on. The trailer—"

"I have to go," Weldon said again.

"They won't let you back in," his father said, frowning. "You leave this area and security won't let you back in the hall. You'll miss the trailer. You'll miss everything."

"Someone's here," Weldon said, "and I have to go see her. I'm sorry."

"Is this your mother's doing?" David Warrick hissed, taking a step toward Weldon. "Is this more of her bullshit—"

"It's not her," said Weldon, turning away. "It's Mir. She's here."

"Who?"

But Weldon had already run out the exit door.

———

Outside the exhibit hall, Mir gaped at the whirlwind of geekdom around her. To her left, a short man in yellow-and-black spandex, an unlit cigar hanging out of the corner of his mouth, posed with a group of teenagers wearing postapocalyptic *Sailor Moon* outfits. Mir was impressed with the attention to detail, although she wasn't sure how practical ripped fishnets would be for surviving a zombie-infested wasteland. Beside her, Weldon's mother watched the interaction, her gaze disapproving.

"Most of that stuff you can buy online," Emma said with a wave of her hand. "When I cosplayed, you had to make your costumes by hand. That was real cosplay."

"I think they look nice," Mir said, feeling protective of the postapocalyptic *Sailor* squad. The group looked like they were having fun, laughing and posing theatrically while taking pictures with their phones. One girl held up a wand with a crescent moon attached to it and proclaimed, "In the name of the moon, I shall punish you!" The rest of the group dissolved into giggles.

Mir pointed at the doors to the exhibit hall.

"Can we go in?"

Emma glanced at her, then down at the phone in her hand.

"Just a minute. I'm waiting to hear back about something."

Mir turned away to hide her impatience. She wanted to find the Warrick Studios booth. She wanted to find Weldon. She wasn't sure why Weldon's mom was so reluctant to go inside the exhibit hall, but she didn't want to go by herself. Mir had the sneaking suspicion that some people went into Comic-Con and never came out. She didn't want to lose track of Emma in this mass of people. She stared longingly at the entrance to the exhibit hall. *Weldon*, she thought. *Weldon, I'm here. Find me!*

———

Weldon dodged a clot of people gathered around a display for anime figurines, stepped carefully over a pack of children playing with a large bin of superhero-themed Lego, and rolled under a poorly constructed booth advertising geek online dating: GUARANTEED TO BE 100% FAKE GEEK FREE. The booth's owner spluttered an indignant "Hey!" as Weldon's foot caught the edge of his display, sending a pile of key chains tumbling to the ground.

"There's no such thing as a fake geek!" Weldon shouted over his shoulder as he tore away from the booth. Ahead of him the exhibit hall doors gaped, and he pounded through them, eliciting a glare from a nearby security guard. He stood panting in the convention center's front foyer, looking for Mir. He had made it through the exhibit hall in less than ten minutes.

Weldon circled to his left and began trotting along the foyer. Several people eyed him curiously. Ahead of him he saw an explosion of color as a large group of what appeared to be postapocalyptic schoolgirls milled around, taking pictures and posing with other cosplayers. The crowd around Weldon slowed to admire the cosplayers and Weldon was forced to slow as well. He dodged to his right to try to move around the group, and then—

He saw Mir.

He saw the top of her head, her hair twisted into a bun, curls escaping and tumbling down her back. She was wearing a red shirt, and the color against her dark hair was like a beacon.

Weldon tried to wind his way through the crowd of cosplayers, dodging between three of the postapocalyptic schoolgirls posing like Charlie's Angels, spinning around a man dressed in a tuxedo and cape, whose appearance elicited shrieks of delight from the cosplayers. Then he was through the crowd and she was there in front of him, her back still turned. He stared at the back of her head, noticing for the first time the way her ears stuck out a little on the sides. *If I say something, it'll ruin everything*, Weldon thought. *She'll vanish in a puff of smoke.* His fingers reached out and brushed the nape of her neck.

She turned, and when she saw him, she smiled. Her eyes were looking straight at him and her mouth was smiling and her hands were reaching for him. Her hands slid over his shoulders and around his neck and clasped where they met at the back. Her forehead was against his and his chest was filled with so much light he thought he would explode and wipe them all out, him and Mir, the convention center, San Diego itself. Wiped from this plane of existence. He wrapped his arms around her and felt her body press into his, filling every space between them. Mir tilted her head up and her mouth met his, and it was weird and sloppy and wonderful. When she pulled away, her face still turned up toward his, a disbelieving laugh bubbled out of Weldon.

"I'm sorry," Mir said.

"I'm sorry," Weldon said. Mir smiled and blinked in a way that might have meant her eyes were watery.

"So Canadian," she said. Behind them, the postapocalyptic schoolgirls screamed with approval.

"COMIC-CON!" howled a blue-haired girl in a tattered leather jacket, flinging her wand into the air. "YEAAAHHH!"

Mir giggled and ducked her head, pressing her face against Weldon's chest. Weldon bent his cheek to the top of Mir's hair bun and slid his hands around her back, closing his eyes. She was here. He could explode with light and everything would be fine.

Mir squirmed a little and he let her go. She pushed a stray curl back from her forehead.

"A little tight."

"Sorry," he said. Mir laughed again.

"Canadian."

"I can't help it," Weldon said. "It's in my blood."

"Now the vengeful and patriotic ghost of Farley Mowat will pass by you, recognizing you as one of our own," said Mir.

"Thank god," Weldon sighed. "That guy was getting on my nerves." He looked up and saw his mother standing a few feet away, watching him and Mir. The heel of her hand was pressed to her mouth, and her eyebrows were drawn downward. For a moment Weldon thought she was angry, but then she smiled.

"I'm happy for you, kiddo," said Emma.

"You did this," Weldon said, astonished. Emma shrugged, still smiling.

"I don't trust the post office," she said. "Makes more sense for her to come out here and pick up her grandfather's artwork in person. Besides—" Emma gestured, taking in the convention, the cosplayers, the entrance to the exhibit hall. "I thought she should see all of this."

Emma smiled, looking down. Her silvery-blond hair fell forward, partially obscuring her face.

"It's a part of who she is. Who you both are." She looked up at Weldon and Mir, and laughed. "Both of you, total nerds."

Mir moved to stand beside Weldon, looping her arm around his waist. He slid his arm around her, thrilling at the feeling of her so close to him. Emma turned away, starting to walk toward the convention exit.

"Enjoy the con, kids. Mir, give me a shout when you want to come back to my place. I'll come pick you up. Don't stay out too late."

"I—I don't have a cell phone," Mir said, her voice suddenly alarmed.

"I have one," Weldon said. "I'll call her. Mom—" Weldon's fingers itched to reach out and prevent his mother from leaving. He kept his hand firmly wrapped around Mir's waist.

"You don't want to stay? Just for a bit? You have a badge."

"I've seen it all before," said Emma, waving a hand over her shoulder. "I was a geek before you kids were thoughts in the universe."

Weldon watched her go, his heart aching a little. But Mir was beside him, and that was enough.

"Holy shit," said a guy dressed as Wolverine. "Was that

Emma Sanders? I had her poster in my room when I was twelve. She still looks amazing!"

Mir slipped her hand through Weldon's and tugged him toward the exhibit hall entrance.

"C'mon," she said, her face shining. "I've never been to Comic-Con. Show me what it's like. Show me everything."

Weldon allowed himself to be pulled toward the hall doors, his hand tangled in Mir's. They wove through the small crowd that had gathered by the entrance, a knot of people holding up badges for security guards to inspect. Mir paused, reaching in her bag to pull out a comic. Weldon saw the title as she turned it toward him: *New TomorrowMen #68*.

"I need this signed by the guy who drew it. Stuart Samuel. Otherwise I might be out of a job. The signature is payment to Holly for getting today off."

"Amazing how everyone is secretly a nerd at heart," Weldon said. He squeezed Mir's hand and held up his badge for the security guard to see. "I'll make sure he signs it."

They stepped through the exhibit hall doors and into the world beyond. Weldon felt Mir's hand tighten around his own as she took in the exhibit hall, her eyes wide. In a flash he saw everything as she saw it, the madness and energy but also the joyful heart of the convention.

"Oh, wow," she whispered. "Comics made all of this."

They walked the length of the convention hall, Weldon's arm around Mir when the crowd thinned, hand in hand when the paths became too crowded and they had to move single file through a group of gawkers shouting for freebies at the Marvel booth. Mir stared at everything, mouth hanging open. They passed by booths for smaller comic publishers, tables stacked high with hardbound graphic novels with beautifully designed covers, the artwork strange and complicated. There were so many comics, the artwork strikingly different from how the TomorrowMen comics were drawn. Mir lingered over the books, her hands brushing the embossed cover designs.

"I think my grandfather would have loved all of this," she murmured. She looked at the rows of covers stretching out to her left and right. "All these comics, and they're all so unique."

They reached the end of the exhibit hall, then looped back toward the Warrick Studios booth. Mir's hand tightened around Weldon's hand and she hung back, her expression unsure.

"It's okay," said Weldon. "Stuart's signing now. I don't think my dad will be around."

"I'll have to meet him someday," Mir said. "If, y'know"— she looked up at Weldon—"if this is going to work."

"No 'ifs,'" Weldon said. Mir pulled on Weldon's hand and he stopped, turning toward her.

"Okay," she said. "No 'ifs.' But if this is going to work, you can't act like you're Tristan Terrific and you can change my mind with a smile."

Mir's expression was bright and fierce, direct on his face. Weldon nodded, feeling like he might melt under the intensity of her gaze.

"Okay," he said. "And you can't blame me for something that happened forty years ago."

Mir nodded too.

"We all have things to work on," she said, then laughed, shaking her head.

"This is the least practical thing I've ever done. What's even going to happen after the summer? Are you going back to LA? We both have another year of school. And then what?"

"We'll figure something out," Weldon said. He looked at Mir. "Skylark was from a galaxy a million miles from Earth. She came here to warn us of impending doom, and then decided to stay because she fell in love with Skybound. If an alien queen and a soldier with superhuman strength can make it work, so can we."

Mir shook her head again, smiling.

"You read too many comic books."

They stood in line for Stuart Samuel, Mir's arm wound around Weldon's waist. Standing behind them was a woman with a pink Skylark T-shirt; in front of them were two teenage boys wearing the same Skybound T-shirt. The Skybound T-shirt was the design from the movie, an impossibly sculpted Skybound standing impassively with arms folded, glowering at anyone nearby. Mir pointed at the T-shirt and stood on her toes to whisper in Weldon's ear: "I miss the cape."

Weldon nodded. "I miss it too."

When they reached the front of the line, Stuart glanced up at Weldon, then did a double take, surprised.

"What are you doing in line, Weldon? You're the boss's kid. You don't have to put up with that nonsense."

"It's okay," Weldon said. He gestured toward Mir, who held out Holly's copy of *New TomorrowMen #68*. "This is Miriam. My—" He froze, suddenly unsure.

"Girlfriend," said Mir. "I'm Weldon's girlfriend. Miriam Kendrick."

Stuart took the comic from Mir, then smiled as though he'd figured out a puzzle. He pointed a finger at her.

"Micah Kendrick. Your dad?"

"Grandfather," said Mir.

"Of course. You're much too young. I met him, you know. Years ago."

"What was he like?" Mir said softly.

Stuart leaned forward, his hands grasping the comic he'd drawn.

"He was kind to me," he said. "I was just a kid who wanted to make comics, and he was my hero. He encouraged me. No one draws the TomorrowMen like he did. Not even me." Stuart leaned back and dug in his pocket for a moment, pulling out a battered wallet. He handed Mir a business card.

"There's my info. You ever want to get in touch about comics or whatever, give me a shout. I owe your grandfather that. All right?"

"I will," said Mir, tucking Stuart's business card into her bag. "Thanks so much."

"Hey, no problem at all," Stuart said, signing his name on

Holly's comic with a dramatic flourish. They stepped out of line, Mir blowing on the signature before placing the comic carefully in its plastic sleeve.

"He was nice," Mir said.

Weldon nodded.

"Yeah, he's cool. Don't ask him about boob windows, though."

Mir frowned. "What's a boob window?"

Weldon grinned, shaking his head. When he looked up, he saw his father standing at the edge of the Warrick Studios booth, watching him and Mir. David Warrick was close enough to have overheard the conversation with Stuart, and from the somber look on his face, he had. The energy that had radiated from him earlier was all but gone. Weldon tensed as his father walked toward them. Mir turned to see what Weldon was looking at and Weldon felt her stiffen as she recognized his father.

David Warrick stopped an arm's length from his son. Weldon waited, his hand laced through Mir's. Weldon's father glanced at Mir, his gaze tired.

"So I guess you're staying in Sandford," he said.

"If that's okay," said Weldon. His father nodded, stuffing his hands into his pockets.

"If it's what you want, son," he said. "If it's right for you."

"It is," said Weldon. "Maybe even for my last year of high school, if that's possible."

David Warrick smiled, almost wistfully.

"I always hoped you'd join me at Warrick Studios," he said. "Maybe you will, someday."

"Maybe."

"I hated Sandford," David Warrick said with a sigh. "But if that's where you want to live, I guess I'll be visiting it over the next year. We'll have to see what your aunt and uncle say, though."

"You should come to our house for dinner," Mir said. "My parents have a vegetable garden, so there are always a million vegetables to eat. I'm sure they'd love to have you over."

David Warrick looked at Mir, and the lines on his face softened a little.

"I'd like that," he said.

"How did the trailer premiere go?" Mir asked.

Weldon's father brightened.

"Really well," he said. "It's trending worldwide on Twitter. It may have been worth it, after all."

Weldon's father turned and walked away from them, toward the same group of suited men and women that Weldon had seen him with earlier. As he approached the group, David Warrick spread his arms wide and the suits turned toward him, smiling their unnerving, perfect smiles.

"You're coming back," Mir said.

Weldon turned to face her.

"Yes," he said. "Well, hopefully. Like my dad says, gotta see if it's okay with my aunt and uncle."

Mir grinned.

"You are going to be so Canadian by this time next year, your dad won't even recognize you." And she stood on tiptoe, kissing him on the mouth. It was a little less sloppy than the first time, but still weird and still wonderful.

"YEAHHH COMIC-CON!" someone yelled from outside the booth.

Mir rolled her eyes.

"Is that going to happen every time we kiss?"

Weldon reached for her hand.

"C'mon," he said. "Let's go exploring."

They walked together into the swirling mass of humanity.